EVERY SHADE OF WINTER

CARRIE ELKS

Her chest was burning, her legs aching, and she was running out of breath. She thought despairingly of that gym membership she'd paid for monthly but hadn't used since she'd taken it out two years ago, in an unusual fit of optimism, believing that this time she'd get those rock hard abs she'd dreamed of for years.

But she wasn't going to stop running. Not yet. She hadn't put enough distance between herself and the *incident*. She wasn't sure she ever could.

Because all she could think about were those words she'd said in front of everybody. And the way Shaun had stared at her, a mixture of hurt and anger dancing in his eyes.

She ran past the Cold Start Garage and the Jingle Bell Theater. Both were closed, the same way every small business in Winterville was closed today. Their owners were all sitting in pretty linen seats with pink ribbons tied to the back right now, gossiping with each other about the spectacle she'd made of herself.

And of Shaun, too.

She wanted to close her eyes and scream, but with her luck she'd catch her foot in the hem of her long, white dress and tumble head over heels into the road.

Or maybe that would be a good thing. Because right now, all she wanted to do was disappear.

"Amber!"

She ignored the shout. There was nobody she wanted to talk to right now. She was too embarrassed, too shocked at her own behavior.

All too aware that she'd caused the biggest scandal in Winterville for years.

She reached the town square and almost collapsed against the fence. She could feel her dark waves curling around her face, having escaped from the elaborate updo the hairdresser had spent almost an hour creating that morning.

Back when she hadn't been the town pariah.

"Excuse me," a man said. "Do you know what time the café opens?"

"Not until tomorrow," she told him. "They're closed today for a wedding."

He blinked, as though he'd just noticed what she was wearing.

A white lace gown that was dirty around the hem. No shoes because she'd kicked them off as she'd run from the Winterville Inn. And she was pretty sure her mascara was smudged under her eyes, from how much she'd cried when she told Shaun she couldn't go through with it.

She couldn't marry him.

"Is it your wedding?" the man asked. He was slowly backing away, as though she was a wild animal about to attack.

"No," she lied. "I just like wearing long, white dresses."

The man turned on his heel and practically ran away.

"Amber!"

She knew that voice. Did she have enough time to run away from it? Her chest tightened, because she'd let him down, too.

She'd let everybody down.

Dammit, she was going to make a run for it. But she'd barely had time to pick up her skirt before she felt two strong arms wrap around her waist. "Will you hold up for a minute?" His voice was rough.

"I'm sorry," she said, and it came out as a sob. "I'm so sorry."

"You don't need to apologize to me. I'm not the chump you left hanging at the altar."

That made her cry harder. She dropped her face into her hands but he spun her around and hugged her tighter.

"You shouldn't be here," she told him.

"Where else would I be? You're my friend. You need me."

Finally, she tipped her head up to look at him. North Winter. Her best friend, her co-worker, the one man who knew her inside and out.

His eyes met hers and all she saw was sympathy. She hated it and she loved it.

"Is it mayhem back there?" she asked him.

Still holding her close to him with one arm, North ran his thumb along his sharp jaw. "Put it this way, the free bar has already been drunk dry."

"And Shaun? Is he okay?"

North lifted a brow. "Define 'okay'."

But she didn't need to. Of course he wasn't okay. She just stood in front of their friends and his family – family who'd traveled from New York to see him get married – and told him she couldn't go through with it.

That she couldn't be his wife.

"He must hate me," she whispered.

North took her hand and led her to one of the benches that surrounded the tall fir tree at the center of the square. She sat down heavily and he took the seat beside her, still clasping her palm in his.

"Yeah, I'm pretty sure he hates you," North said. "I'm not his biggest fan, but even I feel a little sorry for the guy."

She blinked. "You do?"

He wrinkled his nose. "Nah. He's an asshole."

It almost made her laugh. "He's not that bad."

"Uh, you're the one who just left him hanging."

Amber let out a long sigh. "I know. I'm awful. I can't believe I just did that."

"Better now than when you're married with two kids," North said pointedly.

"Room for one more?"

Her other best friend, Kelly, was standing in front of the bench, still wearing her pink maid-of-honor dress and holding what looked like two cocktails in her hand. She offered one to Amber, who shook her head.

"North?" Kelly asked.

"I'm good."

"Well okay then." Kelly downed both glasses and put them on the grass, before sitting on the other side of Amber.

And for a moment none of them said a word. It was so quiet she could hear the birds chirping in the trees and the rush of blood as it pulsed past her ears.

"So that was the most exciting wedding I've ever been to," Kelly finally said, breaking the silence.

"Please don't." Amber shook her head. "I want to pretend it didn't happen."

Kelly shifted next to her. "Um, so you don't want to talk about what happens next then?"

"Next?" Amber repeated.

"Like should I tell everybody to go home?"

Amber frowned. "Haven't they already left?"

"Nuh uh." Kelly shook her head. "They're all in the bar getting sloshed. Especially Shaun and his friends."

Ugh. Shaun's friends. They'd disliked her before today, now they must hate her. The same way his parents must hate her, too.

"We should tell them to go home," Amber said. "I'm not going back there."

"I've got this," North told her. "I'll go back in a minute and explain."

His eyes were soft as he looked at her. And it made her want to cry again. She should have told him she was having doubts. Hell, she should have told Shaun.

Not waited until they were standing in front of the whole town, ready to pledge their troths, whatever the hell they were.

"Personally speaking, I think you've done the right thing," Kelly said. "He's an asshole."

"That's what I said," North agreed.

Kelly looked shocked. The two of them rarely agreed on anything.

"Well blow me down with a feather."

North rolled his eyes.

"But now you have a small problem," Kelly said. "Like where are you going to sleep tonight?"

"Sleep?" Amber wasn't sure she'd ever be able to sleep again.

"You know, put your head on a pillow and close your eyes," Kelly said slowly. "Because you can't stay at Shaun's place."

Oh God, she hadn't thought of that. They were supposed

to spend tonight at the Inn, but her home was his house. The house they rented from the Walker family was in his name.

"Um..."

"She'll stay with me."

"Hmph." Kelly shook her head. "Can you imagine if Shaun finds that out? He'll think the two of you eloped."

The stupid thing was, he would. Since the moment Amber and Shaun had started dating, he'd hated North with a passion. And unfortunately the feeling was mutual. Amber had spent most of the past year tiptoeing the tightrope that traversed the gulf between them.

Maybe that was one good thing about her messing up so badly. At least she wouldn't have to play peacemaker anymore.

"Just for one night. Or until you've sorted yourself out," North said softly.

"I guess I could move back to the old farm house," she said, frowning. She'd grown up in the farm house attached to the Christmas Tree Farm her dad had founded.

She still worked at the farm – she and North owned it together, but the house itself had been empty since her mom died a couple of years earlier, but at least it had a roof and walls.

"It needs too much work," Kelly said. "You could always stay at mine."

"Where would I sleep?" Amber asked her. "With Cole?"

Kelly had a two bedroom house, where she lived with her nine-year-old son, Cole.

"Actually, where is Cole?" Amber asked her.

"He's back at the Inn. Eating your wedding cake."

Well at least it wasn't going to waste.

And ugh, what a waste this all was. Of time, of money, of friendship.

She'd messed everything up.

Her lips parted and a long, ragged sigh escaped. North

looped his arm around her shoulder and pulled her against him. His chest was strong, his skin warm, and if it had been any other time or place she'd probably be enjoying this right now.

Because once upon a time she'd had a huge crush on North Winter. Nowadays, she joked that it was an illness every woman in Winterville suffered from at least once in their lifetime. And why wouldn't they? With his dark hair and piercing blue eyes he was jaw-dropping. Then add to that his strong, farm-honed body and his brooding nature and he was dynamite.

Good thing she was inoculated against him now.

Because his arm around her felt too good. She wanted to melt into him and let him protect her. And she knew he would if she asked him to. That was what North did, took care of those he loved.

North's phone buzzed in his pocket. Without releasing his hold on Amber, he reached into his pocket with his other hand and pulled it out, scowling when he read the screen.

"Can you take Amber to my place?" he asked Kelly.

"Sure." Kelly nodded at him. "Why?"

"Because a fight just broke out at the Inn. They need me back there."

"A fight? Between who?" Amber pulled herself out of his hold and stood. "I should go back there. This is all my fault."

North stood, too, towering over her. Gently, he took her face in his palms and tipped it until her eyes connected with his. "Baby, grown men fighting isn't your fault. Now go back to my place, take a long bath, and borrow some of my clothes, okay?"

"Okay," she breathed.

He pressed his lips against her brow. "Good girl."

And weirdly, that made her shiver.

"It's over. They've left," North's brother told him as he strode into the Winterville Inn.

"All of them?"

"Shaun and all his cronies, yeah?" Gabe nodded. "They're heading over to Marshall's Gap." That was the next town over, where Amber and Shaun lived.

Or at least Shaun did. Amber didn't live there anymore, thank God. Or she wouldn't once he helped her move everything out.

"Did they cause much damage?" Along with his brothers and cousins, North owned a part of this Inn and this town. It was built by their grandmother years ago, and she'd left it to her children when she died. They'd tried to sell the town, but North and his cousins had bought it from under them.

"Just a few glasses broken." Gabe shrugged. "Nothing that can't be replaced. Holly and the others are cleaning up now." He leaned against the wall. "How's Amber doing?"

"Not good." North let out a long breath. He hated seeing her so upset. Amber had never been the kind of girl who cried at anything. She was stoic. Even when her mom died, she'd held it in until the two of them were alone.

To see her weeping so openly made him feel useless.

"Did she tell you why she did it?"

"Did what?" North asked.

"Left Shaun at the altar."

"Because he's an asshole."

Gabe laughed. "Yeah, but that's old news. So she didn't tell you why she ran away at the last minute?"

"No." North frowned. "Do you know?"

"No, but I heard Shaun's mom shouting at him. Just before she left."

So his mom was gone? Good. He wasn't a fan of her either.

"What did he say?"

Gabe shrugged. "Weirdly, he was defending Amber to his mom. She was angry and wanted to hunt her down. So he told her some of this was his fault. That he told Amber this morning what went on at the bachelor party."

North's blood turned cold. "What went on?"

"There was a stripper." Gabe shifted his feet. "Apparently he got close with her. Um, like real close."

For a moment, North said nothing. It was a good thing that Shaun had left. A great thing. Because otherwise North would be pounding his damn face in right now. "And he waited to tell her until today?"

"Yep. I guess the guy does have one decent bone in his body."

"The motherfucker," North spat out.

"Calm it." Gabe put his palm on North's chest. "It's done. She walked away from him. He isn't your concern anymore."

But the fury was hard to ignore. Amber was a good person. She didn't deserve to be treated like crap. And she definitely didn't deserve to find out about it on her wedding day. Yes, he hated Shaun, but he'd tolerated him because he thought the man loved his friend.

It turned out he didn't. And North's tolerance had waned.

"I mean it, North. Let it be. Amber won't appreciate it if you interfere."

No, she wouldn't. She hated fuss and she hated being at the center of it more.

"I'm not doing anything," North said.

"Yeah, but you're thinking about it."

That was the problem with having brothers so close to your own age. They knew you better than you knew yourself. And Gabe knew North sometimes had an anger problem.

Though he was working on it. Like right now.

"I'll go help clean up," North muttered, because he needed something to do. Anything, really, that didn't involve curling his hands into fists and pummeling Shaun Summers' face.

"It's okay, it's nearly done. Go home to Amber," Gabe told him. "She needs you."

She still couldn't quite believe it had happened. Twenty-four hours ago she was putting the final touches to the table decorations – tiny Christmas trees from the farm she and North ran, decorated with pink flowers, to represent her mom and dad who'd died and couldn't be there with her. She'd been drinking champagne and laughing with her girl friends, turning down the tasty food they'd ordered up to the suite in the Winterville Inn because she was determined to fit into her wedding dress.

And now she was sitting in North's living room, wearing a t-shirt and sweatpants that swamped her, trying to work out where it all went wrong.

You know where it all went wrong.

Well okay, finding out on your wedding day that your husband-to-be had done the dirty with a stripper was definitely a kicker. But the truth was she'd been having doubts before today.

She'd been having them for months, actually. All those late nights when he'd roll in from the bar smelling of alcohol and cigarettes. All those mornings when he hadn't come home at all because he'd spent the night at Kyle's or Dean's or at another of his friends.

And all the times she'd lent him money because he'd gambled his wages away at a poker table.

Ugh. She rubbed her now-clean face with her palms. She was such an idiot. For some reason she'd really thought she could make it work.

Because when Shaun wasn't being an ass he was sweet. Those first few months together he'd been so kind and loving, she really thought he was her soulmate. Like her, he'd lost his dad when he was young and they'd bonded over it. He'd made her laugh when she wanted to cry, stroked her hair when she did and held her tight all night.

He'd been the one port in her storm that she'd clung onto. But it turned out he wasn't a port at all.

He was a damn shark.

"Pizza," North said, sliding a cardboard package on the table. "Meat feast for me, Hawaiian for you.

Once upon a time they'd spent most Friday nights eating pizza together. Watching a movie or a TV show until one of them fell asleep. And then Shaun had come along and things changed.

She hadn't realized how much she missed her friend until now.

"I'm sorry." She grimaced. "I can't eat it."

"You want me to get you something else?"

She shook her head. "I'm not hungry."

"You gotta eat something," he told her. "You'll waste away."

Oh if only that were true. Shaun had always told her she needed to lose a few pounds.

"I'll try in the morning."

"Okay." North shoved a slice of pizza in his mouth. "Want to talk?"

"Not really."

"Want to watch a movie?"

"Um yeah." She blinked.

He passed her the remote. "You choose."

So she did. A Netflix movie, based on a Jane Austen novel. If Jane couldn't make her feel better about life, nobody could. The title sequence came on and North stretched his legs out, setting his feet on his coffee table. She nestled into him, finding the perfect cozy spot in the crook of his arms. His fingers drew reassuring patterns on her arm, making her sigh softly.

Thank goodness for friends. Especially Kelly and North. If she didn't have them, she wasn't sure she'd have gotten through today.

"Don't you want to know why I did it?" she asked North as the lead actress began a monologue. Okay, so maybe she did want to talk after all.

"I know why you did it."

"You do?" Her cheeks flamed. "Who told you?"

"Gabe heard Shaun talking to his mom. Said he'd been with a stripper."

Her stomach flipped. "I only found out this morning. I went to give him some cufflinks as a wedding gift. The STD results were on our hall table."

"He took an STD test?" North looked surprised.

"Yeah. I guess that's a good thing, right? It was negative."

North's jaw tightened but he said nothing.

"He was truthful when I asked him about it," Amber continued. "I guess I should be thankful for that, too."

"So why didn't you end it as soon as he told you? And not turn up to the wedding at all?"

"He begged me not to." And like the stupid people pleaser she was, she'd agreed.

She'd almost made it to the altar before the full force of

his confession hit her. And she'd realized she couldn't go through with it. So she'd started crying, her hand in the crook of North's arm as he'd walked her down the aisle.

And when she reached the front she'd broken down. Said she was sorry, that she couldn't marry him. In front of everybody they cared about.

And then she'd run.

"I'm glad you changed your mind," North said, his voice thick.

She met his gaze. "Me, too."

He tightened his hold on her and she liked it. She could feel the warmth of his breath on her cheek. She was trying not to beat herself up about this, too. About him being the one to save her the way he always was.

Even his smell made her feel safe. It was warm, and full of pine. Like the farm on a summer's day. He'd changed out of his suit, thank goodness, into a black t-shirt and gray sweats.

They looked better on him than they did on her, that was for sure.

She tried to bring her attention to the television screen. But Anne Elliott was being belittled about not getting married and it made her feel worse.

"I guess at least I haven't got my parents around to disappoint," she whispered to North.

"They wouldn't be disappointed in you." His voice sounded thick. "They loved you."

And now they were gone. "I thought I was going to have a family again." And wasn't that the kicker? The hope of a future. That she'd found her person, somebody always on her side. That they'd grow together, blossom, and have children.

It was gone.

"You've got a family. Me." He was frowning now. "And my family. They all love you. They keep messaging to check on you."

She tried not to sniffle. There was wallowing and there was *wallowing*.

"I know, and I'm thankful for you."

The lines between his eyes smoothed out. "And I'm thankful that you're not married to an asshole."

This time, she smiled. Because he always made her feel better. That was one of the reasons she loved him. He made her feel safe, made her happy.

And sometimes he made her want things she couldn't have. But she wouldn't think about that right now.

A sudden yawn pulled at her jaw. "I'm sorry," she murmured.

"Enough of the apologies, okay?" He looked at her through those sea-blue eyes. The intensity of his stare made her chest tighten.

Okay, so *maybe* she still had a little crush on him. But right now, that was the least of her worries. She was homeless, husbandless, and the whole town was gossiping about her.

"Stop thinking and go to sleep," North murmured. "You look exhausted."

Even asleep, the shadows beneath her eyes were prominent. Her breath was even, at least, and the tears had stopped, which was something.

He wasn't good with tears. Never had been. They made him want to punch the person who'd caused them.

She was still curled around him, her head against his chest, her arm stretched around his waist. He didn't dare move because he wanted her to sleep.

Her lips parted as she exhaled and he tried to not look at them. He tried to ignore the way her fingertips were brushing against the sliver of skin exposed between his t-shirt and the waistband of his joggers, too. But it was becoming impossible, because his body was responding to her.

In the most inconvenient of fucking ways.

Christ, she looked beautiful. Smelled good, too. Her hair was still damp from her shower earlier, her skin scrubbed clean. If you looked at her now, you wouldn't believe she'd run away from her wedding only hours earlier.

She let out a sigh, her breath tickling the base of his neck. It sent a pulse of excitement down his body. A rush of blood, too, until he was hard.

What the hell was wrong with him?

He was supposed to be taking care of her, not getting turned on from a brush of her fingers.

Rationally, he knew it was just a reflex reaction from a man who hadn't gotten laid in way too long. Maybe he should have. But the fact was, he didn't want to. He was thirty-six, and sometimes he felt it. Casual hookups didn't have the same lure for him that they did when he was younger.

And relationships had even less allure.

It was so much easier to take care of himself than to find somebody else who also had needs to fulfill. His dick didn't ask for cuddles afterward, or get upset if he wanted to break things off. It didn't sulk because he had to work late at the farm or tell him it hated his friends.

Quite the opposite. Right now his dick was very interested in his friend instead.

Shaking his head at himself, he turned his attention to the television, then winced when he realized the couple were getting it on. The man was unfastening her dress, button by button, kissing the soft skin on her back and damn if it didn't make him harder.

Her breath tickled his skin again and she let out a little moan. Dear God was she punishing him?

He needed to get out of here. Because this was just weird.

She was his friend. He wasn't attracted to her. Yes, she was beautiful, and sure, people used to make assumptions when they saw them together. She was one of the few people who could make North laugh, who could tease him without it annoying him.

One of the few people who knew all his secrets. Or most of them.

"Oh."

He turned to look at her. Her eyes were open and wide. She snatched her hand away from his waist.

"Sorry," she breathed. "I didn't mean to fall asleep on you. Tell me I didn't drool."

"You didn't." He adjusted himself. Thank God she wasn't looking down.

"You should have moved me," she told him, her cheeks pink.

"It's fine," he said, his voice thicker than he'd hoped. "You're exhausted. You should go to bed."

"Did they reconnect yet?" she asked him.

"Who?"

"Anne and Wentworth."

He shook his head, not understanding her question.

"In the movie," she said, giving him a strange smile. "Did they get back together?"

"Ah, yeah. I think so." He glanced at the screen.

"I'll have to watch the rest of it another time."

"You should probably rewind to the beginning," he said wryly. "You fell asleep after ten minutes."

"Rewind," she repeated, smiling. "Like I'm watching a video tape."

He loved that she was smiling. He couldn't get enough of it. "What else would you call it?"

She wrinkled her nose. "I don't know, old man."

He lifted a brow. "Less of the old. You're only two years

younger than me." He liked the way her eyes were lighting up. Damn, she was beautiful. His gaze dropped to her lips. Full, pink, so damn kissable.

What the heck, Winter?

He pulled her arm from around him, standing up, needing to put space between them. "I should go get the guest bedroom ready. Let you get some sleep."

"Oh sure. Okay." She sat up straight, lifting her arms up to stretch. "I guess it's been a long day, right?"

"You could say that."

"This wasn't exactly the wedding night I had planned," she murmured. And he felt his throat tighten, because he was so glad she wasn't with Shaun right now.

And yeah, that made him as much of an asshole as Amber's ex.

"Come on," he muttered. "Let's get you to bed."

She slid her hand into his and he tried to ignore how much he liked it. "Tell me something to stop me from thinking about what a mess I've made of my life."

"You haven't made a mess. You prevented one."

She lifted a brow. "Humor me. Come on, tell me something fun."

"I want to buy a helicopter."

Her mouth dropped open.

"For the farm. For harvesting. All the big Christmas tree farms have one."

"We're not getting a helicopter." Her brows pinched. "We're not made of money."

He bit down a smile because he'd distracted her. And yeah, he did want to buy a helicopter but that was a discussion for another day. He pushed open the guest bedroom door and pointed at the en suite. "There's a spare toothbrush in there. Along with some toothpaste."

"Thank you."

"And if you need anything, you know where I am."

"I do." She nodded.

"Come get me if you wake up in the middle of the night, okay? No more crying. Not in my house."

"It's my messed up wedding. I'll cry if I want to."

He reached for her face, cupping her jaw with his palm. "If you want to cry, come get me," he repeated.

"Okay." She looked at him for a moment, then threw her arms around his waist. Thank God he'd managed to get himself under control. "Thank you," she whispered against his chest. "For everything."

"Go get some sleep," he ordered, trying not to breathe her in.

"I owe you."

"Then let me buy a helicopter."

She started to laugh and he loved it.

"It's not going to happen." She pulled away and walked over to the bathroom, yanking the door open before stepping inside. He pulled the guest bedding out of the closet and made up the bed.

And then he left, making his way to his own room and stripping his clothes off to take a long shower.

But when he stepped inside the spray all he could think of was her flushed cheeks. Her soft lips. The way her breath felt against his skin.

Dammit, he needed to get laid. And in the meantime, he'd do it himself.

Because there was no way he was going to fall in lust with his best friend.

$\mathscr{F}$ 3 $\mathscr{F}$

"**O**kay, hear me out," Kelly said through the phone line. "I just saw Dolores and the apartment above the café is available. She says it's yours if you want it."

"Doesn't her son live there?" Amber asked. She was in her car that North had rescued from the Inn parking lot, driving to her house.

Or Shaun's house. *Whatever*. All she knew was that he'd asked for them to meet and she owed him that much.

"He moved out a month ago. She says it's yours if you want it."

"I do." Amber nodded, a wave of relief washing over her. She knew she wouldn't be homeless, but she hated relying on other people. "I can't stay at North's forever."

"Of course you can. You know he'd be happy to have you."

Yeah, he probably would. But she couldn't impose on him. He'd done enough for her already. The last thing he needed was for her to move into his spare bedroom.

"I'll call Dolores this afternoon," Amber said. "I just have to go to the house first."

"You picking up some things?" Kelly asked her.

"Yeah. And meeting with Shaun."

"Why?"

Amber turned left onto the road toward Marshall's Gap. When she and Shaun had agreed to move in together he'd persuaded her it was better for her to move into his place. Sure, it meant a thirty minute commute every day, but it had made him happy.

"Because he wants to talk and I owe him that much." He'd messaged her at five that morning begging for a chance to explain.

"You're not planning on getting back with him, are you?" Kelly asked..

"No. But we need to end things properly. Not in front of everybody in town." She was still mortified about that. "And we have to send the gifts back." Not to mention pay all the bills they owed. It was a giant mess and she had to start untangling it.

"Thank God." Kelly sighed. "Because I'd hate to have to lock you up in my beer cellar." She lifted a brow. "Though I would if I thought you were going back to that loser."

When Amber pulled into the space outside the house—the space that used to be hers—she noticed the curtains moving in the front room of the neighbor to the left. Everybody had to know about their wedding by now. There was nothing for it but to face the music. She grabbed her purse and stepped out of the car, taking a deep breath because she wasn't ready to see Shaun.

Wasn't sure she ever would be.

In the space of a day this place had gone from being her home to being bricks and mortar. She pulled her key out of her purse and then folded her fingers around it, using her other hand to press the doorbell.

"You doing okay?"

She looked to her left to see Ria, their single-mom neighbor, hanging out of the doorway.

"Hi." Amber attempted a smile. "As good as I can be. I'm guessing you heard what happened."

"Yep." Ria shot her a sympathetic glance. "And for what it's worth, I think you did the right thing. Last night was hell."

"Hell *here*?"

"Yep. Shaun brought everybody back. I had to call the cops at four AM." Ria grimaced. "If he does it again tonight I'm calling them again."

"I'm sorry."

"Not your fault," Ria told her. "Anyway, I'm late for work. Good luck, honey."

Amber had a feeling she was going to need it.

After a minute, it was obvious Shaun wasn't coming to answer the door. She knocked again and still there was nothing. And when she tried to call him there was no answer.

She'd walk away, but her things were in there. She needed clothes, she needed shampoo. And then there were the sentimental items. Photographs of her parents, the collection of snow globes her dad had given her every time he went away for business.

Taking a deep breath she slid the key in the lock, turning it open and stepping inside. Silence overwhelmed her as she looked around the white washed hallway.

"Shaun?"

There was no reply. She pulled her shoes off and walked into the kitchen. Every surface was covered with glasses and dishware, full of drinks and half-eaten food. For a moment she considered cleaning up, because she'd loved this kitchen.

But it wasn't hers. So she walked back into the hallway.

"Shaun?"

"Huh?"

He was upstairs. "It's me. You wanted to talk."

"I'm sick. Come back later."

Her heart sank. She wasn't sure she'd have the courage to come back a second time. She wanted to get this over with. End things properly.

Move on.

"I have to go to work." That wasn't quite true. She should be on her honeymoon right now. She'd taken two weeks off that North had been happy to cover. But since she wasn't married and she wasn't going to a beach in Hawaii, it only felt right to go and start her summer planting.

It was an anchor to a life that seemed to be drifting away from her.

"Christ." Shaun appeared at the top of the stairs. His hair was mussed up, there was a dark growth of beard on his jaw. He was wearing what looked like his wedding pants and nothing else. "What time is it?"

"Almost eleven."

He rubbed his eyes with the heels of his hands. "I need water," he muttered, stumbling down the stairs and brushing past her. He groaned when he walked into the kitchen.

"There's Advil in the cupboard," Amber told him. Old habits died hard. Shaun didn't blink, just opened the door and grabbed the bottle, dumping two pills out.

When he'd drunk the glass of water he poured, he turned to look at her. "You need to move all your things out by Saturday."

Thank God for Dolores' apartment. "Okay."

He blinked at her easy acquiescence. "Don't you want to know why?"

"I assume it's because you hate me and don't want any trace of me left in your house."

His nostrils flared. "Close. I'm leaving town. Kyle's moving in while I'm gone."

Amber blinked. "You're leaving?" Horror washed over her. "Because of me?"

"No, babe, not because of you. Because I'm free and I want to enjoy it. Dean and I are gonna do some traveling."

Oh. "You never mentioned traveling before."

"That's because you held me back. But I'm not letting you do that anymore. I'm gonna screw my way around the world, get a little taste of what I've been missing out on."

She didn't bother to point out that he already got more than a taste at the strip club.

He was leaning over the sink now, taking deep breaths. The whole kitchen stank of alcohol, making her stomach turn. She was afraid she'd start heaving.

"Can I pick up a few things now?" She had no idea why she was asking so nicely. "Then I'll arrange to have everything moved out by the weekend."

"By Saturday," Shaun said again.

"That's what I meant."

"Take what you want." He waved his hand. "I don't give a damn."

But she did. And she was only planning on taking what was hers. The things she had when she moved in, the clothes she'd bought since, and the few pieces of kitchenware she knew Shaun would never use.

"Do you know when you'll be back?" she asked him.

"Not for a while." He looked over his shoulder at her. "We're going to Thailand first. Then down to Australia."

"I hope you have a good time," she whispered. But he didn't reply. It felt like another end, and her heart hurt a little. She let out a long breath and walked to the hallway, opening the closet to grab her overnight bag.

She'd take enough for the next few days, then once she'd signed a lease with Dolores she'd move everything else out.

"I'm sorry," she whispered, but it wasn't loud enough for Shaun to hear.

She wasn't sure she wanted him to, anyway.

The sun was beating down as she drove to the Christmas Tree Farm. The smell of pine wafted through her open windows on a light breeze, filling her senses, giving her a sense of belonging she was so sorely missing.

She'd grown up on this farm. Her dad had built it from nothing to a thriving but small homestead that filled orders for local shops. But then he'd died when she was twelve years old and for the next ten years she and her mom had struggled to keep it open. By the time she graduated from college – with a degree in agriculture – the accounts were so far in the red it looked like they were going to lose the place.

And then North had bailed them out. Or more correctly, he'd become their major investor, working with them to build up their stock and widen their customer base. In the decade since, The Stone Christmas Tree Farm had become the number one supplier of trees in West Virginia, and their trees were shipped all along the east coast from New York to the Carolinas.

And yet it still felt like home. The two of them ran it together, and in the summer they only had a skeleton crew. It was mostly North and Amber who planted the new trees, who shaped the ones that would be cut and sold later that year.

She'd always loved this time of year on the farm. It was when it felt a part of her. Filled her with warmth.

Made her feel like she still had something to cling to.

The farm shop was empty when she let herself in. They only used it as a base in the summer for their paperwork and orders – they wouldn't open it to the public until October. She looked out in the distance, spotting the ATV North used at the far end of the six-year-old trees. She grabbed the keys to the second ATV and climbed on, feeling the wind rush through her hair as she drove down the aisles between trees.

He looked up when he heard the engine, a smile pulling at his lips. He was using a blade to shape the trees. It was old fashioned but the only way to get the runaway branches under control. He swept the long, thick blade down in an easy movement and tiny sprigs of pine went flying.

"You okay?" he asked as she climbed off the ATV.

"Yeah. I've found somewhere to live." She'd visited Dolores before she came to the farm. Taken a quick look around the apartment and agreed on a price. The key was already in her pocket. One of the bonuses of living in a small town – she didn't have to provide two references and a print out of her bank balance because Dolores knew she was good for the rent.

"Dolores's place?"

"Kelly told you."

"Yep." He lifted a brow. "You don't have to move out, you know."

"I know," she said softly. "And I'm grateful. But I'm also thirty-four years old. I should be standing on my own two feet by now."

He shrugged and swept the blade down again, his shoulder muscles knotting beneath his thin t-shirt. Her stomach did a little flip and she rolled her eyes at herself.

Okay, he was a fine looking man. But she was supposed to get married yesterday. Now wasn't the time to be ogling his muscles.

"Is it okay if I use the van on Saturday?" she asked him. "Shaun needs me to move my things out by then."

He stopped sweeping and looked at her. "I hope you told

him to go fuck himself and that you'll move out at your own convenience."

"I didn't, actually." She bit down a smile at his outburst. "He's going to travel and Kyle's moving in, so Saturday it is."

"I'll help you. We all will."

"I don't have that much stuff."

He lifted a brow at her and she tried to not smile again. He knew her so well. She wasn't a hoarder, but she had a lot of things. "Okay." She nodded. "Thank you. I'll buy you all a few drinks at the tavern afterward."

"Sounds good to me." He winked at her, and she felt it again. That little stomach flip. It had to be a reaction to running away from her own wedding. She wasn't attracted to North. She hadn't been for years.

"Did Shaun say where he was going?" North asked her.

"He and Dean are flying to Thailand this weekend." She still felt weird about it. Guilty, really. He was leaving because of her.

And yet there was relief, too. Because she wouldn't have to bump into him in town. The space between them was what she needed.

"For how long?"

"He didn't say. I got the impression it would be weeks not days. Months, maybe."

"Halle-fucking-lujah."

"Shut up, Winter." She narrowed her eyes at him, but there was still a smile playing at her mouth.

"Yeah, well I would if you'd stop bothering me," he teased. "Some of us have work to do."

"I have work to do, too," she protested. "I've got seedlings waiting in the greenhouse to be planted."

"So what are you doing here, talking to me about your ex?"

She rolled her eyes at him. "Sorry for boring you."

"Apology accepted." His expression was soft. "By the way, you're gonna be okay. More than okay."

Her throat tightened. "You think so?"

"I know so." His lip quirked. "You've done the right thing. The hardest part is over."

She let out a long breath. "I hope so." Because she never wanted to go through that again.

"Go play with your tree babies," he told her, that smile still playing around his lips. "I'm busy."

She touched her fingers to her brow. "Yes, sir." Walking over to her ATV, she slung her leg across it and started the engine.

And as she drove away from her gorgeous but aggravating best friend, she couldn't help but grin.

He was right. Things were going to get better. The sun was shining and life would be good again. She just had to get through the next few days.

4

"Honey, can you talk to your dad?" North's mom asked him three days later, her voice echoing down the phone line. "He's in one of his moods and I can't shake him out of it."

North glanced at his watch. It was almost midnight, the same time as it was in Florida where his parents lived. "What happened?"

"It started this morning. The people next door bought this new sprinkler system, and it keeps hitting our path. I told Daddy they were watering our yard for free, but he thinks it's rude."

"He's pissed about a sprinkler?" North didn't know why this surprised him. His dad could get riled up by anything given the chance.

"He's more so angry because it's an expensive sprinkler system. He thinks Rhian and Geoff bought it to show off."

Yeah, that sounded like his dad. He always thought the world revolved around him. As kids, North and his two younger brothers had tiptoed around his dad's bad moods, but it was North who'd suffered most from them.

"Mom..." He sighed loudly. How many times did they have to have this conversation?

"I know, I should leave him. You've told me enough times. But I'm not going to, North. Your father's a good man. He just has his... problems."

"He won't do anything about them unless you tell him it's enough," North told her. "Come back here. There's enough space for you on the ranch."

"Oh honey, I wish I could."

But she wouldn't. North knew that much. "I'll talk to him. Where is he?"

"In the basement. Don't tell him I asked you to call."

"I won't." He took a deep breath. "Do you feel safe?"

"Don't be silly. You know he wouldn't hurt me."

He knew nothing of the sort. He'd hurt North enough times until North got big enough to hurt him back.

"You'd tell me if he did, right?"

"He never has, honey."

North tried to hide his sigh. "I'll speak to him."

"Thank you," she whispered, and a moment later, the line went dead.

Leaning back on the chair he'd been sitting in, contemplating going to bed, North brought up his father's contact on his phone, hitting the green call button. His dad picked up after three rings.

"It's late. Why are you calling me now?" his dad grumbled.

It's great to talk to you, too, Dad. "I just wanted to check in. You doing okay?"

There was a pause. Then a huff. "Not really. The Sandersons have been ruining my lawn."

"What have they been doing?"

"They got a sprinkler. It hits the edges of my grass."

"That sucks. What are you going to do about it?" North asked him, weariness suffusing his body. He wanted to go to bed. Wanted to not be the one that everybody called when there was a problem.

Wanted to take a hundred years to sleep.

"What *can* I do? If I complain they'll think I'm crazy. Even your mom thinks I'm making a mountain out of a molehill. She keeps going on about us getting free water for our grass. But she doesn't understand, I water the grass when *I* want to, not when the Sandersons see fit. It doesn't belong to them."

"Maybe you can talk to them tomorrow, suggest they change the angle of the spray," North suggested. "They probably don't even know it's happening. Imagine how annoyed they'll be when they find out they've been paying to water your lawn."

For the first time his dad chuckled. "Ha, yeah, I hadn't thought of that. Sanderson'll be fuming. He hates wasting money." There was a pause. "What was it you called about again?"

"Mom's birthday," North said quickly. "I wanted some ideas for a gift."

"It's not her birthday until next month."

"I know. I just want to choose something nice," North said smoothly. "Any ideas?"

"I'll have to think." His dad sounded calmer.

"Thanks. I'd really appreciate it. Everything else okay?"

"Why wouldn't it be?"

"Just checking," North said lightly. "I haven't heard from you for a while."

"Yeah, well, I'm a busy man."

North looked at his watch. Just talking to his dad for a minute was exhausting. He'd agreed to meet Amber at her old house first thing to help her move out. Gabe and Josh were helping, too. It was going to be a long day.

"I should go to bed," North told him. "It's late. Maybe you should head upstairs to Mom."

"How do you know I'm in the basement?" his dad asked suspiciously. "I didn't tell you I was down here."

"Your voice sounds different. There's an echo. I just assumed that's where you were," North said smoothly.

"Yeah well, whatever. Good night, I'll call you about your mom."

North ended the call and stared at his phone for a minute, before he tapped out a message to his mom to call if there were any more problems.

Then he pushed himself up from the chair and walked to his bedroom, opening the door and stepping inside. It was deadly quiet in here, the same way every room in his house was. Maybe he should get a dog.

Or maybe he should go to sleep and enjoy the fact that he wasn't responsible for anything else, including an animal. He liked living alone. Liked not having to make sure everybody was happy or having to step in to protect them when things went wrong.

Better to be single than end up being like his dad, making everybody's life a misery. Of that he was damned certain.

Somebody had put a country song on the jukebox, and in the corner of the Tavern there were a group of girls Amber remembered from school, dancing and laughing as they raised their cocktails to the roof. A few times they looked over at her and she knew they were talking about her wedding. Or lack of it. She was getting used to that. And hopefully it would pass soon enough and they'd find something else to gossip about.

Every booth was stuffed full, and the line at the bar was three people deep. Through the gap she could see Kelly looking harassed as she tried to work out who to serve next.

They didn't do table service in the Winterville Tavern. It was an old fashioned bar, relying on everybody lining up and taking their turn. But from the grumbles Amber could hear as she joined the throng of people waiting for drinks the taking a turn thing wasn't working.

Kelly looked up from pouring a pint, her eyes catching Amber's through the gap in the crowd and she mouthed 'help!'

"Where's Darla?" Amber mouthed back.

"She quit."

Ouch. Usually the Tavern wouldn't be this busy in the summer months, but more and more visitors were coming to the region at this time of year, thanks to the summer promotions Alaska was running at the Inn, and the sports that the ski resort had during the warm months at the lake.

Kelly was working all the hours she could, as well as taking care of her son and her father. Amber couldn't help but feel sorry for her.

"Excuse me," Amber muttered, pushing her way to the front.

"Wait your turn," a woman in front of her said, pushing her shoulder out to stop Amber from getting through.

"I'm not waiting for a drink," Amber muttered. "I work here."

Yes, it was a small lie, but it was like she'd said a magic word. The bodies immediately parted, giving her a free run to the bar.

"Hey," she said to Kelly who looked like she was about to cry. "Need some help?"

"I would kill you for some," Kelly told her, looking at Amber like she was her savior. "Get behind here."

Amber walked through the gap in the counter and took the apron Kelly was holding out, fastening it around her waist. Her first order was three local ales plus three glasses of wine. Easy enough.

She hadn't bartended since college, when it was the only way to pay the rent. Sure, she'd hung around here with Kelly a lot, but never on this side of the bar.

It took twenty minutes of teamwork to cut the line down to something manageable. Amber was breathless, but damn it was fun. Kelly was an ace at bartending, flirting with the men, complementing the women, all while pouring drinks at lightning speed.

"Can I get the drinks for the Winters now?" Amber asked her. She'd promised them all a drink for helping her move. The family was sitting in a booth at the far end of the Tavern. North was leaning over, telling some kind of story that was making his family laugh uproariously.

He was like a woman magnet. It was great for business at the Christmas Tree Farm, but sometimes she felt weird about it. Like now. She wanted to tell them all to look at something else. Not her best friend.

Ugh. Now she was getting possessive. It must be catching.

"They're on the house," Kelly said. "Thank you for your help, sweetie. I couldn't do it without you."

"Any time." Amber told her, and Kelly hugged her tight. "All you have to do is ask."

Kelly looked at her carefully. "Do you mean that?"

"What?" Amber was still smiling.

"The *anytime* part. Because I've got a job opening and you'd be perfect at it."

"I already have a job," Amber reminded her.

"I know that," Kelly said. "But you don't work on the weekends in the summer and that's when I'd need you. Just until I manage to recruit somebody full time, or until the seasonal staff starts in November."

She leaned over and took another order, grabbing two glasses from the shelf above the bar. "Nobody seems to want to work nights or weekends anymore, and I can't compete with the pay at the Winterville Inn or the ski resort. The tips are better here, but you have to work for them, if you know what I mean."

Amber opened her mouth to tell Kelly thanks, but no thanks. She'd had fun helping but...

"Okay." The word escaped before she could think it through. But then what else did she have to do on weekends now that she and Shaun had split and she didn't have a wedding to plan? She'd spent the last week staring at a wall and wanting to punch her own face in.

Working here could be a welcome distraction. And Kelly was a friend, she'd feel like an ass letting her down.

"Okay as in yes?" Kelly asked, looking Amber in the eye.

"Yes. You're on. I'll help out, but only until you find somebody new," Amber told her.

"I love you!" Kelly flung her arms around Amber. "You won't regret it. And if you wear the right outfits you'll get tips like you'll never believe. Just make them low and sexy."

Amber tried to hide a smile. She didn't need tips. She wasn't doing it for the money. But maybe she could sneak any tips into Kelly's jar. She was a single mom, and although she owned the Tavern — or her family did — Amber knew sometimes she found it hard to make ends meet.

When Amber had poured the drinks for her friends, she stacked them on a wooden tray and carried them over to the booth, impressing herself with her steady hand. North immediately stood to help her, but she shook her head. "If you touch this I'm probably gonna spill them all."

She slid the tray onto the table and started handing out the drinks. Beers for North, Gabe, and Mason. Vodkas for Alaska and Everley, and a glass of wine for Holly. Holly's husband, Josh, and Everley's husband, Dylan, were both at home on babysitting duty.

"Where's your drink?" North asked once everyone was holding their drinks.

"I'm helping Kelly behind the bar. Darla quit."

"Oh no," Alaska groaned. She knew how hard it was to recruit new staff. "Poor Kelly. Has she put any feelers out?"

"Yeah but no takers. I said I'd help until she finds somebody."

North blinked. "You're working behind the bar?"

"Only on weekends," she told him. "You don't have to worry, I'll still be at the farm during the week."

"I wasn't worried. Not about the farm anyway," he told her. "Is it money? Do you need more now that you're on your own? We can take a look at the books."

"It's not about money," Amber told him. "It's about helping Kelly. And about me not sitting at home on my own every weekend. Working here will make sure I get out." She was already feeling better. Bit by bit she was coming back to life again.

"I think it's a great idea," Holly said warmly. "I know Kelly will be grateful."

"So will all of Winterville," Gabe agreed. "We might get served within the first hour of getting here now."

"Don't be rude," Alaska said, shaking her head. "Kelly does her best."

From the corner of her eye Amber could see the line at the bar starting to lengthen again. "I should go back," she said. "You guys let me know when you want another drink."

"You already bought us this one," North said. He hadn't sat down yet, so she had to lift her head to look up at him. "You don't need to buy another."

"This round is on Kelly. For stealing me away," Amber told him.

North looked her in the eye for a minute. He wasn't smiling, he wasn't doing anything really, except looking.

And yet it made her heart hammer against her chest.

"Take it easy," he said softly. "You've had a long day."

She leaned up to kiss his cheek. "Don't worry about me. I've got this."

5

"I always thought you and Amber would end up together one day," Everley said to North. Then she wrinkled her nose. "Well, I did until she ended up getting engaged to Shaun."

North frowned. "Why would you say that?"

"You're best friends. You're both good looking and you make each other laugh." She shrugged. "All that's missing is the sex. I guess I thought there was more to your friendship than met the eye."

"Yeah, well you were wrong."

North glanced over at the bar. Amber was leaning over, smiling at a man who was giving her his order. Then she looked across the tavern to where he was sitting, her eyes meeting his. Her smile widened, and he smiled back.

"See?" Everley lifted a brow. "You two would be couple goals."

"There's one slight problem," North told his cousin. "We're not into each other."

"Oh, shut up." She shook her head. "You're into her. All we ever hear about is Amber this and Amber that. Come on, tell me you haven't imagined what it'd be like to be with her."

Thank God the rest of his family were busy discussing a movie they'd seen last weekend.

"It's never gonna happen," he told her.

"Why not?" Everley sounded sad.

"Because we want different things. Amber wants a long-term relationship, kids one day. I don't."

"Yes you do." Everley narrowed her eyes.

"You think you know me better than I know myself?"

Everley ran her finger around the rim of her drink. "No, I think I can tell when you're lying to yourself. I've known you my whole life, North. I've never met a man who cares about people as much as you do. You just try to hide it behind this gruff bravado."

He shook his head, smiling. "I'm not hiding anything. I am what I am."

Everley rolled her eyes. "Amber's a catch. You were pissed when Shaun proposed to her. I saw that with my own eyes."

"I was angry because she deserves better. And I was proved right, by the way."

"Somebody better like you?" Everley asked him.

"Can we change the subject? Tell me how Finn is doing."

Everley lit up at the mention of her eleven-month-old son. "He's wonderful. And exhausting. Now that he's crawling I feel like I've run a marathon by the end of every day. But then when he's asleep I can't stop staring at him for hours. I never thought I'd be that sort of person."

"I knew you would be," North said. "And you know what? That's what Amber longs for, too. And she won't get it from me, so that's the end of that."

"I think you're making a mistake."

He knew better than to mess up a wonderful friendship with messy feelings. Yes, he loved Amber as much as he loved anybody. But love didn't mean shit if the two of you wanted different things. Watching his mom deal with his dad showed him that.

"She'll get snapped up soon enough and you'll be pissed all over again," Everley said.

North shook his head and took another mouthful of beer, annoyed that Everley had hit him right in the weak spot. Not that Amber was interested in guys right now. She'd already told him she'd sworn them off for life, though he knew it was just the sadness talking.

But Everley was right. One day Amber would try again. And maybe he would be pissed. But he had no right to be. He should want her to be happy.

And he did. Just not with an asshole like Shaun.

By one AM the Tavern was almost empty. And every muscle in Amber's body ached. She thought longingly of that unused gym membership again. She'd thought she was fit, thanks to the physicality of running the farm, but working behind the bar used all different kinds of muscles. Even her cheeks ached from smiling too much. She was going to be useless in the morning.

At least she had six days to recover before doing this all over again.

During a quiet moment, Kelly had gone over the Tavern's schedule with her. Amber would come in at six on Fridays and Saturdays and work until close. Which was usually one, but could stretch to two or three if they couldn't get people to leave.

"Which happens more than you'd think," Kelly told her. "And I don't really mind because the later it gets, the more the tips flow."

"Don't you get exhausted?" Amber asked her. "Doesn't Cole get up early even on weekends?" She'd heard Kelly complain that her son never slept in.

"Yeah. But he just crawls in bed with me and puts on the television. I can sleep through anything after working here." Kelly shrugged. "Then we get up at eleven and I run around the house like a chicken on acid trying to get all the housework done."

"If you ever need me to close up on my own, I can do that," Amber told her. "Give you a break."

"You're such a sweetie," Kelly said. "But I've got it. Now let's start cleaning up. If you can bring all the empty glasses over I'll start tidying the bar. Hopefully we'll be out of here soon."

"Sure." Amber grabbed a tray and walked over to the nearest table, loading the dirty glasses onto it. When they were all on the tray she grabbed the cleaning spray from the pocket of her apron and covered the table with it, then wiped it over with a fresh cloth.

"You need help?"

She almost jumped at the sound of the low voice in her ear. Turning, she saw North standing there, looking amused at her shock.

"I thought you'd all left," she said. "You came over and said goodbye."

"The others left but I thought I'd stay. Walk you home."

She blinked. "I live across the square. I don't think anything's going to happen to me between here and there." That was one advantage of moving into the apartment above the Cold Fingers Café. It was less than a two minute walk to her brand-new weekend job. It wasn't exactly luxurious up there, though. The rooms were small and the iron staircase up to the door was rickety and steep. But it was somewhere to call home.

"Yeah, well a lot can happen in a few hundred yards," North muttered.

"This is Winterville," she pointed out. "Nothing happens."

He lifted a brow and she knew exactly what that meant. Stubborn North had arrived. The one who was like a rock, and everything you said would bounce back to you.

"Okay. While you're waiting you can make yourself useful," she said, thrusting the cloth and spray in his hands. "I'll clear the glasses, you wipe the tables."

His lips twitched. "Yes, ma'am."

"You're enjoying this, aren't you?" she said, picking up the tray.

"Enjoying what?"

"Me not arguing with you for once." Truth was she was too tired to argue. If North wanted to waste his time by hanging around the Tavern until she was finished he could have at it.

"I always enjoy arguing with you," he said smoothly as she moved onto the next table, stacking the glasses higher on her tray. "Especially when I always win."

"You don't always win."

He smirked. "I beg to differ."

Ignoring him, she started to load the dishwasher, pulling out the trays and stacking the glasses inside.

"I see your guard dog's still here," Kelly said, looking amused.

Amber looked up at her. "What?"

Kelly inclined her head at the tables. "North. I should have known he'd stay. There's no way he'd take the risk of you walking alone."

"He's just being a friend," Amber said.

Kelly gave a chuckle. "Sure. The same way he's a friend when he tells guys to stop flirting with you."

Amber blinked. "He doesn't do that. And anyway, who do I flirt with? I've just run out on my own wedding."

"I'm talking about before Shaun. And even when you were with Shaun he was in a permanent bad mood. I couldn't figure out whether it was because he didn't think Shaun was good enough or if it was because he wanted to get into your panties."

"Ugh." Amber grimaced. "Can you stop?"

"Honey, we all know men and women can't be friends. Not like you and North think you are. You gonna tell me you've never thought about it? Never looked at those thick muscles of his and wondered what they'd be liked wrapped around your body? Because you'd be the only woman in Winterville who hasn't."

"Of course I haven't. I wouldn't have agreed to marry Shaun if I felt like that."

It didn't stop an image of North from flashing into her mind. Him topless the way he often was in the summer, a blade in his hand as he shaped the trees. His skin was naturally tan, his muscles coiled and twisted the way they could only be from hard work. No gym could sculpt a body the way North's was.

Her cheeks flamed. She let out a long breath.

"You okay?" Kelly asked her.

"Um yeah. Fine. And no, there's nothing going on with us. There never will be. I've decided to stay an old maid until I die."

Kelly bit down a smile. "Okay. I hear you."

Taking a deep breath, Amber stood and grabbed the tray again, walking out of the bar area and back to the tables that still needed to be cleared.

North was waiting for her, still holding the cloth and spray. "You may want to hurry up," he suggested, his voice light. "Otherwise you're not gonna make it home until morning."

She looked up at him, taking in the dark shadow of his beard growth across the strong lines of his jaw. His hair was cut short, the way he always preferred it in summer, and she could see the scar he'd had since he was a child across his brow.

But it was his lips she couldn't stop looking at. Full, sculpted, the kind of lips that you knew would kiss you until you were breathless.

Why? Why was she thinking that? She wanted to slap herself.

"Amber?"

"Yeah?" Her eyes were wide.

"Aren't you going to argue with me?"

"What about?"

"I told you to hurry up. You're supposed to snap back at me and tell me you'll take your damn sweet time and I'll have to live with it."

"Okay." She nodded, reloading the tray with glasses. "Yeah, that."

He gave her a quizzical look. "You sure you're okay?"

"I..." She took a deep breath. "You're right. I need to hurry. I'm tired and I need to get some sleep." She piled the glasses faster. She needed to get home, where she could be alone because Kelly's stupid words had discombobulated her. Her friend was wrong. North didn't look at her like he wanted to get in her panties.

And now she was picturing him tracing the fragile lace of the white lingerie she was wearing with his practiced fingers, curling them around the fabric and yanking them from her body.

Shaun never did that. Nobody ever had. But North was strong. He was passionate. And he had a caring heart he didn't want anybody else to know about. She needed to stop this train of thought, now. She literally just ran away from her own wedding. It was just a physical reaction to being single once more, that was all.

The one thing she knew was that she didn't need to make any more bad decisions.

"While you're here, big boy, can you help me change a cask?" Kelly asked, her eyes dancing as she watched North clean the next table.

"Sure." He shrugged. "You still keep the spares in the basement."

"Yep, I do. If you bring it up I'll show you how to attach it to the pump." Kelly was grinning, and as North walked over to the door that led to the basement stairs, she turned to Amber and lifted a brow.

"I know what you're doing," Amber said.

"What?" Kelly's expression was the epitome of innocence. "I'm just asking a strong man for help."

"You just want to watch his muscles flex." The way all the women did when they came to watch North chopping wood. But this time Amber felt different.

Almost... jealous?

"The nights can get lonely when I get home." Kelly shrugged. "Don't blame me for needing a little visual of a hot guy to keep me company." Her smile was so big Amber could count her teeth. "And I don't know why you're being so pissy about it. He's just a friend, right?"

6

The skies were clear and blue, the sun a golden disc of fire warming up the town as Amber loaded her truck at the back of the café with a cooler full of food and drinks, along with a blanket and a chair. Five weeks had passed since she fled her vows and changed her life forever, and it felt like she was finally getting settled into her new way of life.

Today was one of those glorious early summer days that most visitors to Winterville didn't get to see. The town was famous for its snow and festive displays. But in the summer, it was beautiful in a whole other way.

She was wearing a bikini and some denim shorts, her hair scraped back into a bun, because it was too warm to have it tumbling around her shoulders. Climbing into the cab of her truck, the heat of the small space immediately hit her, so she turned on the engine and opened the windows to let the breeze in.

Not that there was much, but her air-conditioning needed a repair and she'd forgotten to take it to the garage. She'd been too busy working at the tree farm and Tavern. But she was pleased that she'd kept herself busy.

Shaun and Dean were in Phuket, according to Kelly who knew everything about everybody. She'd also told Amber they were planning on traveling for at least the rest of the year.

That's all she knew, and all she wanted to know. By the time Shaun came back, whenever that was, hopefully the bitterness between them would have abated.

She backed out of the space behind the Cold Fingers Café. A day at the lake was just what she needed to take her mind off things.

Some jet skiing, swimming, and lazing on the beach that skimmed the edge of the sparkling water. Later, they'd barbecue and watch the sun as it dropped below the horizon before they all packed up and headed home.

Yeah, this was what most people didn't get to see about Winterville. How relaxed it was in the summer.

How it belonged to the locals for those few precious months and how they made the most of it.

It only took ten minutes to drive to the lake. She parked in the lot next to all the trucks and cars she recognized, huddled together the same way the Winter family would be huddled on the beach. Pulling the cooler out of her truck bed, she went to join her friends on the sand.

North jumped up and took the cooler from her, kissing her cheek. Damn, he smelled good. He always did. Like pine trees and musk and something indefinable and yet completely North.

And yeah, her body reacted to him. It was aggravating and all Kelly's fault. Since she'd made those comments about North wanting in her panties, Amber had felt weird whenever he was around. She was behaving weird, too. In the last four weeks – since Kelly had teased her about North, Amber's body felt tingly whenever he was close.

At least they were surrounded by people now. All his cousins were here – sans Kris, North's brother, who was currently living in London. And as soon as they saw her they rushed over to hug her, to help her unload the rest of her truck and then to pour her a drink. Candace and Finn – Holly and Everley's children – were here too, Candace was making sandcastles with a bucket and her hands, while Finn was crawling around the blanket Everley had set up.

"Beer?" Gabe asked her, rifling in his cooler.

"No thanks. I'm driving."

"Amber doesn't drink anymore," North said wryly. "Watching Shaun get wasted put her off."

"I'm just trying to be healthy," she told him, grinning. "If I want to find a new man I need to get this body in shape."

He rolled his eyes at her. Okay, she could do this. Pretend that Kelly had never said anything. That she felt nothing toward him but friendship.

That the sight of his bare chest in front of her wasn't making her body ache.

"I'm going for a swim," North muttered. "Who's coming?"

"Me." Gabe pulled his shirt over his head. "Nic, you wanna get wet?"

"Nope. I'm going to sit here and ogle your body from afar," she teased.

"Your loss, baby."

In the end, the guys all went into the glass-clear lake, laughing and splashing as they goofed around. North and Gabe, along with Josh, Dylan, and Mason. Amber joined the girls and children on the sand, leaning down to tickle Finn's cheeks.

"You sure you don't want a drink?" Holly asked Amber. "We have lots."

"Nah, I'll get some water soon. I brought a big bottle." She really was trying to get healthy. She'd even dug out her gym membership card.

She hadn't used it. But still...

"You don't need to lose weight you know. You're beautiful."

Amber smiled at Holly. "Well thank you. I'm just enjoying feeling good about myself. It's been a while, you know?"

Holly nodded. "Yeah. Bad relationships can make you feel bad about yourself."

"Oh yeah." Nicole nodded. "I had one of those myself. Best thing I did was leave. I just hate that it took him cheating on me to do it."

"Yeah, but look who you ended up with," Amber teased. "Gabe is a catch."

"Right?" Nicole let out a sigh as she stared at him throwing a ball straight at North. "Damn we got us some good men."

"Easy on the eye, too," Amber said, wryly, as North dove under the water and made Gabe laugh, before surfacing again, his hair slicked back, his face splitting into a grin.

"That's us Winters," Everley said. "Born and bred to be perfect."

Amber chuckled, because Everley wasn't far from wrong. They were a beautiful family, thanks to the genes they'd inherited from their grandmother. With their golden hair and tan skin, Everley and her sister, Alaska, looked like they'd be at home on a movie set. And then there was Holly whose dark hair was a perfect contrast to her striking features.

Candace shouted and they all looked over. Finn had crawled off the blanket and over to her sandcastle, which he was trying to grab with his chubby fist. Everley rolled her eyes and grabbed him, pulling him onto her lap and he started smacking his lips as though he was hungry.

"You still nursing him?" Holly asked her.

"Yep, though we're down to two a day now," Everley said,

distracting Finn with a toy she grabbed from her bag. "And I got my first period this month." She grimaced. "I miss not having to worry about them."

"Ugh I'd love to not worry about periods," Alaska said. "Mine are just getting worse.

"Wait until you have a baby," Holly warned. "It's like Armageddon straight after."

Amber caught Nicole's eye. They both grimaced.

"And you can stop looking so smug," Holly told Nicole. "I know you and Gabe will have a houseful of kids."

"Not yet. I think we'll wait a little while longer," Nicole told her. "You've made me want to be celibate for life."

Amber sniggered.

"What I want to know is if you get more regular after pregnancy," Alaska said. "I really hate getting taken by surprise."

"I'm always regular," Amber said, shrugging.

"I wish I was," Nicole said. "I'm always getting mine at the worst of times. Poor Gabe ends up having to buy me tampons and then has to call to go through the entire shelf to decide which ones are the best."

"I can't imagine Gabe buying tampons," Holly said, looking amused. "He's too squeamish."

Everley started describing the day she started her own period and Kris had to go find their grandma because she couldn't leave the bathroom. Amber leaned back on her blanket, zoning out a little, because the sun felt too good and the guys were swimming in the lake and maybe, just maybe, she was busy watching them.

"You okay?" Holly whispered to her.

Amber pulled her eyes away from North. "Yeah. Just tired. We had a late one at the Tavern last night."

"Are you enjoying working there?" Alaska asked her.

"Yeah, it's fun. Being with Kelly is always a blast." She was loving spending time with her friend.

"She's hilarious," Alaska agreed. "And I hear North's been walking you home every evening as well."

"Yep." It wasn't a one-off. He arrived just before close most nights, taking a spray and cloth from Kelly before cleaning the tables. She kind of liked it.

"Oh Lord, it's like a real-life cologne ad," Nicole said, fanning herself dramatically.

The guys were all walking out of the lake, their chests gleaming, their hair wet, their shorts plastered to their legs.

Amber's gaze swept over North's muscled calves, taking in the dark hair smattered over his skin, the thick muscles, the blue shorts that were so wet they revealed everything.

Damn.

Warmth suffused her as she allowed her gaze to rise up. Past the waistline of his shorts, low on his hips, and then to his flat stomach and the thin line of hair there.

By the time her eyes reached his face her whole body was overheating. Not least because she shouldn't be ogling her best friend.

And then she realized he was looking right at her, his smile crooked like he could read her mind.

Somebody threw a towel at him – Gabe, probably. North caught it easily and rubbed it over his chest and then through his hair, leaving the strands mussed and pointing in different directions. He ran his fingers through his wet hair to push it out of his face, squatting on his haunches to look at her.

"Okay?"

She nodded.

And then he winked and shook his wet hair over her and everything felt normal again.

The sun was halfway through her descent to the horizon and the beach had thinned out. Everley and Dylan had left earlier with Finn when he'd started to get sleepy, and Holly and Josh had taken Candace home less than an hour later. Alaska and Mason were having dinner with Mason's brother, Ty, who was home from college for the summer, so they were packing up their cooler.

"Can you believe this place will be covered in snow soon?" Nicole said, pulling a t-shirt over her bikini top as she sat on the blanket next to Gabe.

"And we'll be working nonstop." He pulled her into his arms, nestling her between his legs. "So let's enjoy the summer while we can."

"Some of us are working like crazy already," North pointed out. Though summer at the Christmas Tree Farm wasn't as full-on as the festive period, he and Amber were still working every day. Planting trees, ordering new samples, shaping the trees they'd be selling this winter. And it was mostly just the two of them without their seasonal staff to help, so they didn't get a break from morning until evening.

A cool breeze danced in from the lake and Amber shivered.

"You cold?" North asked.

"Yeah. I have a sweater in my truck. I'll go get it in a sec."

"Come here." He held his arms out to her. She smiled and crawled over to where he was sitting, nestling her back against his chest. He curled his arms around her and she let her head tip back, her body enjoying the heat of his skin against hers.

He kissed the crown of her head and it felt good. She let herself relax into him and he held her tighter.

The sun was a ball of orange now, the color staining the still lake in an amber hue. Some kids on the far side of the beach were building a fire, laughing at each other as they struggled to carry logs from the surrounding trees. North trailed his fingers down her arms, and her body responded, her nipples hardening.

She was getting used to this weird response to his touch. She didn't even bother to wriggle out of his hold. Maybe she liked this feeling. Maybe it was a distraction from everything else in her life.

Whatever. Let him touch. She craved human contact and knew it didn't mean anything more than that.

From the corner of her eye, she could see Nicole and Gabe laying on their blanket together, their eyes closed. Had they fallen asleep? She wasn't sure.

North put his hands on her stomach, pushing her t-shirt up so his palms were flat against her bare skin. His fingertips brushed the waistband of her shorts, and warmth pooled between her legs.

Did he know he was having this effect on her? She didn't dare crane her head to look at him. She didn't want to break this spell, whatever it was. It felt too good, too exciting.

Amber leaned harder against his chest, and he kissed the soft skin between her ear and neck. She waited, breathless, to see what he'd do next.

And he kissed her again. This time at the dip between her neck and her shoulder. Every part of her body felt like it was on fire. He nudged the fabric of her t-shirt away with his nose, then kissed her shoulder, his fingers tracing a line along the skin right above her waistband.

Then he moved them lower.

"North." It was just a breath.

"You want me to stop?" His voice was thick.

"No," she managed to squeak.

"Then hush."

He wanted her quiet. To not disturb Gabe and Nicole, who were definitely asleep. And yeah, with the way they were sitting nobody could see where his hand was. But she knew.

It was almost where she needed it. So close yet so far away.

"You *should* tell me to stop," he whispered, pushing one finger beneath her waistband. He paused, waiting, but she shook her head. Wasn't she supposed to be quiet?

"Don't stop," she managed. She could feel the thick ridge of his excitement against her back.

He breathed into her ear and flicked the button of her shorts open, then pushed his hand inside. It was tight, because every part of him was big, but then she felt him brush against her bathing suit bottoms and her body shuddered.

Then he slid his hands underneath them, his finger finding the part of her that needed him most.

She couldn't remember the last time she felt this turned on. Couldn't remember a single touch from a finger sending her pulse soaring to the sky. He circled her most sensitive part, making her body clench with need. His fingers were practiced, setting a rhythm that could only end in one thing. He placed an open mouthed kiss on her neck as her breath quickened.

She could feel the pleasure pooling in her belly. Her nerve endings were on fire as North slid two fingers inside her, his thumb maintaining the steady circling his fingers had stopped.

Her thighs clenched. "North…" she whispered, placing all her weight against him. He kissed her neck again and it sent a million shivers through her. She was close, so close, her hips matching the cadence of his touch, his free arm wrapped around her waist to keep her steady.

"Christ, where am I?"

Her eyes widened in horror as Gabe sat up. North slowly withdrew his hand, putting his arm over her waist to hide the fact that her shorts were gaping open.

"You fell asleep. You snore like a pig, by the way," North said.

How could he talk? How could he say anything? She felt like her world just tipped upside down.

"I don't fucking snore. Nic, on the other hand..." Gabe slowly released his hold on his wife, sitting up and stretching his arms. He finally looked over at Amber and North. "You two look cozy."

"Amber's freezing," North told Gabe, his voice easy. He was holding her tight, and she was thankful for it. She felt like a ragdoll, like she'd fall to the side if he let her go. "We would've left but we thought somebody might come and rob your sleepy asses."

"I'm grateful for your protection," Gabe said, a grin in his voice. Leaning over Nicole, he shook her gently. "Baby? Time to wake up."

"Uggh," Nicole moaned.

"Come on, sleepy," Gabe whispered, a smile playing on his lips. "Let's get you home and back to bed."

"Don't make promises you can't keep, Winter," she growled.

"Oh, I intend to keep this one. You look hot in that bikini."

She finally sat up, blinking the sleep from her eyes. While the two of them were busy talking to each other, Amber felt North carefully button her shorts back up. "We should be getting home, too," he said, his tone light. "Let's pack up."

She finally turned to look at him, and he stared back at her, almost innocently. "Um yeah, okay." She nodded.

Between the four of them it took a couple of minutes to pack up their coolers, roll up the blankets, and make sure nobody had left any trash on their section of beach. In the distance she could see flames flicker from a fire.

North took her cooler and his, stuffing their blankets under his arm. "I can help," she protested.

"You can, but you won't." He gave her a lopsided smile and ambled toward the parking lot where they'd left their vehicles. At least he let her unlock her own damn truck and open the tailgate before he slid the cooler and blanket inside. She grabbed her sweater from where she'd left it and pulled it over her head, thankful for the warmth of it.

"Okay then. We're off." Nicole hugged her. "It's been a great day. We should do it more often."

"Yeah, we should," Gabe agreed, kissing Amber's cheek as soon as Nicole released her. "It's been good to see you."

He turned and held his fist to North, waiting for a bump. North hesitated, then curled his left hand into a fist. That was weird, because he was right-handed like Gabe.

Wait. Oh God, she knew exactly why he wasn't using his right hand.

His fingers were still covered in *her*. How embarrassing.

Gabe didn't seem to notice the change in hands, or if he did he ignored it, just winked at them both as North kissed Nicole's cheek and she climbed into the cab.

And then it was just the two of them. Amber pulled the sleeves of her sweater down over her hands, letting it dangle like she was a teenager again. And that's how she felt. Confused and like she didn't know the world she was living in. That she wasn't sure she fit in where she was supposed to anymore.

"You want to come back to mine?" North asked, his voice low.

She did. She didn't. This was so bad. She was so scared about what would happen next.

"I..." She took a deep breath. "I'm sorry. I have to go to work." And then she practically ran to get into her truck.

✻ 7 ✻

She managed to avoid his calls for the rest of the weekend. It was stupid because she knew she'd have to see him at the farm on Monday, but right now she couldn't face him.

She was too embarrassed. She was barely out of her relationship with Shaun and she was throwing herself at her best friend. He was the one good thing in her life, and here she was, sabotaging that, too.

He'd sent her a message last night. Then two this morning. And then the calls started. Every hour on the hour. So she'd gone grocery shopping to take her mind off things, and now she was putting them all away in the cupboards, and trying to not think about what an idiot she was.

She'd let North touch her. No, more than that. She'd wanted it. Encouraged him, told him to not stop.

She'd almost come around his hot fingers. Been a breath away from it when Gabe woke up.

Mortification was still washing over her as she carried the toiletries she'd bought into the small bathroom at the end of the hallway and opened the cabinet to put the shower gel and extra tampons in there for when she needed them.

But there was already a box in there. She frowned. Had she bought some the last time she went to the grocery store? Pulling them out, she turned the package over, as though it might contain all the answers.

I'm always regular. That's what she'd told her friends at the lake. And it was true. But this carton was unopened. How long had it been in here unused without her noticing?

Had she even had a period since she'd moved in?

Her hands trembled as she tried to think back, but everything in her brain was too messed up. Between Shaun and her finishing things, and her stupid performance at the lake yesterday she couldn't remember the last time she'd bled.

It was the middle of the month which meant she was due now. And last month she'd been moving into this place. So her last period...

It had to have been two months ago. Before she and Shaun split.

"No." No, no, no. Hadn't the universe done enough? She couldn't be pregnant. Not on top of everything else. Surely she wasn't that much of an idiot.

Her period would come tomorrow for sure.

She left the bathroom and sat down heavily. Was it possible to bring on a period through wishful thinking alone?

Her phone buzzed again. Another message from North.

Call me. We need to talk. - North

She put the phone down and swallowed hard. She couldn't talk to him right now. Couldn't tell him what she was thinking. Couldn't let him know what a mess she'd made.

Instead she stood and grabbed her keys. There was only one way to solve this. She needed a test. Once she knew she wasn't pregnant, she'd talk to North. Smooth things over. See if they could go back to how things were before she knew how his fingers felt inside her.

Before she knew how easily he could give pleasure with his touch.

She drove over to Marshall's Gap, not wanting to go back inside the small grocery store in Winterville, where everybody knew your name.

There was a pharmacy there that had self-checkouts. She'd run in and out and get over this weird sicky feeling in her stomach for once and for all.

It was getting dark as she pulled into the parking lot of the twenty-four hour drugstore in Marshall's Gap. Grabbing her purse she climbed out of the cab, the cooler evening air hitting her bare legs and face. There were a few people inside, a couple bickering over in the corner, a mom and her baby in the diaper aisle. Some kids pawing at the candy near the check outs.

Walking down the fourth aisle, Amber found the item she needed – rectangular and white. They had names like First Response, ClearBlue, and Pregmate. Seriously, Pregmate? Who came up with that name? How about Pregenemy? She shook her head.

She had no idea how she was supposed to choose, so she took two boxes and put them in her basket, surreptitiously glancing along the aisle to make sure nobody she knew was here. When she knew the coast was clear, she headed for the self-checkout, scanning and paying for them without anybody noticing.

Clutching the brown bag with the pregnancy tests against her side, she rushed back to her truck. She was pulling the door open when she saw a familiar truck next to hers.

Kyle Walker climbed out, his eyes widening when he saw Amber. Then a mean look stole over his face. He was Shaun's best friend, and he'd barely liked her when she and Shaun were engaged. Right now he probably loathed her after fleeing the wedding.

"Thought you were living in Winterville," he said, accusingly.

She curled her hands tighter around the bag. Even though she knew he didn't have x-ray vision, she still felt exposed. "Hi Kyle."

"Yeah, whatever."

"Have you heard from Dean and Shaun?" she asked him.

Kyle blinked. "Like you care."

She opened her mouth to reply, but Kyle turned his back on her and stomped off to the store, not bothering to look back as he walked through the sliding doors. Shaking her head, Amber climbed into the cab, putting her purse and the brown bag on the passenger seat before starting up the engine.

When she parked outside her apartment, she could see Dolores emptying the trashcans into the dumpsters in the lot. "Hey," she called out as she jumped down to the blacktop, slamming the passenger door behind her.

"Hey." Dolores gave her a beaming smile. "You had a good weekend? I heard y'all went down to the lake the other day."

Amber smiled. "We did. It was lovely. A nice chance to get together before we all get busy in the fall."

"Ah, I can't wait for that," Dolores told her. "I'm itching to decorate the café. Might do it next week."

Amber grinned. She felt the same about opening the farm's shop. Sure, she loved the easy summers, but the frantic fall and winter traffic were what kept the farm going. "Yell at me if you need a hand."

"Oh I think you have your hands full already."

The smile slipped from Amber's lips. Did Dolores know she'd been to Marshall's Gap to buy a pregnancy test? Sure, she thought she'd done it without anybody noticing, but let's face it both these towns were small.

And gossip was currency.

"I mean with your job at the Tavern," Dolores said, looking confused at Amber's sudden change in demeanor. "How's it going?"

"Oh!" Relief suffused her. "It's going well. We have fun."

"I'm glad. You're looking healthier," Dolores told her. "It's nice to see."

"Thank you." Amber shifted her feet. "I should get inside and let you finish up."

"Sure. I'm about done, anyway. Time to get home and put these old legs up for a rest." She went to pull the lid of the dumpster down, but it was just out of her reach.

Amber leaned over to help her, grabbing the rim, and the brown bag slipped out of her hand, falling to the ground with a thump. A box slipped out, revealing the logo.

Amber quickly picked it up, her cheeks flaming. When she looked up, Dolores' face was wrinkled with sympathy.

"Oh, honey," she said, her voice gentle.

"Please don't," Amber whispered. "Please pretend you didn't see it."

Dolores patted her arm. "Okay, sweetie. But I'm here anytime you want to talk, okay? No judgment, just friendship."

Amber nodded, her throat tight. "Thank you."

"You go on in now."

"I will." She turned and headed for the steps up to the apartment. "Good night, Dolores."

"Good night," Dolores replied. After a moment, she added. "And good luck."

Amber didn't turn up to work the next day. North had tried calling her—again—and messaged her, but all he'd got in return was a one liner telling him she was sick and she'd be back soon.

But she was *never* sick. He couldn't remember the last time she took time off work. It had taken all of his persuasion to get her to take two weeks off when her mom died.

She hated being away from the farm, so he knew she was avoiding him.

He pulled his truck up outside the Cold Fingers Café. It was almost six that evening, and a few customers were still inside, but he knew Dolores would close up soon. She waved at him from behind the counter and he waved back, then walked around the outside to the steps that led to Amber's apartment.

Taking the steps in easy strides, he knocked on the door when he got to the top. It took almost a minute before he heard her voice through the closed door.

"Hello?" She sounded hesitant.

"It's me."

Silence again.

"Can you hear me?" he asked, frowning.

"Yes."

That was a start. "Can you let me in?"

"I'm sick."

"Then let me take care of you."

Another pause. "It could be contagious. I'm just going to sleep it off in bed."

"Amber. Just open the door." He tried to hide the annoyance in his voice.

"I can't."

"We need to talk." He took a deep breath. "Did I upset you at the lake?"

"No!" She sighed. "No, it's not about the lake. I just don't feel good. Please don't make me open the door."

He wanted to. Wanted to demand it. Wanted to make sure she was okay, that she was telling the truth.

That she wasn't mad at him for touching her. Because God knew he was mad at himself.

"I'll call you tomorrow," she promised. "I'm sure I'll feel better then."

What else could he do? Beat the door down? Ask Dolores for a spare key? He exhaled, frustrated.

"If you don't call me I'll be back again tomorrow."

"I'm sorry." Her voice was a whisper.

"You don't need to be sorry." Now he felt like an asshole. "Just try to get better. We all love you."

Was that a sniffle? He couldn't tell through the thick wooden door. But she didn't say anything else, so he walked down the steps to his truck.

It was almost nine by the time North had eaten and cleaned up after himself. Drying his hands with a dish towel, he walked into the living room and grabbed the remote to scroll through his streaming service to cue something up. But before he could hit the button he heard the rumbling of a car engine cutting through the silence of the house.

Bright headlamps swept over the windows – he never bothered to close the curtains because the house was too out of the way for anybody to see in. Putting the remote back down on the wooden table, he turned and walked to the window, looking out with his eyes squinted, trying to work out whose truck it was out in the dark.

And then *she* got out, wearing a pair of black yoga pants and a cropped t-shirt, her hair falling out of a messy bun. He swallowed because she looked beautiful and his body was responding. Remembering the feel of her clenching around his fingers.

Instead of walking to his door, she leaned back on the hood of her truck, her head falling into her hands as though she was about to cry.

His heart hammered against his ribcage. He hated to see her so sick, hunched over and hurting. He stalked to his front door and slid his feet into his work boots, wrenching at the handle and walking outside.

Amber didn't look up, though she must have heard him approaching. As he got closer he could see her body shaking, and he knew she was crying.

Because of him? He was a piece of shit. He should never have touched her. Should never have made her feel that way.

"Amber?"

He heard the ragged pull of her breath and then she slowly looked up, her hands still cupped in place from where she'd buried her head in them. There were tears on her face, her eyes rimmed red.

He couldn't stand to see her like this. Without thinking, he pulled her into his arms and she let him. Her face pushed against his chest, her breath muffled against his t-shirt. She was fighting the tears. She always did.

She hated showing weakness. He understood that. He knew that feeling all too well.

"I'm sorry," he whispered. "This is all my fault."

She shook her head but said nothing.

"I shouldn't have touched you. I shouldn't have pushed you like that. I won't do it again," he told her, stroking her hair, thinking frantically about how he could make this all okay again. "You must hate me."

"I don't," she whispered so quietly he could barely hear it.

"Maybe you should."

She shook her head and looked up at him. "It's not your fault. You didn't make me cry, I did."

"Why?"

"Because I'm an idiot."

He frowned. "No you're not."

"I am, North," she said, the moon catching her eyes, making them shine brightly behind her tears. "I'm the biggest idiot on this side of the mountains. Nobody else runs out of their wedding in front of the entire town. I'm thirty-four years old and I'm the biggest fuck up I've met." She pressed her mouth together, shaking her head again.

He searched for the right words. He'd never seen her like this. So worked up, so hating herself. The Amber he knew was a strong, confident woman. Not this shadow of a person. "Sweetheart..."

"I'm pregnant."

The words reverberated around his head like the aftershock of a shotgun.

"What?"

She let out a harsh laugh. "Can you believe it? I should know better, right? It's like life is trying to shit on my head."

"You're pregnant?" he repeated, like he had to hear it in his own voice. "Are you sure?"

"I took two tests. Both say the same."

He was so out of his depth it wasn't funny. "You want me to call Kelly?" he asked, because she would know what to do.

"No. I don't want to tell anybody." Her voice was plaintive. "Just you." She pulled her lip between her teeth. "I'm keeping it."

"Okay." He nodded. She was looking at him like he could solve all her problems. Damn, he wanted to. "It's Shaun's, right?"

EVERY SHADE OF WINTER

She laughed again. "Oh yeah, it's his." She looked down at her stomach, as though she could see a baby there.

"Come inside," he said, still reeling. "We can talk in there."

Taking her hand – so cold – in his, he led her into his house. What should he do? What did you do with pregnant women? Make them warm, make them cozy. Feed them?

"Have you eaten anything tonight?" he asked her.

"No. I haven't had a chance."

"I'll cook you something." He paused. "Is there anything you shouldn't eat? I know Holly had to avoid some things when she was..." Pregnant. Why couldn't he say it?

"I don't know. I think I only have to avoid seafood and soft cheese." Her voice echoed against the tiles. "I should know this stuff, right?"

"I'll make you some steak and fries."

"Oh, that sounds delicious."

He looked at her carefully, taking in the tear streaks on her cheeks. "You want to go wash up in the bathroom?" he asked her gently.

She touched her still-wet face and nodded. "Thank you."

"Anytime."

He left her to it, striding to the kitchen and opening the refrigerator. He wasn't the best cook in the world, but he knew how to grill a steak and put some fries in the oven. Wait. She should probably have some vegetables, too. Didn't pregnant women need those? He tugged at the crisper drawer at the bottom of the fridge. A half-wilted head of lettuce and an onion stared up at him. Damn. Dropping to his haunches he searched through his freezer, finding a frosted bag of peas.

He was tenderizing the steak when she walked into the kitchen. Her hair was tied back neatly, her face shining from scrubbing it.

"Just about to put the steak on," he told her. "You want a

drink? There are sodas in the refrigerator." Then he frowned. "Wait, are you allowed to drink soda?"

"What are you?" she asked him. "The food police now?" At least she was smiling. Looking healthier, too. More like the Amber he knew. "I think I'm allowed non-caffeinated soda but I promise to review my diet tomorrow."

She watched as he put the fries into the oven then seasoned the steak.

"Aren't you eating?" she asked him.

"I thought we could share."

Her mouth dropped open and he couldn't help but grin. "I'm kidding, I ate earlier."

"Thank God. I was going to fight you for it. It's weird, because I haven't been able to eat all day but now I'm so hungry it isn't funny."

"I thought the hunger didn't start until the second trimester," he said.

"Look at you using all the technical words. How do you know about trimesters?"

He rolled his eyes at her. "I have a niece and nephew."

"Yeah, but that means you actually listen, too. I'm impressed."

"Whatever." He shook his head, secretly pleased that the tears had stopped. He could deal with a sassy Amber. A tearful one not so much. "Do you want a soda or not?"

She walked over to his oversize refrigerator. "I'll get it. You want one?"

"Yeah, sounds good."

"Caffeinated or non-caffeinated?" she asked him.

"Non," he said, turning up the flame on the grill. "I'd like to sleep tonight."

She grabbed two cans and threw one at him. He caught it easily. "You're so rock' n' roll," she told him. "No caffeine after eight."

"Shut up and sit down."

"Yes, sir." She slid onto the stool at his counter, popping the can open and taking a long sip.

He had this kitchen remodeled three years ago, adding an indoor grill with five burners. He preferred his meat barbecued to fried or broiled, and it had seemed like a simple decision to have it installed here.

Sliding the pan of frozen peas onto the stovetop, he turned to check the timer on the fries. Fifteen more minutes. That gave him enough time to broil the steak and let it rest—the most important part of the process, in his opinion. "You should probably start taking prenatal vitamins," he said, putting the stake onto the rack. Juices sizzled as they met the hot stones underneath.

"Oh my God, are you going to turn into Doctor Spock now?" she asked him.

"Just trying to help. I remember Holly and Everley taking them. Everley said they were important."

Amber took another sip of her drink. "Yeah, I guess they are. I have a lot to learn."

"You'll do just fine," he told her.

"Don't you need to turn the steak now?" she asked him. She'd watched him grill enough times to know the drill.

"I'm cooking it to well done," he said.

"But we like them rare."

He kind of liked the way she said 'we'. They had a mutual love of steak.

"Meat can have parasites. Nasty little things. I'm making sure I nuke them."

"Parasites. Sure." She rolled her eyes.

After another two minutes, he flipped the filet over, the warm aroma filling the kitchen. Flipping the stove on, he boiled the peas as the steak sizzled and spat. Another minute and he checked on it by pushing down on the middle of the meat.

Yep, it was good. He slid it onto a board to rest, then grabbed a plate from the rack. The peas were almost at a boil. He turned them down and looked at Amber to make sure she was okay.

She was staring right at him.

"What is it?" he asked her, a smile playing at his lips.

"You're so domesticated. Maybe you're the one who should be pregnant."

He laughed. "Can you imagine? The poor kid."

"The lucky kid," she said softly. A weird pang pulled at his chest.

Then the oven timer rang, letting him know the fries were ready. Glad for the distraction, he opened it up and grabbed a towel, sliding the tray out and loading her plate with fries. The peas followed – overboiled to heck – and then he checked the steak again. Even cooked to death it still leaked some juice and his mouth watered.

"Wow. There's green on this plate," she said when he slid it in front of her. Then she grinned. "Thank you for cooking for me."

"Yeah, well I'm the food police now, remember? I expect you to eat all of it up."

She touched her fingertips to her temple. "Yes, sir."

She ended up falling asleep on his couch after she ate. They'd spent the evening talking about the baby, and though they were both still getting used to it, weirdly knowing the truth was a relief.

He'd slid into his usual role of protector, listening to her talk, stroking her hair, telling her everything was going to be okay.

None of it was a lie. She would be a great mom. And she would get through this. He knew her like he knew himself. She was the strongest person he knew, even if she didn't believe it right now.

It was getting toward midnight when he finally decided she wasn't waking up. He had no idea how much sleep she'd lost this weekend, but she wasn't losing any more. He scooped her into his arms and carried her to the spare bedroom, laying her gently down on the mattress and pulling the covers over her.

She muttered something then turned onto her side. He reached over her to pull out her hair tie, pushing the stray hairs out of her face. Then he stroked her cheek, and she sighed softly.

He was still pissed at himself for losing control at the lake. For allowing himself to know what it was like to touch her. If he thought about it enough he'd get hard again, but he wasn't planning on getting aroused by her.

Not now. Not ever.

What Amber needed was a friend. And he wasn't going to stir things up between them again. Because if he hadn't messed up at the lake, she would have come to him on Saturday when she found out about her pregnancy.

And she wouldn't have suffered at home alone for two goddamned days, panicking over two tiny lines on a stick.

8

Climbing out of her truck, Amber looked up at the non-descript office building in the center of Gorton, twenty miles from Winterville. She'd found the obstetrician through Google – she hadn't wanted to use her usual ob/gyn, too many chances of bumping into people she knew.

She was slowly getting used to the fact that she was going to have a baby, but she still wasn't ready for people to know yet.

Taking a deep breath, she pushed the door open and followed the sign to Doctor Cavanagh's office. It was starting to feel real. She was having a baby. And the weirdest thing was that she was beginning to get excited.

When she reached the reception desk she gave her name.

"Oh yes. Mrs... ah, sorry, Miss Stone," the receptionist looked Amber up and down carefully. "Please take a seat over there. Will your, um, will the father be joining us?" There was a bitchy tone to her voice. It reminded Amber of being in high school.

A million different answers – all of them inappropriate – rushed through her brain. "No, it's just me."

The receptionist handed her an iPad. "There are some forms we need you to complete. Once you're done please bring this back to the desk."

"Of course."

Amber walked over to the waiting area. It was almost full, but she found a seat in the corner, next to a woman, her husband, and two children. The children were sitting on their father's knees while he read them a story from a picture book. The mom had her eyes closed, her hand resting lightly on her bump. From the size of it she looked like she wasn't far from her due date.

Turning her attention to the tablet, she scrolled through the questions on the screen, ticking the boxes as she did. Then she got to the ones about her partner's medical history.

She tried to skip them but they were required boxes. She felt her chest contract, because she knew she'd have to talk to him soon. Would he come back? Want to be there when she had their child?

The thought of him watching as she went through birth made her skin feel cold. Of course he could be involved, he should be.

She just couldn't picture Shaun being supportive in there. Plus it felt wrong to put his name on the form when he didn't even know she was having a baby. And of course she knew that North and Kelly would be there if she asked them, but she hated being dependent. It was all too much.

Taking a deep breath, she answered what she could and added 'don't know' into the ones she couldn't.

The rest of the form was simple. She completed it and pressed the submit button then carried the tablet back to the receptionist.

"Thank you. The doctor won't be long now."

As Amber sat back down, the door to the exam rooms opened and a couple walked out arm in arm. The woman was leaning into him and he was proudly holding a black and white printout. He leaned down to kiss the woman's cheek and she sighed.

"Anne Marie?" the receptionist called out. "The doctor is ready for you now."

The woman next to Amber opened her eyes. "What did she say?" she mumbled to her husband

"That's us, sweetheart." He put the book down and gathered up their children. "Remember what I told you?" he said to the kids.

"Be good and we get ice cream afterward," the oldest – a little girl of around four – piped up.

"Are we gonna see the baby?" the younger one asked.

"Yep. Come on, let's go."

The children ran ahead, the dad putting his arm around the mom and helping her walk. She looked like she was in pain every step. Amber looked down at her still-flat stomach and wondered how the heck it was going to grow that big.

She tried to imagine having to work at the farm with her stomach protruding outward. Trying to kneel down and tend to her saplings. She wasn't sure she'd even be able to reach the cash register if she got huge.

"Amber? Right this way."

Amber picked up her bag and walked over, to the nurse.

"Amber? I'm Nurse Alex."

"Pleased to meet you." She shook her hand.

"Are we waiting for somebody or have you come alone?" Alex asked. She was smiling at Amber, as though it was her job to make her feel at home.

"I'm alone. The father... he's not available."

Nurse Alex didn't blink. "No problem. Let's go to the exam room and I'll take your vitals. Then Doctor Cavanagh will come in to take a look at you. Sound good?"

"Works for me." Amber nodded.

Alex directed her to the exam room where Amber changed into a gown before sitting on the table to answer more questions and have her blood taken. Then she called in the ultrasound technician who did a scan of the baby to check gestational age.

When everything was done an older man walked in, his eyes crinkling as he smiled at them both.

"Amber Stone?"

She nodded.

"I'm Doctor Cavanagh." He slid some glasses on his nose as the nurse passed him the iPad. "Can't read anything without these damn things." He looked up at her. "How are you feeling?"

"I'm good."

"Excellent." He took some gloves from a dispenser on the wall. "Are you okay for me to examine you?"

"Of course."

He was gentle as he carefully examined her – asking permission before every touch – and talked her through what he was doing.

"We palpate your stomach to see where the womb is. It'll move up with each week as the baby grows," he told her.

"Does it feel okay?" she asked.

"Absolutely fine. You're doing great." Dr. Cavanagh smiled. "I just wanted to confirm something. You're measuring a little big."

Amber's heart did a little stutter. "Is that bad?"

"No. I think you might be a little off on your dates, that's all. You say your last menstruation was nine weeks ago?"

Amber nodded. "That's right."

He glanced at the tablet he was holding again. He didn't look concerned. But she couldn't help the worry pulling at her brain. If the baby was too big, did that mean there was something wrong? The thought of it made her want to be sick. She didn't want her baby to feel any pain.

"Was it a heavy one? Do you remember?"

She thought back. It was before her bungled wedding and she'd had so much on her plate at the time. "I don't think so. But I'm usually quite light."

He nodded. "It may have just been spotting. That happens sometimes during a pregnancy."

"You think I was pregnant before my last period?"

"Yes. You're measuring somewhere between twelve and fourteen weeks according to the ultrasound. Is it possible you might have got your dates wrong?" he asked her.

She remembered the closed pack of tampons in her bathroom. Her confusion. "Maybe? I don't know. Does this cause any problems?"

"Being four weeks further along?" He smiled. "No, just means you get to meet your baby four weeks earlier than you thought." He tapped at his laptop. "We're looking at a due date of January twelfth."

She let out a mouthful of air. That was six months away, but it still sounded soon. Too soon. She wasn't ready for this.

But she was going to have to be.

"I'll make some changes to your future appointments," the nurse said, giving her a warm smile. "We'll need to bring everything forward by a few weeks."

"And you're still taking prenatal vitamins, right?" the doctor asked.

Amber nodded. She'd started them as soon as she'd left North's last week.

"Great." The doctor gave her a reassuring smile. "Let's get you sitting up and we can talk next steps."

"Have you thought of using a homing pigeon?" Kelly asked her, picking up a pint glass and pulling the beer handle. It had been three weeks since Amber had her appointment with Doctor Cavanagh, and she'd spent most of them trying – and failing – to get a hold of Shaun. She'd also confided in Kelly – she couldn't continue to keep this a secret from her. Especially one as big as this.

It was Friday evening, and the bar was already filling up with the usual locals and a few out-of-towners. The only people making any noise were a bachelorette party in the corner. Alaska had called ahead to warn Kelly that they were already a few bottles of sparkling wine into their celebrations. Amber felt sorry for them. They probably thought Winterville would be more exciting than it was.

She would have told them they'd be better off grabbing a cab to Marshall's Gap, but Kelly was delighted they were spending so much money. And Amber had learned long ago not to piss her friend off.

"Can homing pigeons fly all the way to the far east?" Amber held out the card reader to her customer. "Thank you, have a great evening," she told him when he pressed his phone against the screen.

"I have no idea," Kelly said, "But at least you might hear from him this side of Christmas."

It turned out Shaun had blocked her on everything. She'd tried to call and text, and message him on social media. She'd even tried email, but that had bounced back as though he'd closed his account.

"It doesn't matter, I guess," Amber sighed. "There's not much he could do to help anyway."

"He could pay for half your medical bills," Kelly pointed out. "What are you having?" she asked a stressed looking man who'd managed to get to the front of the counter.

"I don't need anybody to pay my bills. I have health insurance." Amber shrugged.

"Yeah, but you're gonna want him to provide financial support once the baby's here, won't you?" Kelly asked as she grabbed a glass.

"Two beers, two sauvignon blancs, and a gin and tonic please," Amber's next customer shouted out.

"Coming right up." She turned to pull two bottles from the glass-doored refrigerator, popping them open and putting them on the counter. "Shaun's never been able to pay his way for anything," she told Kelly, as she picked up the bottle of Sauvignon and measured out two medium glasses. "The only reason I'm trying to contact him is because I think he should know."

"Well at least you tried. A lot of women wouldn't."

She grabbed two beer glasses. "He deserves to know he's going to be a father."

"Yeah, well maybe it's for the best," Kelly suggested, looking around for the card reader. Amber picked it up and passed it to her. "This way he gets to have a good time traveling without worrying about being a deadbeat dad, and you get to go through pregnancy without having to deal with his crap."

The door opened and a group of men walked in. Amber felt her back stiffen when she saw who it was.

Kyle Walker and his friends stumbled through the door. From the way they were talking she could tell they'd already been drinking.

"Great," Kelly muttered.

"Do you want me to disappear?" Amber asked. She didn't want any trouble.

"No. Let's just watch and see how they behave." Kelly lifted a brow. "And if anybody's leaving, it's them, not you."

From the corner of her eye she noticed Kyle looking

straight at her. The way he was staring made her feel uncomfortable.

Luckily a moment later, one of his friends noticed the bachelorette party, and started calling over to them, pulling Kyle's gaze from hers.

"North coming in tonight?" Kelly asked Amber, holding up the card reader for a customer.

"I think so."

Kelly winked. "I know so. I wish I had my own personal rottweiler. Especially one that looked that good. And at least he'll be around if there's any trouble later."

"He's actually being very sweet," Amber told her. He knew her so well he could tell when she needed his support and when she wanted to be independent. Thank God she had him.

"Sweet. Hmm." Kelly smiled.

"What?"

"I don't know. I've seen him angry, I've seen him silent. I've just never seen him sweet. I imagine it would be devastating."

"Six Buds." Kyle's voice sounded rough, like he'd spent the day shouting the loudest he could.

"Can you get those?" Kelly asked Amber. Amber nodded. "There's gonna be no trouble tonight, right?" Kelly lifted a brow at Kyle.

"Not unless somebody causes us trouble first."

Amber could feel Kyle's eyes on her as she leaned down to grab the bottles.

"Even then," Kelly said. "You're on your last warning. And I know for a fact that you're still barred from every establishment in Marshall's Gap."

Kyle said nothing, but she could still feel the heat of his stare. "Yeah well, if you treat us right, we'll treat you right."

Amber slid the bottles in front of him. Kyle's gaze flickered to her and away again.

"How's your brother doing?" Kelly asked.

Kyle's jaw twitched. "Having a fucking ball. He and Shaun are living like kings, fucking their way through the female population."

Amber winced. She knew that one was aimed at her.

"Shaun's phone working okay?" Kelly's voice was light.

Kyle frowned. "What do you mean?"

"Nothing," Kelly said. "That'll be thirty-five dollars please."

Kyle held his phone up.

"You can pay Amber," Kelly told him.

"I'd rather pay you," he said gruffly.

"Yeah, well you don't get the choice. Pay Amber or get out. It's up to you."

Amber shifted her feet. She hated this so much.

"Fuck it." Kyle put his phone on the reader as Amber held it, then as soon as the transaction went through he snatched it away like he could catch something from her.

"Have a nice evening," Kelly called out as he grabbed the bottles of Bud and stalked away.

As soon as he was out of earshot, Amber turned to look at her. "What was that about?"

"Just making sure Kyle knows who's boss around here," Kelly said. "I'm not having him ignore my staff because he's throwing a hissy fit."

"I didn't mean that. I meant the bit about Shaun's phone."

Kelly grimaced. "Sorry. It came out before I thought it through."

"Please don't do it again. Things are hard enough," Amber told her. "There's no way I want Shaun's friends finding out about this before he does."

"I hear ya," Kelly told her, patting her hand. "But the

problem is you might not have a choice. What are you gonna do when you start showing?"

***

These bachelorettes had stamina. They were on their fifth round of drinks – cocktails now, instead of champagne, and Kelly was so delighted with their bar spend that she'd asked Amber to be their own personal waitress.

She'd also given them some chips to soak up some of the alcohol. "Let's see if we can get them back to the Inn without any medical emergencies."

"Good idea. We don't want to upset Alaska." As the Inn's manager, North's cousin was protective of her guests. She also liked them to have a good time. Because good times meant repeat customers.

When Amber carried the tray over to where the bachelorette party was sitting, she noticed Kyle and his friends had left. They'd probably gone back to his place – her old home. Poor Ria. Amber's old neighbor was probably pulling her hair out right now.

"You guys having fun?" she asked the women as she handed out their cocktails.

"Yep. Last chance for her to enjoy the single life," the blonde sitting nearest Amber – Karla - said. She was the maid of honor according to the pink satin sash that hung from her shoulder. "Say, do you know anywhere we can go after this?" she asked, looking hopeful.

"We're not going anywhere else," the bride, or at least Amber assumed she was from the veil pinned on her head, slurred. "I want to go back to my room and call Damon.

"You can't talk to the groom during your bachelorette party," the blonde said. "It's bad luck."

"I thought that was the night before the wedding." The bride frowned.

"Nope. It's the party." Her friend had a completely straight face. "Anyway, you won't want to talk to him after we find you some hot guys to spend some time with." She looked up at Amber. "There are some hot guys around here, right?"

"We're in the middle of nowhere," a beautiful redhead to her right said. "There's just mountains and deer. I told you we should have gone to Vegas."

Amber's lips twitched. It was getting harder to not laugh.

"I didn't want to go to Vegas," the bride said. "I wanted to come here. My dad used to bring me here as a kid."

"Her dad's dead," Karla whispered, way too loudly. "She's kinda sentimental."

"I get that," Amber said. She'd felt the same knowing her dad wasn't around to walk her down the aisle. "You all set, or can I get you ladies anything else?"

"Do you know any male strippers?" Karla asked her.

This time Amber couldn't hide her laughter. "No, sorry."

When she got back to the bar, Kelly was serving two waiters she knew from the Inn.

"You working here now?" the older one asked Amber as she slid the tray beneath the counter.

"Just for a while, until Kelly recruits somebody permanent."

"Good for you."

When Kelly finished serving them, there was nobody left in line. It was the first time all night they'd not been rushing to serve the next customer. Letting out a sigh, Kelly leaned on the counter and kicked off her heels, circling her feet in the air one at a time.

"How are my favorite customers doing?" Kelly asked her, glancing over at the bachelorettes.

"They asked if I know any male strippers," Amber told her, still smiling.

"Ah, damn. I hope they don't move on to Wild Sally's." Kelly lifted a brow. "You didn't tell them about that place, did you?"

"Nope. Pinky swear."

"Good." Kelly nodded.

The door opened, and North and Gabe walked in, both wearing jeans and t-shirts, the two of them laughing about something as they stepped inside.

The Maid of Honor let out a low whistle.

"Okay, they're gonna stay now for sure," Kelly said, grinning. "I wonder if Gabe and North would do a little striptease for them."

Amber rolled her eyes.

"You could ask them," Kelly said, looking straight at her.

"Are you serious?"

"No." Kelly shook her head. "Well, maybe. A little. I don't know, these girls just deserve a good time, you know?"

"Amber!" The maid of honor was beckoning her over. "Can we get some more drinks?"

"I just took them some," Amber muttered.

Kelly winked. "The customer is always right, honey."

Grabbing her pad from her apron pocket, Amber walked back to their table. She couldn't see North and Gabe from their table, but she assumed they were at their favorite booth. The one in the corner where the lights were dark.

"What can I get you?" Amber asked Karla.

"Those guys over there," Karla said, pointing at the other side of the room. "Are they single?"

Amber's chest felt weird. "One of them is married."

"Which one?" the redhead asked, leaning to the left so she could look at them.

"The shorter one with the slightly longer hair."

"And the other one?" Karla asked.

"You wouldn't like him," Amber told her. "He's moody."

"I love moody guys." The redhead clapped her hands together. "Let's send them over some drinks."

"I don't know if they're drinking," Amber told them. Her chest still felt tight.

"Of course they are. They're in a bar. What shall we send them?" Karla asked her friends.

"Sex on the beach? A long hot screw?" Her redheaded friend was laughing.

"No. Something masculine. Whiskey," Karla said, looking up at Amber. "What's your best single malt?"

"We have a nineteen ninety black label," Amber told her. "But it's something stupid like fifty dollars a glass."

"Ah to hell with it, it's cheaper than a stripper." The maid of honor looked at her friends. "Shall we add it to the tab?"

The answer was a resounding yes, and Amber walked back to the bar as laughter from the bachelorette table filled the air.

"They want to send two nineteen ninety black labels to North and Gabe," she told Kelly, trying not to sound churlish.

"Did you tell them how much it is?"

"Yep. Apparently cheaper than a stripper." Disdain filled her tone. Okay, she was losing the battle. She wasn't sure why she was so annoyed.

At least North would be more annoyed. That thought soothed her.

"Oh, I wish they'd come back every week. Maybe we can persuade her to do a runaway bride thing like you and she can do it all over again."

"Great idea," Amber said dryly.

"Just a thought." Kelly rolled onto her tiptoes to reach for the bottle. Dust particles rose into the air as she pulled it down, the light catching them as they danced in the air. "I guess it's been a while since we opened this one," she said. "Not a lot of demand for good whiskey here. Unless there's a conference in town and the guys are trying to one up each other."

Amber passed her two whiskey glasses and Kelly measured them carefully. "Can you take them over to the guys?"

"Can't you?" Amber asked her.

Kelly looked at her for a moment. "Is everything okay?"

"It's fine." Amber nodded. "Just a long night, you know?"

"You want to leave early?" Kelly asked. "Now that your rottweiler's here? I can manage the customers who are left."

Amber shook her head. "It's okay, I'll help you close."

"Well, all right then." Kelly turned to start emptying the dishwasher.

Lifting the tray up, Amber carried it over to the booth. That's when she saw the maid of honor and her redhead friend had already sat down with North and Gabe. They were gesturing and Gabe's eyes were crinkled like he was amused.

But it was North that caught her eye. The redhead was sitting next to him, her thighs touching his. She leaned in to whisper in his ear and North smiled.

It felt like somebody had kicked Amber in the gut.

What was wrong with her? North could smile at whomever he liked. He was a free agent.

But an image of him tangled with the redhead flashed into her brain. Her stomach swirled like she was about to be sick.

"Two black labels. Courtesy of your friends," Amber said, putting the glasses down in front of Gabe and North. "Enjoy."

"Everything okay?" North asked. The redhead was rubbing his arm.

"How's Nicole?" Amber asked Gabe pointedly.

"She's good. Waiting for me at home."

"He was just showing us her picture. She's pretty." The maid of honor smiled up at Amber. Ugh, she wanted to hate her, but she couldn't. She seemed nice.

A little over the top, maybe, but that was the alcohol talking.

"She's lovely," Amber said. "One of my good friends."

The maid of honor caught her eye and nodded, as though she understood what Amber was trying to say.

"So North, you got any other brothers that aren't attached?" the redhead asked him. So he'd already told her his name.

Even that made Amber want to punch something.

"Actually, we do," Gabe said, grinning over at North. "His name is Kris."

Amber tried to not roll her eyes.

"Is he as handsome as you?" the redhead asked North.

She couldn't listen to this anymore. Amber picked up the now-empty tray and stomped back to the bar, gritting her teeth when a wave of laughter came from the other table where the rest of the bachelorettes were sitting.

"I'm gonna put on some music," Kelly said. "See if we can get them dancing so they will stay longer."

"There's nowhere for them to dance." Amber glanced back at the room. Most of the tables were empty now, but they still covered most of the floor.

"They'll find a way. Let's see," Kelly said, scrolling through her phone. "Yeah, this will work."

"What is it?"

"Shania Twain. 'Man! I Feel Like a Woman!' It's perfect." Kelly hit the play button and a catchy riff filled the air. "Come on, let's see you dance, girls," she shouted out, as Shania's voice echoed from the speakers, singing about going out tonight.

"I love this one!" the bride stood up, unsteadily. "Come on, let's do it."

"If they're dancing they're not drinking," Amber pointed out.

"If they're dancing they're getting thirsty, and they're not leaving," Kelly replied, swinging her hips to the beat. "Come on, cheer up. The tip jar is already overflowing. Everybody loves a bunch of pretty women in the bar."

Most of the women were in the middle of the room now, their arms up and bodies swaying. The maid of honor went to join them, and Gabe headed to the exit holding his phone, sliding his finger across it as he headed out of the door to take the call in silence.

The redhead was still with North, her hand sliding up and down his bicep as they talked.

Amber couldn't watch anymore. She felt sick and light-headed and so stupidly jealous it wasn't funny. And yeah, she knew she was being stupid, but she was about a breath away from finding herself in tears.

"Can I take you up on that offer to head out early?" she whispered to Kelly. "I'm not feeling so good."

Kelly glanced at her then over to the booth. "You taking North with you?"

She shook her head. "I'll just slip out. It looks like he's having... fun."

Kelly looked at her carefully. "Sure. Okay. Just text me when you get in. That way if he shouts at me I can show him you're fine."

Amber leaned in to hug her. "I will. See you tomorrow? I'll come in early to make up for it."

"Sounds good. I'll divide the tips up and have them ready for you."

"Keep them. I'm the one who's ducking out early."

"Nope. They're yours fair and square."

She'd fight Kelly about that later. Right now she just needed to get out of there. Before she had to watch North touch the redhead back. Or even worse, watch him kiss her.

She grabbed her purse and walked out of the bar, keeping to the edge of the room as she headed for the door. The cooler evening air washed over her as she stepped outside, and she took a deep breath, trying to forget about her best friend and the beautiful redhead.

"You okay?"

She'd forgotten Gabe was out here. He was still holding his phone, giving her a quizzical look.

She forced a smile onto her face. "It's gotten quiet so Kelly's sent me home. You don't have to hurry though, she's happy to stay open as long as you're all in there."

His eyes skimmed her face, then looked behind her at the closed door. "Is North walking you back?"

"No. I think he's busy." She kept her voice light. "I didn't want to disturb him if you know what I mean. See you later, Gabe. Have a good night." She lifted her hand in a wave and walked across the road to the town square. Though there was a fence and gates around the grass and trees, it was never locked and it was much quicker to walk through than to traipse around the perimeter. In the winter this square was full of festive decorations. The eighty-foot fir tree that her dad had donated to the town so many years ago, would be lit up and decorated with ornaments and garland, surrounded by candy cane lights.

But for now it was just a tree. One that needed some TLC from what she could see on the moonlit fronds. She'd bring some fertilizer home from the farm next week.

"Amber."

She froze at the sound of North's voice. *Please don't follow me.* She wasn't sure she could deal with him right now. Didn't want him to walk her home and then go back to the beautiful redhead who looked perfect next to him.

It wasn't his fault he was a good-looking man. And it definitely wasn't his fault she was feeling jealous. She'd blame it on the pregnancy hormones but she knew it wasn't them.

It was her. Being mean. She didn't like herself for it.

"What are you doing?" he asked, jogging easily across the square. He wasn't even breathless when he reached her.

"Going home."

"Why didn't you tell me?"

She stopped walking.

"I didn't want to disturb you. You looked like you were having a good time. I'm perfectly able to walk myself home," she reminded him. "I'm a big girl."

"What do you mean you didn't want to disturb me?" he asked, his voice low. "You're the only reason I'm at the damn bar."

"Yeah, but that was until you met the bachelorettes. You and the redhead were getting close. I didn't want to get in the way."

"What?" He frowned.

"Go back, North. She's pretty and she likes you." Every word felt like a pain in her gut. This was so stupid. Amber had seen him with women before, the same way she'd had boyfriends. Hell, she'd almost had a husband. She was used to half the women in the town coming to watch him chop down trees on days when he was shirtless and sweaty and she laughed at it.

So why was she hurting now?

Maybe it's because she knew what it was like to be touched by him. To feel his lips on her neck, his fingers sliding through her. Neither of them had mentioned that day at the lake. Her finding out about her pregnancy had overridden everything.

It was like it never happened. And that was for the best, or at least she thought so.

But now it was like her muscle memory was protesting. He was supposed to be hers.

"I'm not interested in her," he said, still looking confused.

"Of course you are. You're male and you're single and she's throwing herself at you. I saw you whispering in her ear. I saw you smiling."

"So I'm not allowed to smile now?"

She huffed. That's not what she meant at all.

"And I was whispering because the music was loud. She wanted to know about the farm."

"You don't need to explain yourself to me. You're a free agent."

He ran his hands through his hair. "I know I am. And I'm not explaining. I'm correcting you, because you're wrong."

An irrational wave of fury broke over her. "Of course I'm wrong. I'm always wrong. I know that." She shook her head. "And now I'm going home *alone* and you can go back and make Miss Redhead's night."

She started walking again, not bothering to say goodbye. She'd have to call him in the morning to apologize for being so irrational, maybe buy him a coffee and donut and explain that it was all her hormones.

And more than anything she'd have to get used to seeing him with other women.

She could still hear his footsteps behind her. He wasn't bothering to catch up, just following at a distance in case she lashed out again. Fine. Whatever. Let him follow her back to her house if it made him happy.

God knows one of them deserved to be.

She wrenched open the gate that led to the back of the café and took a deep breath, turning to look at him once more.

"Thank you for making sure I got home."

He said nothing, his eyes wary as they roamed her face.

"I meant what I said." Her voice was soft. "The girl is pretty. Go have fun. You're not the one who's gonna be tied down for the rest of your life."

He reached up to pinch the bridge of his nose. "You're so damn annoying sometimes."

"The feeling's mutual."

His lips twitched. "Let me tell you again. I'm not interested in her. I'm not interested in an easy lay or an uneasy lay and I'm not interested in complicating my life more than it already is."

He meant her, she knew that. *She* was his complication. "I'm not your mess to clean up," she said softly.

"I know that. I didn't..."

"You can go now, North. I'm tired and my feet hurt and I want to go to bed."

She wasn't sure how it happened. She didn't even hear him close the distance between them. But he was right in front of her, his fingers softly holding her chin, tipping her face so she could see his.

There was a softness in his expression that made her chest ache. But there was a darkness, too. The same kind of darkness she felt inside. A fight against something that shouldn't happen.

Something that could ruin everything.

He'd been her friend for so long she couldn't picture her life without him. Even now, when her future had changed so much, he was still part of every thought she had. Him playing with the baby. Showing him or her how to walk. Carrying them around the farm explaining what each tree was, the same way her dad used to do for her.

But he's not your baby's dad.

No, he wasn't. But he'd be some kind of uncle. And she knew he was great at that.

"Gabe's gone home," North told her.

"Okay."

"And I'm not going back to the bar."

She nodded, not trusting herself to say anything. She was such a self-saboteur she'd probably urge him to change his mind.

"I'm not interested in anybody else." His voice was gruff. "Because all I can think about is how soft you felt when I slid my fingers against you when we were at the lake."

Oh. Her lips parted, but still no words escaped. His eyes caught hers once more, and then he was slowly lowering his head, his mouth a breath from hers.

And then he pulled right back up, a frown on his face.

"Did you leave your door open when you left for work?"

Amber blinked. "What?"

"Your door is open."

She turned to follow the line of his gaze. He was right, her door was wide open. "I closed it," she said, trying to think about earlier that evening. "I always close it."

"Well it's not closed now." He lifted himself up to his full height. Any softness in his expression was gone. He looked almost menacing as his jaw twitched. "Stay here. I'll go check it out."

His boots hit the metal of her stairs as he took them two at a time. Ignoring his command, she followed him up, still trying to remember if she really did close it.

But then they walked into the hallway and she saw the devastation.

Her things were flung everywhere. The hall table was knocked over, her jackets had been pulled from the rack, the hall closet was swinging open just like the front door, and somebody had rummaged through it and thrown her shoes all over the floor, too.

"Fuck." North turned to look at her. "Don't move. They could still be here."

She nodded, her chest tight.

He looked in each room while she stood glued to the floor, her blood rushing through her ears.

"They left the taps running. The bathroom's flooded." His voice echoed through the hallway. It galvanized her into action, running to join him. Whoever had been in here had put the plug in the bathtub, along with her clothes from her closet, and turned the tap on. Water was spilling over the edge and onto the tiled floor. North turned the taps off and pulled the plug, letting the water escape.

All her favorite clothes were in there. Some of them dry clean only. They'd be shrunk and unusable.

"Okay," North said, his voice on the edge of control. "We need to call the police and then Dolores. This water might have seeped through to the café."

"Oh God." She put her hand over her mouth. "Poor Dolores."

"I know. But we need to tell her."

"I'll call her now."

"Let's go outside and do it. That way we won't touch anything. In case the cops need to take fingerprints."

She took a deep breath, trying to not think about all her things ruined and damaged – and no doubt some of them stolen, too.

"You don't have to stay," she told him. "I can wait for the cops alone."

He gave her a withering look and she shut up. Maybe now wasn't the time to be Miss Independent. And deep down she was so glad he was here.

9

"Can you think of anybody who might have a grudge against you?" the cop asked, holding her notepad and a tiny pen. Amber had known Marie for years. She was one of a group of four cops who served Winterville and the surrounding area.

It was two hours since she and North had walked home from the bar and found the apartment door open. They were sitting in the Cold Fingers Café – Dolores had rushed over as soon as Amber had called her, even though she'd clearly been asleep from her groggy voice. There was some minor water damage to the ceiling, and she'd need to call an electrician in the morning to make sure no light fixtures were damaged, but Dolores didn't seem worried about that at all.

Amber was, though. She couldn't help but feel this was her fault.

"I can't think of anybody," she said. "It has to be an out-of-towner. Nobody else would do something like this."

"What about Kyle Walker?" Kelly asked. She'd come over as soon as the bar had emptied. Amber still had no idea how she found out about the break in. And she'd urged her to go home but Kelly refused.

"Kyle?" Marie asked. "Hmm."

"It's not Kyle." Amber shook her head. "He wouldn't do this."

"He was pretty pissed at you tonight at the bar."

"What?" North looked pissed now, too. "He was there tonight? What did he say to you?"

"Nothing," Amber told him. "It doesn't matter."

"Of course it matters," North replied, his eyes stormy. "What did he say?"

"He refused to pay her at first, until I made him. Wanted to ignore her completely," Kelly told North, ignoring Amber's furious gesturing. "And he told her Shaun was fucking his way across the Far East."

North's mouth was tight.

"He's an asshole, not a criminal," Amber said softly.

"Well, it won't hurt to pay him a little visit," Marie said. "Rule him out."

Great. Now he was going to hate her more.

"I don't know about you all, but I'm ready to hit the mattress," Dolores said. "Amber, I don't think you can stay in the apartment tonight. The lock is busted and the water damage is going to take a while to clean up."

"She's coming home with me," North said.

Amber looked at him and he stared right back. *Try me.*

Yeah, she didn't have the energy to do that right now.

"I'll come over first thing," Amber told Dolores. "Start on the cleanup."

"I'll get a crew in. What with..." Dolores gestured at her stomach.

"What with what?" Marie asked. "Is there something else I should know?"

"Nothing," Amber said. "Nothing at all."

Dolores grimaced, as though she knew she'd spoken out of turn. She hadn't mentioned Amber's pregnancy since the day she'd seen the pregnancy test fall onto the ground, but she'd given Amber plenty of sympathetic looks.

"I think I have everything I need for now. Y'all stay safe, okay?" Marie slid her notepad back into her shirt pocket. "We'll find out who did it," she told Amber. "Try to not worry."

North pulled his front door open to see Gabe standing on the doorstep. He looked exhausted, and no wonder, since it was almost three in the morning. But North had called and Gabe headed right over.

"There'd better be a good reason for dragging me out of bed," his younger brother muttered. Then he frowned, his eyes scanning North's face. "You look like shit. What's up?"

"I need you to stop me from getting in my car and driving to Marshall's Gap," North said. "Or I need you to stay here and look after Amber while I do it."

"Amber's here?" Gabe looked around. "Why? I thought you were walking her home."

"I did. But somebody broke into her apartment."

"Shit." Gabe's mouth dropped open. "Was it bad?"

"The assholes put all her clothes in the tub and the faucets were running. It flooded the room. The café has water damage, too."

"Is she okay?"

"Pretty shook up," North told him. "She tried her best to hide it, but I could tell." The fury was making his muscles tight and his heart speed. "Come in," he said, stepping aside so his brother could get through the door.

Gabe gently pulled it closed behind him. "Where's Amber now?"

"Asleep on my bed. She took a shower and just kind of collapsed there. I got her tucked in without waking her." She was only wearing a towel wrapped around her body, but Gabe didn't need to know that.

She'd looked so fucking vulnerable laying there. Her wet hair wrapped in a towel, her face shiny from scrubbing it with hot water. He'd left her a t-shirt to put on in case she woke up and was cold.

Tomorrow, they'd get anything they could salvage from the apartment. Because she sure as hell wasn't living there anymore.

"So why do you want to go to Marshall's Gap?" Gabe asked. "Or why don't you? I'm kinda confused."

"Apparently, Kyle Walker had been an asshole to Amber at the bar. Kelly thinks he might be involved."

"Walker?" Gabe's eyes widened. "Seriously?"

All North wanted to do was beat the shit out of him. It was like the red mist had descended, pushing out all rational thought. Thank God he'd had enough insight to call his brother before he stalked out of his house.

Or thank his need to stay here and make sure Amber was safe. Whatever.

"Makes sense, doesn't it? He and his cronies were in the bar and got pissed when Kelly made them pay Amber. So then they go and take it out on her stuff."

"But you don't know for sure?"

"Who else could it be?" North asked him. "Winterville isn't exactly known for its crime waves."

"Was anything taken?"

"A few things. Amber's laptop, some jewelry, some cash she had in a drawer."

"Why would Kyle take that stuff? He has enough money,

or his daddy does." Gabe followed North to the kitchen and leaned against the counter.

"To hide his tracks. He doesn't want to get caught so he took a few things."

"You realize this is all just conjecture, right? You can't go drag him out of bed just because you think he might have been involved. Leave it to the police."

North sighed. "There's still the matter of him being an asshole to Amber."

"I get that." Gabe nodded. "And you can talk to him about that when you're calm if you so choose." His mouth twitched. "Or calm-er. I know calm isn't exactly your thing."

He didn't sound accusing. Just stating facts. North had never been the calm one of the family, Gabe took that role.

"I just hate that she's hurting."

"Of course you do. She's your friend." Gabe ran his finger along his jaw. "You *are* just friends, right?"

"What do you mean?"

"I dunno. At the lake you looked close. Happy. Nicole thought there might be something going on between the two of you."

"Me and Amber?" North lifted a brow. "Nah, you got that wrong."

"Have I?" Gabe asked quietly. "You hated it when she started dating Shaun."

"Because I knew he was an asshole."

"You didn't know Shaun at all. You barely gave him a chance. At first I thought it was because you didn't want to lose your friend, but it was more than that. You acted like a man who was in love with her."

"I love her as a friend," North said. "That's it."

"Okay." Gabe shrugged. "If you say so."

North opened his mouth to tell his brother that it didn't matter anyway. That Amber was having Shaun's baby. That he'd missed his chance long, long ago, and now he couldn't be the one who got to sweep her off her feet.

Not when he knew she needed somebody better. Somebody who could be a father to the kid she was having. Somebody who was calm, understanding, who didn't have the same red mist North's dad suffered from.

But he couldn't tell his brother about that. He'd promised Amber. She still wasn't ready to tell people about her baby and he understood that. She was still getting used to the idea herself and she wanted to wait until she'd spoken to Shaun before she shared. For now the only people who knew were him, Kelly, and Dolores.

"You've got it wrong," North told him. "I don't see her that way. She's just a friend and that's it. And I'd appreciate it if you didn't say anything to her and give her the wrong idea. She's been hurt enough. I don't want to see her being hurt anymore."

Gabe was silent for a moment. Then there was a squeak from the floorboards in the hallway.

"Hello?" North called out.

Amber popped her head around the door, rubbing her eyes. "I woke up and couldn't find you," she said softly. "What time is it?"

"Three."

"In the morning?" Her eyes widened.

"Yeah," he said softly. "Go back to bed."

Her gaze swept over to Gabe. "Is everything okay? Did the police call?"

"Everything's fine," North said. "Nobody's called." She hadn't heard their conversation, had she? She certainly didn't look like she had.

"North told me about the break in," Gabe told her. "I'm sorry."

She gave him a small smile. "Not your fault."

"I know. But I wish... anyway, I'm glad North was with you when you were there. I'm glad I went in and told him you'd left."

North's eyes caught hers and she blushed.

"Oh, and by the way, Nicole's giving me hell for drinking that whiskey," Gabe told him. "She's wanted to try it for years. So tomorrow I get to buy her a fifty-dollar glass."

Amber's brow lifted. "I'll be working tomorrow. I'll give you a discount."

"Nope. I gotta pay or I don't get laid."

She started to laugh and damn if it didn't make North's chest feel tight. She was wearing his t-shirt and nothing else, her hair all sleep mussed. She was fucking adorable. Beautiful.

Pregnant.

Yeah, that too.

He'd expected that knowledge to stop him from wanting her. But there was something so sexy in the way she was blooming. Growing another life inside of her.

It was fascinating. And so very attractive.

"So listen," Gabe said. "I hear that Kyle Walker's being an asshole."

Amber looked at North. "You told him."

"Only that," he said softly. She nodded, knowing what he meant.

"He told me because he wants to beat the shit out of him and asked me to stop him. Or help. I'm not sure."

North rolled his eyes at his brother. So much for family loyalty.

"Don't you dare beat up Kyle Walker," Amber told him. "I can fight my own battles."

"I know that. And I wasn't going to beat him up," North said, shooting his brother a dirty look. "I was just going to talk to him. Still am."

"No." She shook her head. "Definitely not."

Gabe looked amused. "Okay then. The woman is the voice of reason. Nobody talks to Kyle Walker except the cops."

"I guess it doesn't matter," North muttered. "Kelly will ban him from the Tavern anyway."

"Not on my behalf she won't. His money is as good as anybody else's. I'm gonna have to get used to seeing him around. Maybe it'll be easier after the first time."

North's eyes caught hers again. They both knew that wasn't true. If she thought it was bad now, it would get so much worse once she started showing. It was only a matter of time and North had no idea how Kyle would take it.

"Well if that's it, I think I might head back home to bed," Gabe said, running his hand through his hair. "And you should go to bed, too." He gave North a pointed look.

"I will."

Gabe ruffled Amber's already messy hair. "Stay strong, kid."

"Doing my best."

"I know." He turned to look at North. "You good?" he asked.

"Calmer."

Gabe grinned. "Then my work here is done." He brushed his hands together like they were full of dirt then walked to the hallway. North followed him, Amber still in the kitchen, and slapped his back.

"Thank you."

"You didn't need me," Gabe said. "You already knew it was a bad idea." His eyes flickered over North's face. "You should learn to trust yourself."

"Sure."

"I mean it. You're not *him*." Gabe could see right through him. "Now go to bed and get some sleep. I know that's what I'm gonna be doing for the next five hours."

He watched Gabe climb into his truck, then closed the door and turned around. Amber was standing right behind him, and it shocked him.

"You okay?"

"Fine."

"You don't look it. Go back to bed. I'll sleep in the spare room."

She shifted her feet. "I'll take the spare room. I'm not kicking you out of your bed."

"Christ, are we gonna argue about this, too?" he asked her, pulling at his hair. "Because I'm too tired."

She laced her fingers into his. "Come to bed, North."

He wasn't sure what she meant until she led him into his bedroom and climbed beneath the duvet. "There's enough room for two and I don't want to be alone tonight."

She was still wearing his t-shirt. An old college one that swamped her. It made him feel weird to see her in his bed. She looked at home, like she was supposed to be there.

And yet so very fucking enticing, too.

She's just had the shock of her life, you idiot.

Yeah, he knew that. She needed comfort, and he could give her that, at least. "I'm gonna take a shower and brush my teeth." He pulled his drawer open, grabbing a pair of shorts. He usually slept naked but... yeah.

"Sure." She nodded. "I'll probably be asleep when you come out."

"Then I'll try to not disturb you."

He was the one who'd be fucking disturbed. He already was. She was in his bed, in his t-shirt, and he couldn't have her.

There was only one thing left for him to do. He'd have to beat off in the shower. That way he might actually get some sleep.

❦ 10 ❧

A mber wasn't asleep when he came to bed, but she pretended to be. She was on her side, her eyes closed, as she faced away from North's side of the bed.

The cover lifted and cool air touched her skin. A second later the mattress dipped, telling her he was beside her. North flicked off the light, the orange glow through her eyelids disappearing.

His bed was big, but so was North, and his knee brushed her calf as he tried to get comfortable. It sent a shiver down her spine.

An unwelcome one.

Amber hadn't told him she overheard him talking with Gabe.

"I don't see her that way. She's just a friend, and that's it."

She took a deep breath, ignoring the pang in her chest. There was a time when he might have seen her that way. On the beach at the lake. She still thought of that moment. Still got hot remembering the way his fingers had slid over her, inside her. In a different life she would have gone home with him.

She squeezed her eyelids tight. No, she couldn't think that way. He saw her differently now. Of course he did. She was carrying another man's baby. Growing him or her inside of her.

She wasn't somebody he desired.

It didn't stop her wanting to turn over and curl into his body. To feel the hardness of his chest and the tightness of his biceps as he held her tight. The stupid thing was, she knew he would if she asked. He'd hold her so tight she'd feel completely safe.

He'd do anything for her. And she'd do the same for him.

Including getting over this stupid crush she had on him.

She wanted to just be his friend again. Have that light, easy banter they always had. Tease him about wanting to buy a helicopter and the women who flirted with him.

Not feel a stab of jealousy every time he talked to them.

Yeah, she'd let this go. She had bigger things to concentrate on anyway. Like getting the apartment back into shape and growing a baby inside of her, as well as contacting Shaun somehow to let him know he'd be a dad.

And then there was Kyle. She wasn't lying when she said it wasn't him who'd ransacked her things. That wasn't his style. He was big and brash and told you openly if he didn't like you. He was mean but he wasn't underhanded.

No, this was done by somebody else.

"Go to sleep," North murmured.

Her brows pinched. "How did you know I was awake?"

"I can hear you thinking." His voice was thick.

"You can't," she scoffed.

"Yeah I can."

She turned to find him closer to her than she'd realized. It was dark but she could make out his features. His eyes were looking right at hers, his face at ease. He hadn't shaved after his shower, and the darkness of his stubble peppered his jaw.

"I was just thinking that you're a bed hogger," she told him, trying to sound light.

"It's my bed," he reminded her.

"I can go..."

"Shut up and come here." He pulled her toward him. And damn if she didn't like the way he was all warm from the shower, his muscles hard, his skin taut. He was wearing shorts but his top half was bare beneath the covers. She nestled her face against his chest.

"I've never slept with you in the same bed before," she whispered.

His chest moved like he was chuckling. "There's a first time for everything."

"I'm probably the only woman in Winterville who hasn't."

"Shut up."

She smiled against his skin. This was better. "Thank you for being here tonight."

"Wouldn't want to be anywhere else." He stroked her hair. "Now go to sleep. We have a lot to do in the morning and we're gonna be exhausted."

"You don't have to clean this up," Dolores said, fussing with her hands as she watched Amber on her hands and knees, scrubbing the bathroom tiles. "Not when you're..." she trailed off. "You know."

Dolores was the worst secret keeper, but Amber couldn't blame her. She'd had the shock of her life, too, with the apartment being ransacked.

"I already told her that," North said, looking through the bathroom door. She didn't have to look up to know he was frowning. She was pregnant, dammit, not injured. She could clean her own floor.

"Did you dump those clothes?" she asked him. They'd sorted through what was salvageable and what wasn't. He was taking the ones that needed to go through the washer and dryer back to his place. There was an electrician downstairs in the café checking the lighting. He'd already given her apartment the thumbs up.

It was going to be okay. Yes, it was upsetting and she hated the thought that somebody had broken in, but the world hadn't ended.

"I saw Marie down there," North said. "She's waiting to talk to you, Dolores."

"Does she have any news?" Dolores asked hopefully.

"Kyle has a rock hard alibi apparently." North shrugged. "And two more places in Winterville were hit. They think it was an out-of-towner. They've ran the prints but she doesn't think they'll give any leads."

"I knew it wasn't Kyle," Amber told him.

He scrunched his nose up at her. She'd been right and he knew it.

She'd save the ribbing for later.

"Well then I better go see her." Dolores bustled past him, her heels clipping against the floor. "Find out what I need to do to claim it on the insurance."

"She wants to talk to you after she's finished with Dolores," North told Amber. "So why don't you get up and grab yourself something to eat and I'll finish up in here."

"It's okay," she said, dipping the cloth in the bucket of water next to her. "I got it."

He knelt down, gently taking the cloth from her. "Baby, I know you got it. But let me help."

"You *are* helping. You've done nothing but help," she told him. "And I'm not hungry."

"You didn't eat breakfast. And it's not only you that you need to think of," he said, his voice still gentle. It sent a shiver down her spine. "So go eat then pack a bag. We should probably get to the farm sometime today before the trees all wither."

"Pack a bag?" she asked. "Why?"

"Because you're staying with me."

She blinked. "No I'm not."

North sighed and started scrubbing at the tiles. "Yes you are. You can have the guest bedroom. You'll be comfortable there until you find somewhere new."

"Why would I want to find somewhere new?" she asked him. "I like it here. It's convenient and Dolores charges a fair rent. Anyway, there aren't exactly a whole lot of rental properties in Winterville."

"I'm sure we can find you somewhere. Or build you something."

She wanted to laugh. Like it was *that* easy.

"I don't need any charity."

He glanced up at her, his hands stilling. "I know you don't. But you can't stay here."

"Give me one good reason why."

"It's growing inside of you."

She looked down at her stomach. "What?"

"Think about it," he told her. "In a few months, you'll have a baby. And I don't know if you've been around Everley or Holly recently, but babies have a lot of stuff. Strollers and car seats, for starters. You want to carry those up the stairs every time you come home along with your overstuffed diaper bag, grocery bags full of baby milk or whatever the hell else it is you need to buy. Oh, and a baby too?"

She blinked. She hadn't thought about that. He was right, though. She'd seen Holly struggle under the weight of all the things her daughter needed. And she had Josh's help. Amber would be alone. She'd have to work out whether it was best to leave the baby at the bottom of the stairs or at the top while she carried everything in.

"And that's before he or she starts crawling," North pointed out.

"People manage stairs and babies." She wasn't really arguing. Just thinking out loud. Because he was right, she hadn't thought this through.

"They do," he agreed. "But you don't have to. You've had a hard time. With Shaun and then the baby..." He trailed off. "But you're not alone. We want to help."

"We?"

"All of us. Your friends."

"I could move into my folks' old place, I guess." The old farmhouse still stood on the other side of the trees from North's ranch house.

He frowned. "Nobody's lived there for years. It'll need a lot of work."

She nodded. "Yeah, I know. But it's got good bones. And it's near the farm." And she'd grown up in that house. Been happy. Maybe it was a chance for her to give the same to her own child.

"And near me." He lifted a brow. "In case you hadn't realized that."

A small smile pulled at her lips. "It was the first thing I thought."

"Sure." He smirked.

"It'll be nice. We'd be neighbors. I can call you over to change the baby's poopy diaper."

"I don't do poopy diapers."

She lifted a brow. "I thought you wanted to help."

"I'm cleaning your floors for you. What more do you want?" he asked her.

Amber smiled. "Nothing. Just wanted to watch you squirm."

"I'll head over to your parents' place this afternoon," he said. "Look at what needs to be taken care of."

She nodded. "Sounds good." She looked up at him. "Thank you. For everything."

He winked. "You're welcome. Just trying to butter you up so I can change your mind about that helicopter."

"You're not gonna be able to hide it for much longer, you know?" Kelly said, glancing down at Amber's stomach. "You've done well to get this far without people noticing. I was like a Goodyear blimp at this stage."

Following the line of her gaze, Amber stroked her now-growing bump. Kelly was right, it was getting noticeable. Yesterday she finally had to admit that her jeans wouldn't button anymore.

She'd looped an elastic band through the buttonhole and then around the button to keep them closed, but that would only last for so long. She was going to have to investigate maternity wear.

"I know," Amber sighed. "But I still can't get a hold of Shaun." And she still had this thing about his friends not knowing before he did.

"It's gonna be a moot point soon." Kelly gave her a sympathetic glance. "You might be able to hide it behind the bar, but if anybody sees you in the street..." She shrugged.

Amber was almost twenty-one weeks now. Time was passing faster than ever, thanks to the time she'd spent getting her parents' old house ready. She and North had gone over the day after the break in at the apartment to assess the state of it.

After her mom had moved out a few years ago, they'd rented it out as an Airbnb for a while, but for the last two years it had remained empty.

The floors needed refinishing, and North had insisted on a complete kitchen and bathroom remodel instead of trying to refresh what was there. Once those were done they would redecorate. She'd stayed at North's place over the last month while the house was full of sawdust and workers.

"I'll tell Holly and the others this weekend," Amber said. Kelly was right, people would notice very soon – if they hadn't already. She wasn't usually the type to wear floaty tops and jeans, especially in the summer. She'd always been a tight tank and shorts girl.

Things were changing.

"They still helping out at your place?" Kelly asked her. There were only a few customers in tonight. Schools started back the previous week and there was always a lull between the summer visitors and those who came to Winterville for the holiday season.

"Yeah. We've been trying to get it finished before we open the farm shop for fall." That's the other thing she and North had been doing – restocking the shelves, going through the trees in the farm to work out which ones would be cut down and which ones needed another year of growth.

Once October hit there wouldn't be any let up. And she was all too aware that by mid-December she'd be almost eight months pregnant. Now she'd gotten to know a couple of women at her obstetrician's office she understood what that meant.

Aches, pains, not being able to walk.

And then there was North who already didn't want her

lifting a thing. Last week he'd yelled at her when he walked into her place to find her putting away groceries in the kitchen cupboards.

She'd laughed at him and pointed out that in less than a month she'd be carrying fifty pound Christmas trees.

He'd muttered something about over his dead body, which she'd decided to ignore. They'd argue about that when it happened.

And if she was being honest, she liked the way he was protective. She didn't have anybody else looking out for her.

"Oh boy." Kelly let out a low sigh. "They're back."

Kyle and his friends were walking up to the bar. He leaned his elbows on the counter and looked at Amber.

"You okay?"

She blinked. "I'm fine."

Well hello, Mr. Mercurial. She hadn't seen him since the night they'd argued and her place had been broken into. Marie had told her that the police in Marshall's Gap had arrested a suspect. The nephew of one of the residents who was visiting with friends, but the investigation was still ongoing.

Five houses and apartments had been hit in all. In the strangest way she felt more at ease knowing it wasn't directed at her.

And that Kyle wasn't involved.

"What can I get you?" she asked Kyle when he made it to the bar.

"Four Buds please. I heard about your break in."

Amber let out a mouthful of air. "Yeah. It sucked."

"Have you told Shaun?" Kelly asked him.

"I told Dean. I'm guessing he told him." Kyle shrugged.

"So you're in contact with them?" Kelly couldn't help herself. She just had to keep digging.

"Sometimes. Mostly Dean." Kyle shrugged, holding his

card onto the reader that Amber pushed toward him. "Thanks. See you later."

He walked away and Kelly sighed. "That was your chance."

"I'm not using Kyle as a go-between," Amber told her.

"You're not gonna get a choice soon."

"I'll cross that bridge when the time comes." And anyway, she was just glad Kyle wasn't trying to scratch her eyes out. Even if he was just being nice so he could get served in the Tavern.

It wasn't her fault Shaun was still blocking her everywhere after all this time. She'd tried to call and message him again, heck she even tried to follow him on Snapchat, of all things. Which had involved downloading the app because she wasn't much into social media.

Surprise, surprise, he'd turned down her friend request. Which was probably a good thing because what kind of picture would she have sent him anyway?

A photo of a onesie with 'surprise, Daddy!'

Hell no. This kind of conversation had to be done face to face.

The night went slow, thanks to the lack of customers. She and Kelly used the free time as an opportunity to clean the shelves and glasses along the back of the bar. Amber was wiping the mirror when she felt Kelly shift her feet. It was her tell, she always did that when a good looking guy came in.

"I'm a sexual woman who hasn't had sex for a year," Kelly had told her when Amber teased her about it. "So sue me."

North walked up to the counter and Kelly smiled. "What a surprise to see you here."

"Just trying to make your day." North leaned on the counter, but he was looking at Amber, not Kelly.

Amber caught his eye. "You didn't need to come in tonight, I've got my car, remember?" She'd about managed to wean him off escorting her home while she'd been staying at his place.

"Holly wanted to make sure you go straight to my place and don't stop at yours tonight."

She'd gotten into the habit of checking on her house on her way home to his. She liked to see the day's progress. It made her happy.

"Why's that?"

"Because everything is almost finished and Holly's insisting we do the big reveal tomorrow. She says you can't go home tonight because it'll spoil the surprise."

"I love it," Kelly said, clapping her hands. "It's like one of those house makeover shows on TV. You guys should record it and send it to me."

"You can be there if you like." North shrugged.

"I can?" Kelly's face lit up. "Can I bring Cole?"

"Of course." North nodded. "It wouldn't be the same without you."

"That's why you're my favorite Winter." Kelly leaned forward, her shirt gaping. North was still smiling. And for a moment Amber felt her whole body stiffening.

Why was she getting so annoyed? Kelly flirted with everybody. She meant nothing by it.

"You two can go now," Kelly said, still looking happy. "I'll finish up here."

"You sure?" Amber asked.

"Yep. I'm gonna clean some tables and dream about my own place getting a dream makeover."

North shifted his feet. "It's not going to be a dream makeover exactly. We just put some finishing touches in there."

"Spoil a girl's fantasy why don't you." Kelly batted her eyelashes.

North looked at her from the corner of his eye, his

expression amused. "Shut up." He glanced at Amber. "Are you ready?"

"Yes." She unknotted her apron and hung it on the hook. "I'll see you tomorrow," she told Kelly.

"For sure. Remember to look suitably surprised."

North reached for her hand as they left the bar. There were only a few people left now – Kyle and his friends had left about an hour before. Pushing the door, North held it open for her.

"Oh North!" Kelly shouted out.

"What?"

"Don't forget the blindfold tomorrow." She blew him a kiss.

He was grinning and Amber noticed. "She's blatant," he said, shaking his head. "She never changes, does she?"

"Why would she? Guys seem to like it." Amber shrugged.

He said nothing. Just kept walking with her to her car. Amber fished in her purse for her keys and pressed the unlock button.

"You okay?" he asked as she yanked at the handle.

"I'm fine."

"You don't sound it," he said lightly.

"I just wish you wouldn't flirt with my friends." She regretted the words before they were even out.

That smile was still playing around his lips. It was aggravating. "Was I flirting?"

"Yes." No. Ugh, not really. And it was none of her business, anyway. Why was she being so rude?

"I don't think I was flirting. If you want to see somebody flirting with her, you should have seen her and Kris back in the day."

"Kelly and Kris? They were a thing?"

"Nope. Just drove each other crazy. It was a man-woman thing."

"Men and women shouldn't drive each other crazy," Amber said. "That's not flirting. That's annoying." She was still holding the handle, standing next to her car. North was close enough for her to smell the cologne he was wearing. It filled her senses.

Made her body react like it was at an all-you-can-eat man buffet. Whatever one of those was.

"It depends." His eyelashes swept as he blinked. "That kind of banter can be the perfect prelude to..."

"Fucking." That one escaped unthinkingly, too. She was way too aggravated for this conversation.

He gave a short laugh. As though he hadn't expected her retort.

"I'm right, aren't I? You're not talking about dating or sweet things. You're talking about being down and dirty."

He tipped his head to the side, glancing at her mouth.

"Would you fuck Kelly if she offered?" she whispered. Her chest felt so tight it was hurting. Breathe, she needed to breathe. Why was she asking this? It hurt to just think about.

"What's this fascination with my sex life?" he asked her. He dipped his head as though he couldn't hear her. He was looking at her mouth again.

She pulled her lip between her teeth, then released it. "I'm just fascinated by what I can't have."

"You can have sex." His brows pinched together.

"I'm having a baby," she pointed out.

"Last I heard, that didn't stop you from getting some." He reached out to touch her cheek, his fingers trailing along her skin. It made her whole body tingle. Her nipples hardened.

"Sure," she said, lifting a brow. "I'll put an ad in the paper. Pregnant woman needs a good fucking. All eligible males to apply."

North frowned. "Christ."

"You know the stupid thing?" she asked him. "I think

about it all the time. Sex. Being touched." It was the truth. She'd read that it was hormones, but maybe it was the fact that she hadn't been touched by a man since that day at the lake.

North lifted a brow and her cheeks flamed. Did she really just say that? She wanted to take it back right now. He didn't need to know that. He didn't need to hear her problems.

Didn't need to know she was jealous of one of her closest friends because she could flirt with whoever she liked.

"And then when I have the baby, it's going to be worse. I'll have this label on me and no guy's going to look at me twice. I might as well buy some batteries in bulk."

"Batteries? What for?" He looked confused.

"Do I really need to spell it out?"

His jaw twitched. "You mean a vibrator?"

"Ugh, forget about it."

"You're the one who started this," he pointed out.

"I'm just pointing out the difference between you and me."

He opened his mouth. Closed it again. Then he ran his hand through his hair. "I don't want to fuck Kelly."

She started to laugh. She couldn't help it. What was going on here? She wasn't even sure. They were standing in the middle of the town square, swapping sexual confessions. Now he knew she used her battery-operated boyfriend on regular occasions, and she knew he didn't want to have sex with her friend.

Well, okay then.

She took a deep breath. "I'll follow you back to your house."

"Yeah. I'll make sure you get in okay and then I'll go."

"Go where?"

He shifted his feet. "I need to get back to your place. Everyone's there finishing up."

"Oh. Okay."

His brows knit. "You'll be all right at my place on your own, right?"

"I'll be fine."

He nodded. "Good." He ran his finger along his jaw. "Ah, Holly was talking about putting some new sheets on your bed. You took some stuff over there yesterday didn't you? Do I need to hide anything?"

Now she wanted to laugh, knowing exactly what he was referring to. He was so adorably awkward sometimes. "It's okay. I have good hiding places for my battery operated friends."

"Holly's really good at finding shit."

"Then she'll find out that I'm a grown woman with needs." She wasn't embarrassed about owning a vibrator. "It's fine, North. I haven't taken my collection over there yet, she won't find anything."

He looked at her carefully. "Collection," he repeated. "Okay."

"By the way, I'm going to tell them about the baby tomorrow."

He looked relieved at the change in subject. "You are?"

"Yeah. It's time." Kelly was right, she couldn't keep hiding it because Shaun was being an idiot. She needed to take control of this thing, starting tomorrow. She'd have a new house, a new life, and she wasn't going to be embarrassed about the best thing that had ever happened to her.

He looked relieved. "Good. Yeah, that's great."

She smiled. "Okay then. We should probably get going before Holly turns my house into a sex den or something."

The expression on his face was one she wasn't planning on forgetting for a long time.

North spent most of the night with an annoying hard-on, thinking about the things Amber had said. Picturing her naked, her stomach a soft swell as she lay on her back and slowly slid a thick vibrator along the seam of her sex.

Her eyelids were heavy, her lips swollen, her breath coming out in little tiny pants. He wanted to take the vibrator from her, tease her with it, bring her to the edge again and again. And when he finally relented he'd watch her body lift with the power of her orgasm. Then he'd hold her in his arms until she drifted off to sleep.

What the fuck was wrong with him? She was his friend, this was wrong. He shouldn't be imagining her like that.

Yeah, well maybe you shouldn't have slid your fingers inside her at the lake either.

That was where it had all gone wrong. If he hadn't touched her then he wouldn't know how soft she felt. How her skin warmed when she was turned on. How good she tasted – because yeah, like the fucking creeper he was he'd licked his fingers later.

At least she didn't suspect a thing. That was good, right? He was supposed to be her friend. Her support. The one person she could rely on. Not the guy who wanted to get into her pants.

She'd been asleep in the guest room when he got back from her place. He'd poked his head in the room to check that she was okay, then headed back to his own room to take a shower. They'd spent two more hours getting everything finished up. And Holly had gotten upset because he wouldn't let her style the little bedroom adjoining the master.

It would be the nursery. There was no point in decorating it any other way. But he couldn't tell his cousins that when Amber hadn't told them about the baby, so he'd made some excuse about Amber thinking about using it as an office. Holly had given him a strange look anyway.

It'd be easier when everybody knew. For him at least.

Letting out a long breath, he lay back on his covers, willing himself to sleep. He needed to stop thinking about sex and vibrators and the woman sprawled on the bed in his guest room and then maybe his rock-hard erection might disappear.

Yeah, sure. He shook his head and let his hand slide down his stomach, his fingers brushing the head of his dick. He needed a release.

Maybe then he'd actually get some goddamned sleep.

"Is the blindfold really necessary?" Amber muttered as North pulled the black silk mask from his pocket.

"Holly insists," he told her. "I think Kelly must have gotten to her."

"I'll be having words with them both. I feel like I'm in some kind of BDSM movie." She sighed as he pulled the eye mask over her head. "Where did you even get this? Please tell me you didn't buy it for some kind of deviant sex game."

He swallowed down a laugh. "Hey, like you can talk, Miss Vibrator Collection."

Her elbow shot out, and somehow she managed to catch him in the ribs. He let out a harsh breath. "Shit."

"Oops. Sorry, my arm slipped. And I thought we established, a woman has needs."

"Yeah, well so does a man." His voice was gritty.

The mask was covering her eyes completely, and weirdly he missed seeing her expression.

"What? Did I silence you?" he asked her. "I should have tried this mask thing before."

"Have you ever tried it on anybody else?" There was an edge to her voice. Like she wanted to know but also didn't.

He bit down a smile even though she couldn't see him. "No, baby. I got it for my overnight flight the last time I visited Kris."

She shifted in her seat. Did he say something wrong? Her skin looked all flushed again."

"So can we get out of the car and get this over with now?" she asked him.

"Yeah. Wait there, I'll come around and help you out."

"Good idea," Amber said. "Hurry up."

"Always in such a rush." He pulled at the door handle and jumped down from her truck. Gabe had borrowed his this morning—he had the biggest flatbed, and he'd asked Gabe to pick a couple of pieces up from an artisan he knew just past Marshall's Gap.

When he opened Amber's door, she'd released her seatbelt, but it was clear from the grimace on her face that she couldn't see a thing. Her lips were parted, she was breathing softly.

He wanted to kiss them so badly his body hurt.

"Come on, let's do this. Turn so your legs are toward me."

"I don't know where you are. How can I move them toward you?" she grumbled.

"You have ears. You know exactly where I am."

She huffed again, but did as she was told. He put his hands gently on her hips and leaned forward. "Lean on my shoulders," he whispered in her ear.

Sliding her hands up, she found his chest first. Her pinky finger trailed against his nipple and he let out a hiss.

"That's not my shoulder," he told her, trying to keep the grit from his voice. Maybe he had some kind of fetish for pregnant women.

No. Just her. He had an Amber Stone fetish.

It was her turn to whisper. Her lips brushed his ear. "I know." Instead of sliding her hand up, she moved her thumb over his nipple again. Slower this time, more deliberate.

"What are you doing?" he asked her.

"Enjoying myself. If only I could see I'd be able to find your shoulder."

He curled his hand around her wrist. "You're on thin ice."

"Feels thick to me."

"What's going on here?" he asked, to himself as much as to her. He needed to get her inside. To be surrounded by his family. To take the danger out of these feelings he had coursing through his body.

"I'm playing some kind of deviant sex game." Her face was flush, her lips parted. Her chest was rising and falling as fast as his was. He wanted to bundle her back into the car and take her back to his.

Finish what they started all those months ago.

"Are you coming in or what?"

They both startled at Holly's voice. Amber pulled her hand from his chest and he already missed her touch.

"We're coming," Amber yelled. Then she muttered. "I wish."

He looked at her again, so aware that she couldn't see him. There was a power shift. She was relying on him. He liked that all too much. The one in charge, the one in control.

The man who made the decisions.

Those were his happy places. Maybe he should try the mask during sex.

Yeah? With who?

He blinked that thought away, because there wasn't a who. There was a her. And she was sitting right in front of him.

"I'm going to lift you out now," he told her. "And you're gonna keep holding onto me. Then I'm going to lead you over to the house. There are a few trip hazards and I don't want you hitting the ground. You're carrying precious cargo."

"Precious cargo?"

"The baby."

"Oh."

He gently lifted her down. Despite the extra pregnancy weight she kept complaining about, she still felt light to him. She kept her hands on his shoulders as he'd told her, her head lifted up as though she was staring right at him even though she was wearing the mask.

"You okay?"

She nodded. "Yeah."

"You trust me?"

"I do."

A little firework went off in his chest, but he had no time to think about that because the rest of his damn family along with Kelly and Cole had joined Holly on the porch. He took Amber's hands from his shoulders and held them gently in his hands. "Walk forward until I tell you to stop."

Gingerly she stepped where he told her to, stopping and turning when he urged her. She was slow and maybe not as trusting as he thought. He managed to get her through the gap in the hedge and onto the footpath that led to her new house without any scratches though.

"We're at the front steps."

"Oh for God sake pick her up before I do," Gabe said, rolling his eyes. "We haven't got all day."

"Pick me u—?" Before she could finish the words, North swung her into his arms because there was no way he was letting his brother touch her. Amber started laughing as he carried her up the steps, placing her down in the only empty spot on her stoop.

"Can I take this thing off yet?" Amber asked.

"Nope." Holly stepped forward. "Come on inside though. Mind the step. That's it." North lingered back while Holly and the other girls crowded around Amber. This was their moment. He, Gabe, and Alaska's fiancé, Mason, had done most of the grunt work. Josh and Dylan had helped out where they could.

But it was Holly, Everley, and Alaska who'd added the finishing touches and made it look like a home.

He wanted them to have their moment.

"You coming in?" Gabe asked. There was the strangest look on his face.

"Yeah. I'll follow you."

"Okay," Holly said. "We're gonna take your mask off in one... two... three..." She pulled the silk from Amber's eyes, rolling the mask up in her hands. North couldn't see Amber's face from where he was standing, but he knew she was blinking, getting used to the light.

He knew everything about her. No, not everything. There was more he wanted to know. So much more.

"Oh My God!" Amber let out a soft cry. "You guys made it look beautiful." She threw her arms around Holly.

"We didn't want you to have to do any more work," Holly told her. "Do you like it?"

"I love it." Amber looked around. "I can't believe you made it look like this in one night."

She'd last seen the place yesterday morning, when North was finishing up the tiling in the bathroom. The walls had all been whitewashed and the floors finished, but there were no soft furnishings then.

Holly and her team had worked around him and Mason, hustling them up so they could style each room.

The living room was light and airy, the windows looking out to the west over the fields of Christmas trees lit up by the morning sun and to the mountains that in a few months' time would be tipped with snow. North and Gabe had stripped back the fireplace to its original brick, and whitewashed the walls to make the room look modern and cozy. They'd stripped and oiled the wooden floor, too, but it was Holly who'd found Amber's mom's old rug and had it cleaned, then teamed it with a cream leather L-shaped sofa that was covered with throws and cushions.

There were three framed blown-up photos on the wall. Black and white ones of the farm from when Amber's dad ran it. A picture of her parents in front of the original sign, another of Amber and her dad in the tractor as he drove it through the fields, and a third one of her mom, just before she died, smiling as she held a baby tree in her hands.

Amber's eyes filled with tears as she gazed from one to the next. "Where did you find these?" she asked.

"North found them. He got them blown up and framed."

Amber turned to look at him, and a tear rolled down her cheek. "Thank you."

He wanted to wipe the tear away. Wanted to taste it on his tongue. Wanted to press his lips against hers until the thrum of blood rushing through his ears disappeared.

"Show her the other rooms," he said to Holly.

"We should do the kitchen next," Everley said excitedly, grabbing Amber's hand. "And then the bedroom. You're going to love what we've done in there."

They rushed from room to room, and North watched as his best friend's face lit up again and again. "There's only one room we haven't done anything with," Everley said, pouting. "North wouldn't let us."

"Which room?"

"The little one next to your bedroom. I wanted to make it into an oversized closet but he told me no."

Amber's eyes met his. "There's a good reason for that," she said, her voice thin. He nodded at her, trying to give her strength. Tell them.

"I'm having a baby," she said, her eyes still on his.

"What?" Holly asked.

"A baby?" Everley squealed. "Oh my God."

His cousins surrounded Amber, shooting her with questions and North held back again, hovering to make sure she was okay without interfering. He knew his cousins would be happy for her. He knew she'd feel better now that she told them.

And thank God he didn't have to keep this a secret anymore.

"You knew about this?" Gabe asked.

"Yeah." North nodded. "She told me when she found out."

"When was that?"

"A couple of months ago." He shrugged. Amber was smiling. It made his chest feel less tight.

"So how far along is she?"

"Around five months."

"Seriously? That far? I would never have known." Gabe tipped his head, looking at her. "It's Shaun's, right?"

"Yep."

"How's he taking it?"

"He doesn't know," North told him.

Gabe turned his head to look at him. "She hasn't told him?"

"She's tried. He's blocked her everywhere. That's why she's waited this long to share. She wanted him to know first but... people are gonna be able to tell real soon."

"Yeah, I suppose they will." Gabe's brows knit. "So what are you gonna do about it?"

"What do you mean?" From the corner of his eye he could see Holly touching Amber's stomach, revealing a slither of her skin.

"Well there's the matter of Kyle Walker. When he finds out he's gonna go crazy. And then there's your feelings for her."

North blinked. "What feelings?"

"You're in love with her."

His chest felt tight again. He was getting used to that sensation now. "She's having another man's baby."

"So what?"

"Okay let me rephrase that. She's having Shaun's baby."

"But Shaun isn't here," Gabe said. "And we both know he's an asshole. The guy leached off Amber for years."

"I know that." North lifted a brow.

"So you're just gonna let her slip through your fingers again?" Gabe asked.

"I'm right here, aren't I?"

"But you're not telling her how you feel."

"Because she's having a baby. And I think we both know I'd make a shit dad."

"You're wrong," Gabe said, his voice low. "You'd make a great dad. Remember how you took care of Kris and me all our lives? Don't let her go just because our dad messed up. You're not him."

North let out a mouthful of air. He hated when his brother was right.

Nicole walked over and slipped her hand around Gabe's arm. "Isn't that the best news?" she asked him.

"Yep." He lifted a brow at North and let his wife pull him away.

"So, can we decorate the nursery now?" Everley was asking.

"I'm doing that," North told her.

Everybody turned to look at him. Amber was half-smiling, half-confused.

"My gift to the baby. I want to do the nursery alone."

"Okay." Amber nodded. "I'd like that."

"Spoilsport," Everley muttered.

But he didn't look at his cousin. Amber was all he could see. Standing there surrounded by his family. Part of his family. The woman he'd do anything for.

She was looking back at him, her eyes wide and innocent. Did she know how he felt about her? How he wanted to bundle her up and protect her from the world, except he knew she didn't need his protection.

She didn't need anything. She was amazing. A strong, independent woman who could run a business and be a single mother and anything else she wanted to be. He was in awe of her and in love with her, and he didn't know what to do with all these emotions.

But before he could think of anything, his phone rang. His mom's name flashed on the screen. He slid his thumb across it and lifted it to his ear.

"Mom?"

"Honey. I'm at the hospital with your dad. He's broken his hand."

He groaned. "Tell me what happened."

❧ 13 ❧

"Are you gonna tell Kyle about the pregnancy now that everybody else knows?" Kelly asked her that evening. Unlike last night, the Tavern was full of people, though Walker and his friends were nowhere to be seen.

Kind of like North. He'd disappeared that morning and she hadn't heard from him since. She asked Gabe where he'd gone and Gabe had evaded her questions, muttering something about a family emergency.

Anyway, he'd call like he always did. And in the meantime, she had customers to serve. She leaned over to take an order of three beers and a dirty snowman cocktail. She tried to keep smiling, but dammit, she hated making cocktails.

They took so long to make and that pissed off the rest of the customers because they had to wait longer for their drinks.

She wasn't wearing a loose shirt tonight. Instead, she'd put on the only jeans that still fit around her growing stomach and a tank top that kept her always-heated skin a little cooler. Her apron disguised most of her bump, but if you looked carefully enough, you could see it.

"I'll tell him if he asks, but I'm not gonna seek him out." Amber shrugged. "It's really none of his business."

Kelly grinned. "That's my girl. Tell him to go to hell if he gives you any problems."

Amber started to measure out the liquor for the cocktail. "Don't worry, I intend to."

She knew he'd find out soon. This town was too small for gossip not to spread and although he lived in Marshall's Gap he was here a lot. Dolores had run over to the tavern when she'd pulled in for her shift, grabbing her arm and telling her that people in the café had been talking about her pregnancy.

The look of relief on her face when Amber reassured her everything was fine was kind of funny. And maybe Amber was feeling some relief, too. It was good to stop hiding, to actually enjoy her pregnancy. This was the part where she was supposed to bloom after all.

The lines at the bar didn't let up all night. Before she knew it, the clock was showing midnight.

"North not coming to meet you?" Kelly asked.

"I'm not sure." She pulled her phone out to check her messages but there was nothing.

"Shame. We could have used the help cleaning up. Speaking of which, I was wondering if you'd like to stay on a little longer."

"Tonight?"

"No, I mean until the seasonal staff are all trained and ready to go. Cole keeps getting invitations to sleepovers and parties and it'd be nice if I could take a break from this place every couple of weekends." Kelly shrugged. "You don't have to if you don't want to, but I'd love it if you could stay on for a while longer."

"Yeah, I'd like to. I'm not sure that I'll be able to keep working into December though. Holly warned me that the third trimester can be tiring and the farm will keep me busy."

"It definitely can," Kelly agreed. "How about we play it by ear? Once the staff is here you'll have more flexibility and we'll take it week by week?"

"That sounds good." Amber nodded. "You're on."

The Tavern door opened and Amber looked over expectantly, only to see it was a random customer. A rush of disappointment washed through her. Though North hadn't said he was coming to pick her up, he also hadn't told her he *wasn't* coming. He still hadn't called or messaged and she was starting to get worried.

She should message him. Yeah, she'd do that as soon as she got home.

But then the door opened again and he was there, his tall frame outlined by the street lights shining in from the town square. His gaze immediately swept to the bar, catching hers.

Even though there had to be more than fifty people in here, for a moment it felt like they were alone. He looked different somehow. Like he was sure about something. But there was a darkness in his eyes, too. He walked across the bar, weaving through the full tables, then came up to the counter she was standing behind.

"Hi." His voice was thick. Closer up he looked tired.

"Hey. Is everything okay?"

"Yeah." He nodded. "It's all good."

"I wasn't sure if you were coming tonight or not. I was going to message you when I got home."

He leaned on the counter, ignoring the line of customers beside him. "I'll always come for you."

A little bolt of excitement rushed through her.

"Gabe said you had family problems." She was multi-tasking now, taking orders and talking to North at the same time.

"I'll tell you about them later."

It was right after two when they finally finished clearing

up. Kelly took advantage of having North's help, getting him to change two barrels that were almost empty. And though Amber was supposed to be cleaning, she kept sneaking looks at him hefting the barrels through the doorway that led to the cellar, his thick bicep muscles knotting tight as he carried them down the steps.

Every part of her wanted him. Her blood ran hot through her body whenever he was near. It was like he was the sun and no matter how hard she tried she couldn't stop orbiting around him.

Not that she was trying very hard.

Why hadn't she realized this years ago? Before Shaun, before she got... no. She didn't regret this baby. He or she – and yeah, she'd decided to not find out – was part of her. She felt so protective, so full of love and she hadn't even met her baby yet.

She hung up her apron and touched her stomach, feeling the hard swell of it. It was funny how much she was doing that now. Kelly had said she might feel some movement soon but there was nothing yet.

When she looked up, North was staring at the way her fingers splayed over the sliver of skin between her tank top and her most forgiving jeans. His gaze slowly rose up, over her chest, her neck, her face, finally reaching her eyes. He didn't look shocked that she was looking straight at him.

He just looked... hazy. Like he was caught up in something she couldn't quite understand.

"Are you ready?" he asked her.

She nodded, her throat thick. The way he looked at her was making every part of her tingle. It was so raw. So sexual.

Was she imagining it?

She grabbed her bag and her jacket – needed now that summer was on its way out – and waved her hand at Kelly who was sitting talking to a couple of old timers who came in regularly. Kelly waved back and then North put his hand on Amber's back, his palm touching her bare skin.

She shivered.

"My truck is parked around the corner," she said. Her voice sounded strange. A few notes too high. "It was busy when I got here."

"We'll take mine. We can get yours in the morning."

"Tomorrow's Sunday," she said lightly.

He lifted his brows. "Well good job knowing your days of the week."

"It's your day off, I mean. Don't you want to rest? Kelly and I are driving to the mall to pick a few things up." Maternity clothes, mostly. She couldn't wear these jeans every day until January. And Kelly wanted to get Cole's Halloween costume while there were still some options.

"What time do you need it by?" he asked her.

"I don't know. Ten?"

"It'll be outside your door."

"It'd be a lot simpler if you'd just let me take it now," she pointed out.

"Yeah, well maybe I don't want to be apart from you right now."

Her breath caught in her throat. What did that mean? "Is everything okay?"

"Let's just get you home."

Her heart softened. Maybe his family emergency was bad. He needed her support, her friendship, not her stupid ideas about them being together. "Okay," she said softly sliding her hand into his. "Ten tomorrow will be fine."

He stroked her hand with his thumb. "Thank you."

The roads out of town were empty and they were at her house less than ten minutes later. She smiled at the pretty planters that Holly had put by the front steps – filled with flowers and two tiny Christmas trees that she'd definitely light up when she decorated the house for the season.

She opened the front door and he followed her in, waiting quietly as she kicked off her shoes and hung her jacket and purse on the hook.

"Go look in the nursery," he said.

She looked over her shoulder at him. "Now?"

He nodded. "I was here this evening. Before I came to pick you up. I hope that's okay."

"Of course." She walked to the little room North had set aside for the nursery – the one right next to her bedroom. She pushed the door open and flicked on the light, her eyes widening as she looked around.

They'd whitewashed the walls when they'd done the rest of the house, and North had refinished the floor a week ago. But it was no longer an empty shell. There were stencils on the wall – of trees and animals and a tiny lake that reminded her of the one at the foot of their mountain. And there was furniture, too. An antique mahogany dresser that would be perfect for storing the baby's clothes, and a more modern yet matching crib that had cream bedding inside, contrasting perfectly with the wood.

There was a changing table, too, and cream shutters covered the windows.

"How did you do this so quickly?" she asked, shaking her head.

"I'd bought the furniture already. Gabe picked the rest of it up this morning. And I had the shutters made a couple of days ago. If you hate it, tell me. I can paint over the walls and send the furniture back. I just wanted…" he trailed off. "Wanted to show you I'm part of this thing with you. If you'll have me."

She slowly turned around, taking everything in. And when she stopped there he was, towering over her. There was an almost boyish expression on his face. Like he was hoping for the best but fearing the worst.

So un-North like and yet it touched her heart.

"I love it," she whispered, tears prickling her eyes. "It's so beautiful."

"I want the best for the baby." He glanced down at her stomach again.

"Do you want to touch it?" she asked.

He nodded, still strangely hesitant. "Yeah, I think I do."

"Go on then."

He reached his hand out but then hesitated, stopping inches from her stomach. His eyes caught hers and she smiled softly, then took his hand in hers and placed his rough palm against her belly. His were working hands, strong and calloused, the kind of hands that could hurt if they wanted to. But she knew he didn't want to. He was so, so gentle as his palm caressed her stomach, the feel of him touching her made her breath stutter.

"It's harder than I thought."

"There's a baby in there."

His lip quirked. "Yeah, I get that."

"Everything about my body is changing. Parts that were hard are soft, parts that were soft are hard. I'm still getting used to it."

"You've never looked more beautiful." He traced his fingers over her stomach, his expression intense. "I've never seen a woman bloom like you have."

"Maybe you haven't been looking."

He was still touching her. She didn't want him to stop. The connection was making every part of her feel alive.

"Remember that day at the lake?" he asked her.

She nodded. "I remember."

"Do you think about it ever?" He dragged his fingers to

where her jeans were fastened beneath her bump. How could a brief touch make her feel like she was on fire?

"All the time," she replied honestly. "Most nights when it's just me and..."

"And what?" His eyes met hers.

"And my collection." She didn't look away. "How about you?"

"All the time," he said, his voice thick. "When it's just me and my palm."

"Oh." Her heart was banging against her ribcage. The thought of him touching himself and thinking of her made her thighs ache. He pressed his hand flat against her stomach, the warmth of him leaching into her skin. She imagined him standing in his shower, one hand braced against the wall, the other stroking himself, his eyes closed, his breath harsh.

And then she imagined him standing over her, dominating her, telling her what he wanted her to do.

Demanding, taking.

"North..."

"I need to know how you feel about me," he rasped. "Because I can't stop thinking about you."

She placed her hand on his, stilling his movements for a moment, flicking her jeans' button open with her free hand. Then she pushed his hand down, past the waistband, to the elastic of her panties. With her eyes on his, she pushed his fingers inside.

He groaned. "You're wet."

"I ache for you," she whispered. "That's how I feel."

Despite the open buttons, his hand had little room to move. He slid his fingertip along her, finding the neediest part of her. She gasped as his calloused finger brushed her, making her thighs contract and her nipples harden.

He didn't look uncertain anymore. Or boyish. He was all

man, his eyes dark, his expression full of intent. He pulled his hand from inside her jeans, and her body protested.

"I haven't even kissed you yet," he told her. "Can you believe that? I know what your body feels like but not your lips."

"Then kiss me."

"I intend to." He lowered his head until his brow was against hers. She put her hands on his chest, feeling the hard planes of his muscles. Everything about this man was tough apart from his heart.

She knew that was tender. Even if most people didn't.

He lifted his hand as though to cup her face, but instead of doing that he put the finger he'd touched her with into his mouth, his eyes dark and sexual as he consumed her essence. Then he used the same finger to trace her lips, smearing them, painting them, before he pressed his mouth to hers in the softest, barely there kiss.

Oh so gently, he moved his lips against hers, starting a fire between them she wasn't sure they could ever put out.

His tongue flicked at her, encouraging her to let him in, then he slid his hands down her back and lifted her easily against him.

She could feel his hardness pressed against her. Could feel the heat of his mouth, the teasing stroking of his tongue. Blood rushed through her body, heating her thighs, and tightening her nipples as her chest smashed into his.

He didn't even break the kiss when he carried her into her bedroom and kicked the door shut behind them. She had her hands tangled into his hair, her pulse racing as she kissed him back. He dropped her onto the bed, her ass against the mattress, her legs over the front, him kneeling in front of her. He moved his hands up, his fingers pushing beneath her tank, tracing the base of her spine.

A shiver wracked through her as he brought his hands to

her front, pushing her top up further, until her belly was exposed and so close to him.

For a moment, she wondered if he'd stop. If the proof of her pregnancy would be too much for him. But then he leaned forward, kissing her right there, his lips soft as they traced a line of fire from the base of her swell to her navel.

He didn't stop kissing, as he pushed her top up higher as his mouth trailed toward her breasts. She was wearing a cropped bra–so much more comfortable than the underwired ones that hardly fit her anymore–but it didn't cool his ardor, as he moved his mouth over the fabric, sucking at her nipple through the thin material. Her breath stuttered as the warmth of his mouth closed over her.

He tugged with his lips and she tangled her fingers in his hair, scraping her nails against his scalp. North let out a soft groan that made her only want him more.

"Lay down," he said. "I want to see you."

She did as he asked, dropping her back onto the mattress, her hair splaying out around her shoulders. He was still kneeling. Almost like he was praying except his hands were too busy touching her. Sliding the tank top up and tugging it over her head and outstretched arms.

He did the same with her bra, his eyes drinking in her breasts. He liked them, she could tell that from his expression. And from the way he lowered his head to kiss them all over.

He sucked at her, the tug of his mouth making her wetter still. She moaned and he lifted his head, cool blue eyes capturing hers. "Does it hurt?"

"No," she whispered. "It feels good. So good."

A smile ghosted his lips as he worshipped her other nipple, his tongue teasing and licking until she couldn't stop her back from arching up. She needed him closer. Needed to touch him, to feel him.

To have his body weighing hers down.

"North..." she gasped.

"I know. You've got me, baby."

His lips released her nipple, then he kissed his way back down to her jeans, his hands tugging at them until all she was wearing were her white lace panties. But she didn't feel exposed or afraid. She felt strong. Beautiful, the way he told her she was.

What did he call her? Blooming. Like a flower. Yeah, she liked that. He dragged his palms down her thighs, parting them, then pressed his face against the core of her, breathing her in.

Before she could even start to beg, he slid his fingers beneath the elastic, dragging them down, too. She was naked. Laying in front of her best friend.

Aching for him with every single part of her body.

He slid his finger easily against her, the tip gliding against her clit, making her almost buck off the bed. And then he buried his face between her thighs, his tongue dipping into and lapping against her, the growth of his beard deliciously rough between her thighs as he pushed two fingers inside.

Her breath caught. She was so needy. He licked with his tongue again, his fingers moving inside her, pleasure pooling low in her belly as he brought her to her peak.

She was almost there. Her skin was on fire, her heart was racing, but that teasing tongue of his was all she could concentrate on. Then, feeling that she was on the edge, he sucked her between his lips, and the sensation tipped her over.

She let out a long groan, her fingers raking his scalp, her body arching from the bed as pleasure overwhelmed her. He kissed her softly, his fingers still inside of her, coaxing the trails of her pleasure as she slowly came down.

"I need you," she whispered.

"I'll get a condom."

"No condom." She couldn't bear a barrier between them. Not now. "I'm clean."

"Me too." He gave her a lopsided grin. "It's been a while."

She tugged at him, pulling him over her. His mouth glistened with her, but she didn't care. She needed his kisses, needed his body.

She was naked and he was dressed and that couldn't be. She tugged at his t-shirt, and he lifted his arms to help her take it off him. Then her fingers found his belt, the button of his jeans.

Then he was just in his boxers, this beautiful, beautiful man who she couldn't get enough of. The one who'd always been on her side. Her complex, complicated friend who was so much more than that right now.

She slid her hands inside his shorts, curling her hand around him. He was hard and thick and so warm against her. She moved her hand up and down, trying to work out how he was going to fit inside her.

"If you keep doing that I'm gonna come in my shorts," he whispered.

She grinned, releasing him. Then she tugged his boxers down, watching as his hardness slapped against his muscled stomach.

This man was beautiful. Everything she hadn't known she needed. And somehow he'd fit. He had to.

"Get inside me," she told him.

He gave her a lopsided smile. "Just savoring the moment. Before you rock my world forever."

The tip of him slid against her, finding the place where she needed him. He paused and caught her gaze.

His eyes were a maelstrom of emotions. Desire and need mixed with something softer. The kind of expression he had when he looked at her, thinking she wasn't looking back.

It made her heart ache.

"Kiss me again," she whispered.

"Always." His mouth closed over hers, and she could feel him press against her. Her body parted, and he pushed in, the sensation overwhelming her.

"You okay?"

She nodded. "You're just... it's tight."

"So fucking tight." His voice was a growl. "I'm gonna move now, okay?"

"Yes."

But he didn't move. He just looked at her like he couldn't quite believe he was there. Maybe she couldn't believe it either. All these years and she hadn't realized he could make her feel like this. Just one move of his hips and she'd almost certainly reach the peak again.

Her lips parted, trying to catch a breath. He cupped her jaw, his touch tender. "You're beautiful."

"So are you."

The corner of his lips twitched. Then she felt it, the rock of his hips, the fullness of him inside her, the surge that she couldn't stop even if she tried.

It took less than a minute for her to come again. This time it was sweet, drawn out, like she was rising up even though she was beneath him. He kept moving, his breaths harsh, but his eyes never leaving hers.

Everything but the two of them disappeared. Nothing mattered but him. The way he looked at her, the way he moved inside of her. The feeling of his mouth as it captured hers. She dragged her fingers down his back, digging them into his behind, urging him to go harder, faster, to join her in this oblivion created for two.

And when he came it was glorious. He pulled his head back, a low, animalistic grunt escaping his lips. His eyes were dark but she could see universes in them. There was such a rawness to his gaze it touched her deep inside.

Everything was shifting. Her friend had become her lover. Her body had become his.

Her heart already was.

He stilled, his body still inside of hers, and her chest felt like it was going to explode with emotion.

"North..." It came out plaintive, like a cry.

"It's okay." He cupped her face with his palms, kissing her like she was something precious. "You're okay."

Okay didn't cut it. She wasn't sure words existed that did. The cocktail of emotions running through her made her feel dizzy and high. She was sated. Ecstatic. Scared.

Because what if this was a mistake? She couldn't lose him, she couldn't.

"Baby? Are you still with me?"

Her heart hammered against her chest. "Yeah..."

"Are you hurt?"

She shook her head.

"Can you tell me what's happening? Because I'm still inside of you and you're on the edge of freaking out."

He knew her well. Over the past ten years, he'd seen every expression, held her hand through every emotion. She couldn't hide from him, even if she wanted to.

"I'm scared," she whispered.

His blue eyes blazed into hers. "Of what?"

"Of losing you."

He paused for a moment, his hands still cupping her tenderly. "You'll never lose me, don't you get that? I'm yours. I'm not going anywhere."

She swallowed, nodding.

He brushed his lips against hers, and everything inside of her clenched. "I'm yours," he said again. "You fucking slay me, you know that? You couldn't lose me if you tried. I'm a fool for you. Haven't you watched me recently? Everybody can see it."

"Who can see it?"

"Wait a minute." He gently pulled out of her, rolling over to her side. He dragged his finger over her jaw, then tucked her hair behind her ear. "Everybody can see it." He kissed her lips, her cheek, her neck. "Gabe, Everley, Alaska. All of them."

"Is it because of what happened at the lake?" she asked him. "Was that when you started feeling differently?"

He shook his head and kissed her jaw. It was like he couldn't bear to not touch her. "Before that."

"When I was with Shaun?"

He swallowed. "Yeah," he said. "I think it was when you got engaged that I really knew. I wanted to punch myself because you'd been here all along, but I hadn't realized it."

"Why didn't you say anything?" she whispered.

"Because you were marrying another guy. And I thought you were happy. And I wasn't sure if what I was feeling was real or if it was just... I don't know... wanting what I couldn't have."

"When were you sure?"

The corner of his mouth twitched. "That day by the lake. You were free, I was free. It just felt... Yeah."

"And then I took the pregnancy test."

He threaded his fingers through hers, lifting her hand to kiss her palm. "And then you took the test."

"And everything got messed up."

He shook his head. "I just knew you needed a friend. You didn't need me spilling my guts about how I felt about you. You had enough to deal with. Living in a new place, working a new job on top of the one you already had. And now you were having a baby. Every time I looked at you there was this scared expression on your face. You didn't need to carry my baggage, too."

"Maybe I like your baggage." She kissed his shoulder. It felt warm and tight against her mouth. "Maybe I like everything about you." She yawned, unable to stop it.

"Come here." He pulled her into the crook of his arm. "You're exhausted. You need some sleep."

She inclined her head to look at him. "Will you stay tonight?"

"Not planning on going anywhere." There was a lopsided smile on his face. "Anyway, we need to pick up your truck in the morning."

She'd forgotten about that. She opened her mouth to tell him he should have let her drive it home after all, but instead another yawn stole her words. It could wait until tomorrow. Everything could.

❧ 14 ❧

North couldn't stop looking at her. Couldn't stop touching her either, even though she was asleep and there was no way he wanted to wake her. About ten minutes after she'd finally succumbed to her exhaustion, she'd rolled out of his arms and onto her back. The covers were tangled around her hips, revealing the naked swell of her stomach and breasts. He'd tried to cover them up, but she'd moved the sheets again as though she was too hot to have them over her.

If she'd been awake he'd have worshipped those breasts until she was on the cusp of soaring all over again. Kissed his way down her body and consumed every part of her. The memory of her taste still lingered on his mouth, on his tongue.

The memory of her coming on his fingers made him so hard it was almost painful.

"North."

He looked up at her face, expecting to see her awake. But she was still fast asleep, her eyes closed tightly.

"The trees. We have to save the trees."

She was sleep talking? How did he not know she did that? He leaned over her, fascinated.

"No, not those ones."

The corner of his lips twitched. What the hell was she dreaming about? Was it wrong that he loved that he was part of her dream?

"Stupid," she muttered and he almost laughed out loud. He couldn't wait to tell her about this tomorrow.

Tomorrow. He blinked at the thought of it. It was like tonight was a watershed. That every moment in his life had led up to this one. He was in love with this woman, completely and unreservedly.

He was sick of fighting that feeling. Truth be told, he wasn't sure he could fight it even if he'd wanted to anymore.

The dam had well and truly been breached. He knew what it felt like to kiss her, to taste her, to make her come.

He didn't ever want to stop.

He wanted to spend tomorrow with her. And the day after. And the day after that.

He wanted to watch her stomach grow. Wanted to watch her become a mom.

Wanted to be there with her when she did.

"Not the helicopter again," she muttered.

This time he grinned. Did she have such vivid dreams all the time? He'd thought he knew everything about this woman, but there was so much more to learn. He wanted to ask her everything, to know everything.

Wanted to listen to her muttering every night.

He lay there for twenty more minutes, willing her to say something, but she was quiet now. She rolled onto her side, her hand cupping her abdomen and it immediately drew his eyes to her bump.

He wanted that, too. Wanted to be good enough to be a role model for that baby. He wanted to protect him or her from the world, the same way he protected everything he loved.

He wanted to be the man she deserved.

"You still awake?" Amber's voice cut through his thoughts.

"Yeah." He turned to look at her. Her eyes were heavy with sleep, her lips swollen where he'd kissed her so much. He wanted to kiss them again. "You've kept me awake with your talking."

"I don't talk in my sleep." She looked amused.

"Were you dreaming about the farm?" he asked.

She blinked. "I don't know. I think..." Her eyes flickered up to his. "Did I talk about the farm?"

"So you admit you talk in your sleep?" His lip quirked.

"Depends what I said." She pouted and he wanted to kiss her again.

"You said I could get a helicopter."

Her face was a picture. He wanted to laugh out loud. "I did not," she said. "Even asleep I'd never say that. And anyway, whatever I say when I'm asleep doesn't count."

"You said my name."

A smile played at her lips. "What else did I say?"

"Something about trees. Saving them. I don't know, you're pretty boring when you're asleep."

She swatted his arm. "Shut up."

"You shut up first."

She was grinning now. "Make me."

"You're gonna regret saying that." Curling his hand around her neck he pulled her closer, his mouth capturing hers. Warmth rushed through him. He felt so damn good he wasn't sure he could cope with it.

Then she kissed him back and he was certain he could.

"Don't go." North cupped her face, his thumbs tenderly stroking her jaw. His eyes didn't leave hers. Amber knew this man was intense, but not like this. She could get lost in him if she let herself.

He took her breath away.

They were sitting in his truck, parked next to hers in the square. It was just after nine in the morning – North had groaned when she'd dragged him out of bed.

"I have to go. I promised Kelly. We have to shop."

"You could shop online."

Amber burst out laughing. "Since when did friends go online shopping together? Anyway, we promised Cole we'd find him a Halloween costume."

"Halloween is months away."

"It's six weeks," Amber pointed out. "And since we're opening the shop this week, I won't have time to actually go shopping myself anymore." Between the farm and her still working at the tavern, she wasn't sure she'd have much time to do anything.

"Okay then. Go." He pouted, and she wanted to laugh again. "But come to mine when you're done."

"Why would I do that?" she asked, a smile playing on her lips.

"Because I'm gonna fuck the sass right out of you."

Heat suffused her. "I'd like to see you try."

"I'd like to try now." He leaned forward and kissed her hard. "Climb on top of me."

"We're in the middle of town."

"And?"

"And there are people around. Children."

He glanced out of the truck window as though surprised they were in public. "We never should have left your bed." He feathered his mouth against her jaw and neck, sending shivers down her spine. "Get Cole a costume, come back to mine, and be ready."

"Ready for what?" Those shivers weren't disappearing.

"Me."

She wasn't sure she could ever be ready for that. It didn't stop her grinning like a loon, though. "Goodbye, North." She pulled at the handle and jumped out of the truck, blowing him a kiss.

He looked grumpy, but she liked it. She liked him.

Last night had been so intense she'd barely had time to think about the fact that North, her best friend, was now her lover. That she knew the way he felt inside her—perfect, by the way—and the way his lips opened and the deep resonance of his groans.

Amber knew how he liked to cuddle in bed, how his voice sounded low and thick when they talked in the middle of the night. She'd thought she knew everything about him, but it was like she'd barely scratched the surface.

Grabbing her keys from her purse, she pulled her lip between her teeth. "What will you do today?" she asked.

"I'm heading over to the shop," he said. "I'll get it ready for opening."

A pang of guilt washed through her. "I should do that, too."

"It's a one-man job. And we're almost there. Anyway, it's mostly lifting stuff. And you can't..." he gestured at her stomach.

"I'll cook for you tonight. To say thank you."

"You don't need to thank me. I enjoy doing things for you."

Could he stop being so sweet please? It would be so easy to be overwhelmed by this man. To lose herself and everything else in him.

"Then I'll give you a blow job," she said, smiling when his

brows shot up. "The international language of thanks." She slammed the door closed on him, satisfied that she'd shocked him.

But the stupid thing was, now she was getting turned on. She wanted to climb back into the cab with him, get him to drive somewhere secluded, so she could trail her tongue along his hardness until he let out that soft, aching groan again.

She could live off North Winter's groans. They were a miraculous thing.

Just as she was wavering, her phone buzzed. She pulled it from her pocket and smiled when she saw the message.

Auntie Amber, Mom says you once dressed up as Mickey Mouse's Glove for Halloween. Is that true? (PS mom said I can use her phone.) - Cole

Of course she had to go shopping. She couldn't let Cole down. And maybe a break from this mercurial man would do her good. She found it hard to think straight when he was with her. Like he'd cast some kind of spell on her.

I'm afraid it's true. But we'll get you a much better costume. Tell your mom I'll be at your place to pick you up in ten minutes. Xx – Amber

When she looked up from her phone, North's gaze was still on her. She lifted a brow and he lifted one back and she bit down a smile.

"Bye," she mouthed, opening her truck with her key fob.

"Later," he mouthed back and the thought of it kept her

warm as she walked around and climbed into the driver's seat and started up the engine.

Later she'd be with him again. And maybe that couldn't come soon enough.

"Wow," Kelly breathed. "Wow, wow, wow. So is he good? Was he big? Hey, is he as intense in bed as he is out of it? Man, I have so many questions."

"We're in the Disney Store," Amber pointed out with a whisper. "Let's try to keep this PG rated."

Cole had run ahead of them and was standing in front of a Thor costume, his fingers trailing on the hammer. Another boy came and joined him and the two of them started talking.

Amber turned back to look at Kelly. "Okay, so is he intense?" Kelly said, looking annoyed at having to tone down her questions.

"Completely."

"And good?"

"Absolutely."

Kelly let out a long sigh. "You can't keep answering with one word. I need details. Like descriptive, long details." She wrinkled her nose. "Okay, so let's do this like it's a Disney movie. You're Cinderella and North's Prince Charming. Wait, no that's not right. He's the Beast and you're Beauty." She looked pleased with that. "So tell me how the Beast tamed you with his huge hairy—"

Amber put her hand up to stop Kelly. "I'm not tainting fairytales with dirty talk just to satisfy your curiosity."

"Spoilsport."

"Mom, can I go as Thor?" Cole asked, turning around to look at them.

"Sure, honey. Do they have your size?" She leaned over

him, flicking through the hangers to find the right one. "This is a nice hammer, isn't it?" she asked Amber. "Does North have one like this?"

Dear Lord, was she really going there?

"Does North have a Thor's hammer?" Cole asked. "That's cool."

"Shut up," Amber mouthed at Kelly, but Kelly just grinned.

"Here's your size," Kelly said, pulling a hanger off the rail. "Let's hold it against you." She turned to look at Amber. "What do you think?"

"I think Cole would make an excellent North," Amber said, giving him a wink.

"You mean Thor?" Kelly corrected her.

"That's what I said."

"Nope. You said North," Cole piped up. "But I don't want to dress up as him. He wears flannel shirts and doesn't shave properly."

"He does have a big hammer though," Kelly said. "Apparently."

Amber swatted her arm.

They bought Cole's costume and then headed to grab a snack and drink in the food court. Cole ordered a soda and Amber and Kelly both chose decaf lattes, Amber because it was good for the baby and Kelly because she really didn't need the caffeine – she was naturally on fire.

"I was thinking," Kelly said, lifting her cup to her lips. "Thor is practically an anagram of North."

"What's an anagram?" Cole asked, swinging his legs.

"It's when you mix the letters up from one word to make another. Like hate and heat. They have the same letters but are different words," Amber told him, shaking her head at Kelly.

"Oh." Cole frowned, his lips moving as he tried them both out. "Oh yeah. But North and Thor have different letters."

"Thor's just missing the 'N', honey," Kelly told him.

"Yeah, I guess he is."

"And he's tall and big like Thor, isn't he?" Kelly said, shooting Amber an amused glance.

"Um, yeah I guess. But he's not blond."

Thank God Cole was on her side.

"But he is strong," Cole added. "He has big muscles. I saw them once when we came to the farm and he was chopping wood. He had his shirt off."

Kelly let out a snigger.

"And Mom was really weird because she talked about wanting to eat him for dinner." Cole frowned at her. "You shouldn't eat people."

"You hear that," Kelly said, still grinning as she looked at Amber. "No eating North."

"Hey, Mom, is that Noah?" Cole asked, pointing at a table a few down from theirs. "Hey, Noah!" he shouted.

The little boy turned around and waved madly when he saw Cole. The next minute he was running over to them. "I'm going as Thor for Halloween," he told Cole.

"Me too," Cole said.

"Thor twins!" Kelly clapped her hands together as though it was the most amazing thing in the world and not an oops at all. "That's so cool."

"Yay! Twins," Cole said, holding his hand up for a high five. Noah slapped his palm against Cole's.

"You're fabulous," Amber mouthed at Kelly.

"Shut up."

As they started talking about their costumes, the man from Noah's table came over. "Hi, I'm sorry. He took off before I could stop him."

"No problem. We're almost finished here anyway."

"Dad, can Cole come play with us?" Noah asked. "Please?"

Noah's dad smiled at Kelly. "We were just heading over to the play area," he said, pointing to the indoor playground at the far end of the food court. "Just for half an hour before we head home. Cole's welcome to join us."

"Can I, Mom?" Cole asked, looking excited.

"Are you sure?" Kelly asked Noah's dad. Amber tried not to smile because she might be the most outspoken person she knew, but Kelly hated relying on other people.

"Yeah of course."

"Well, okay then." Kelly leaned over and ruffled Cole's hair. "Be good and come back when Noah's dad tells you."

"I will." Cole beamed and jumped down from his chair. He and Noah chatted animatedly as they followed his dad over to the play area.

"It's not like you to let Cole go off with somebody," Amber pointed out.

"Yeah, well I know Noah's family. They're good people." She turned to her friend. "And now I can grill you without little ears listening."

"Oh God."

"So?" Kelly asked her. "Spill it. Everything. I want to hear all the details from beginning to end."

Giving into the inevitable, Amber filled her friend in, though Kelly grimaced a few times when she skipped over the dirtier details. Luckily, Cole kept calling over and waving from the top of the soft climbing frame, interrupting Kelly's flow.

Amber thanked God for small mercies.

"So now what?" Kelly asked Amber.

"What do you mean?" Amber frowned.

"Does he want to be involved in your pregnancy?"

Amber cupped her stomach. "I don't know. We didn't talk about that."

"What *did* you talk about?"

"We... ah... didn't talk that much." Why was her face getting so hot?

Kelly started laughing. "Well, that's obvious."

"It's new. I don't think either of us wanted to get too serious. At least not last night. It's like a little bubble. Neither of us wants to burst it."

Kelly ran her fingertip around the rim of her now-empty cup. "Thing is, it's gonna get burst. You're having a baby in a few months. You're gonna get huge and grumpy and achy and won't be able to have sex for weeks. Is he up for that?"

A little twinge pulled at Amber's chest. "I don't know."

"It makes sense that you want him to be there for you." Kelly caught her eye. "That you'd want the baby to have a father figure, I mean."

"That's not why..." Amber shook her head. "I don't expect him to do that."

"What else is he gonna do?" Kelly asked her. "If he's around you, he's gonna be around the baby. That kid is going to be hanging off your tits for months. Ask me how I know."

Amber glanced over at the play area where Cole and Noah were throwing balls against a target and laughing uproariously. "I don't need to ask."

"You don't need to look sad," Kelly said, her voice sympathetic. "If a guy like North came along and wanted to be my baby daddy, I'd snap him up in a heartbeat. It's tough being a single mom." She noticed Amber's face falling. "It's great, too. But having a guy on your side." Kelly shrugged. "That would be the dream."

"I didn't sleep with him so he'd be this baby's father," Amber told her. "Shaun's the father."

"I think we both know Shaun's going to be a shit father. And it makes sense, really it does. North would have been around, anyway. You two are best friends. He'd always be an uncle figure to the kid. It's not that big a step to turn him into the daddy."

"I don't think he wants to be the baby's daddy," Amber told her. There was a weird twisty feeling in her stomach. "He's never wanted kids."

"So what's he doing having sex with a pregnant woman?"

Amber wasn't sure she had the answer to that. She hated that she didn't. "I don't know," she whispered.

"Well you need to know." Kelly's voice was soft. "It's not just you anymore."

"I know it's not."

"Then ask him," Kelly urged. "Ask him what he wants from this. Because if he hurts you it's one thing, but if he ends up hurting your baby you'll never forgive him."

"He won't hurt the baby," Amber said. She was sure of that.

"He might not mean to, but just imagine when your baby is Cole's age and is getting all confused about this big guy who keeps spending the night but doesn't want anything to do with him. How do you think that's going to work?"

Amber shook her head. "I wouldn't let it go on that long."

"So how long would you let it go on?"

Another question that made her chest ache. How long would she let this thing between her and North go on if it led nowhere? The thought of not being with him, of not touching him, being kissed by him, it felt physically painful. She wanted him, all of him.

But she was going to be a mother.

She needed to talk to him. But what if he admitted he just wanted this to be physical? That he didn't want anything to do with the baby? It was going to rip her heart in two.

"Oh honey." Kelly took her hand. "Don't cry."

"I shouldn't have slept with him," Amber whispered. "What if I lose him?"

"Then I'll go beat his ass," Kelly told her. "But let's face it, he'll never walk away from you. He's a good man. He'll stay even if he doesn't want to."

That was worse. So much worse. Amber felt physically sick, mostly because Kelly was right. Among the many shades of North Winter, there was honor. The kind of honor that made him stand up for everybody he loved.

"I don't want to trap him," Amber whispered.

"What if he wants to be trapped?" Kelly replied. "Seriously, you two just need a good conversation. Be honest. Tell each other what you want."

Amber knew what she wanted. Her baby and him. But was it too much? There was the small matter of Shaun, who she still hadn't been able to speak to. He was her baby's father.

So where did that leave North?

All her life she'd assumed that when she had a family it would be like the one she was born into. A mom, a dad who loved them. A nuclear family that took care of each other.

Not once had she thought she hoped the baby's father would be a guy who hated her, and that she'd fall in love with her best friend who never wanted children.

"This is a mess." She buried her face in her hands.

"I'm sorry," Kelly said. "I didn't mean to make you feel worse."

"I know you didn't. It's not your fault. It's mine. I keep making all the wrong decisions."

"It could be the right decision," Kelly told her. "The best decision of your life. You just need to talk to each other."

Amber nodded, slowly peeling her hands from her face. "I will."

Kelly smiled. "Come on, let's go over to watch Cole and Noah for a little while. All those screaming kids will remind you that your worst decisions are yet to come."

15

When she drove past the Winterville Inn there were work crews dotted all over the driveway and the huge sprawling building, their yellow vests catching the last of the afternoon sun. They were starting to decorate for Christmas, even though Halloween had yet to come. Time was passing too quickly.

Before they knew it winter would be here.

This would be the last time she watched the decorations go up as a single woman without a child. Next year she'd have a baby. Not even a newborn but a real, big baby who would likely be crawling and pulling decorations down from the tree.

She had so much to do. Yes, she was in the house but she wasn't prepared at all. And next week they'd open the shop and things would get crazy.

"Can you drop me and Cole off at the Tavern?" Kelly asked, looking up from her phone. "Grandpa's there and there's a problem with a delivery."

"You need some help?"

"Nope. There's somebody you need to talk to. No putting

it off by helping me." Kelly smirked and tapped out a quick reply on her phone.

"I don't even know where he is right now."

"There's only one way to find out."

Amber parked outside the Tavern and helped Kelly and Cole unload their bags from shopping. Cole insisted on carrying the Thor costume, his cheeks pink with pleasure as Kelly's dad came out and Cole showed him the hammer.

"Thank you," Kelly said, hugging Amber.

"Shouldn't I be thanking you? I feel like I just had hours of therapy," Amber said, her voice muffled by Kelly's shoulder.

"No. I should be apologizing for bossing you around. It's so much easier when it's not your own life, you know?"

Amber nodded. "I do."

"So next time I get hurt by a guy you can lecture me," Kelly offered.

"It's a deal." It would almost certainly be a while. Kelly rarely dated. Between running the Tavern and being Cole's mom she swore she didn't have time. But there was more to it than that. More than Amber could unravel in a quick mall-therapy session.

Maybe once she got her own life sorted out she'd help Kelly, too.

"Oh no." Kelly's voice lowered to a whisper. "Why now?" She leaned down to Cole. "Go inside, honey. Stay with Grandpa."

Amber followed Kelly's gaze, swallowing when she saw Kyle Walker bearing down on them, his eyes dark and narrow.

"Oh God," Amber whispered, as he stopped in front of them and folded his arms across his chest.

"Is it true?"

Amber swallowed. "What?"

"You're pregnant?" His gaze flickered down to her stomach. She was wearing a long sleeved t-shirt and a pair of yoga pants. Comfortable and revealing her now-rounded bump.

"Yes."

"Is it Shaun's?"

"Shouldn't Shaun be asking that?" Kelly asked. She looked fierce, like she was about to go into battle for Amber.

Ignoring her, Kyle took a step closer to Amber. "What are you doing? Trying to trap him?"

"I'm not trying to trap anybody," she told him. "I'm pregnant and the last I heard it took two to make that happen."

"So why haven't you told him?"

"She has tried!" Kelly threw her hands up. "He blocked her. She's been trying to get a hold of him any way she could before everybody else found out."

"Is everything okay?"

Amber turned to see North standing behind them. He put a gentle hand on her shoulder and it made her want to melt.

"Is there a problem here?" North continued, his voice tight as he and Kyle stared at each other.

From the corner of her eye Amber could see Kelly's eyes light up. She always did like a guy fight. At school she'd be at the front of any crowd if there was a brawl. She loved drama – especially when it didn't involve her.

Right now Amber was wishing it didn't involve *her* either.

She put her hand over North's, where his fingers were almost digging into her shoulder. She could feel the tension in them. "It's okay," she said. "Kyle was just asking about the baby."

North slid his hand down over her stomach, as though protecting her. Her heart did a little leap in her chest.

Kyle frowned. "It is Shaun's, right?" His jaw twitched. "Or is it *yours*?" he asked North. "You two been fucking around behind Shaun's back?"

Amber flinched at the implication. North's chest was firm against her back now, like he was trying to protect her from all sides. She could feel the heat of his skin, hear the tightness of his breath.

He was getting riled and she understood that. Hell, she was getting riled, too.

"I never slept around on Shaun," she said. "I got pregnant when I was with him, but I didn't find out until he was gone."

"So what the hell is going on here?" Kyle asked, gesturing at her and North.

"It's none of your business," North said. He sounded on edge. Amber slid the fingers of her other hand through his. It was okay. They had this. She knew this would happen eventually.

North just needed to not end up in jail right now.

"Damn right it's my business," Kyle said, his face red. "If you're pregnant with my friend's baby you shouldn't be letting another man touch you like you're a whore."

Kelly let out a gasp at the same time North pulled his hand from Amber's. She tried to grab it again, but he was already in front of her, facing up to Kyle.

"Let's get one thing straight," North said, his voice dangerously low. "You don't call her a whore. You don't call any woman a whore. *Ever*." He put his hand on Kyle's chest.

Kyle's mouth twisted into a grimace. "Take your hands off me."

"North..." Amber reached for him again and Kelly came to stand beside her.

"Let him do this," Kelly whispered. "Kyle needs to know he can't talk to you like that. The way they all treat you is so wrong."

Amber knew that. But it felt wrong letting North stand up for her. And she was afraid that he wouldn't know when to stop.

"I say it as I see it," Kyle spat. "She's pregnant with another man's kid. My best friend's kid. She shouldn't be spreading her legs for anybody else."

North's hand shot up Kyle's chest, his fingers digging into his neck. Kyle's eyes widened.

"Tell her you're sorry," North grunted, his eyes narrow, his jaw tight.

Kyle pulled at North's fingers. "Get off me."

"Apologize to the lady."

"North," Amber said, finally reaching out to touch his shoulder. It was so tense it felt like steel. "Stop it."

He shook his head but said nothing.

"Let go," Amber whispered. "Please."

He turned to look at her, blinking, like he'd only just realized she was there.

As if in slow motion, he removed his hand from Kyle's throat. Kyle took a step back, fury molding his features.

"You want to stay away from him," Kyle told her. "He's a fucking maniac."

"He's standing up for her," Kelly said. "Which is more than you or Shaun have ever done. She's gone through all of this alone. Can you imagine that? Finding out you're pregnant and the father won't take your call? He's an asshole."

Amber shot her a look. "I've got this," she said quietly. Kelly wrinkled her nose, as though she didn't believe it.

But the truth was, she *did* have it. She had to. In a few months she'd be a mom and this baby needed her to be strong. To be a protective mama bear who fought off anybody and anything that threatened them.

And if she could do that for the baby, she damn well needed to do it for herself.

"Kyle," she said, pushing between North and him. "If you call me a whore again you don't need to worry about North or

Kelly because I'll knee you in the groin so hard your balls will end up in your throat."

Kelly coughed a laugh.

"So you go tell Shaun about the baby. You can tell him that I'm doing just fine, and if he wants to be involved he can be. But only if he shows me some respect because I'm carrying some precious damn cargo here."

Kyle stared at her, his fingertips dancing on his throat. For a moment she wondered if he was going to lash out at her. He'd never liked her. At first she'd assumed it was because Shaun was spending more time with her than with his friends. The stupid thing was, she'd encouraged him to go be with them. But that didn't make Kyle happy either.

Bailing on their wedding had been the final straw in their fragile détente.

"And now I'm going home," she told him. "This is the last time I'm going to talk to you about any of this. Because North was right. This is none of your business. I don't want you near me so just..." she waved her hand. "Just keep away."

Kyle opened his mouth to reply, but something changed his mind. His eyes flickered over her shoulder, where North was standing.

"Whatever," Kyle muttered and turned to walk away.

"And you're barred from the Tavern," Kelly yelled after him. Kyle didn't even acknowledge her.

A weird sensation came over Amber. Her chest hitched as a cough of laughter exploded from her mouth.

"What?" Kelly asked, as she continued to laugh.

"Nothing."

Kelly put her hand on her hips. "I just don't want him bothering my staff."

"I know. And I'm grateful." Amber was in control now. "It was just funny, in a really unfunny situation."

"Well, I'd better go in before my dad throws a fit over this delivery." Kelly hugged her. "Call me later, okay?"

"Okay."

She watched as Kelly walked inside, her hips swinging as though she didn't have a care in the world. That was Kelly, nothing daunted her.

One of the many things Amber loved about her.

Once her friend was inside, Amber slowly turned to look at North. His expression was wary, his eyes darting over her face like he was trying to read her mood.

"I'm sorry. I shouldn't..." He shook his head as she started speaking at the same time.

"Let's go home. We should talk."

16

They picked up coffees and pastries to go from The Cold Finger Café, mostly because Amber's stomach was growling with hunger, and he knew this was the kind of conversation they shouldn't have on an empty belly.

Not that he wanted to have this conversation. As they walked into her place – she'd insisted they go there because she had to change her clothes for some reason – all those doubts he'd had about himself for years washed over him.

It had been one day since they'd gotten together and he'd already managed to mess things up.

Kyle Walker calling Amber a whore had made every cell in his body react. No man should call a woman that, not ever. But to call the woman he loved that was unacceptable. The red mist had descended so fast it took his breath away.

"Make yourself at home," Amber said, pointing at her new sofas. "I'm just gonna get some fresh clothes on." She wrinkled her nose. "And maybe take a shower."

"What were you doing at the mall?" North asked her, putting their coffees on the low table in the center of the living room. "Working out?"

"It's not because of sweat," Amber told him, lifting a brow. "I might have peed myself a little when I was shouting at Kyle."

An adorable blush stole her cheeks.

"Oh."

"Don't you look at me like that," she warned him, her eyes full of fire. "I'm pregnant and I'm riled up and I peed myself in the middle of Winterville Square. Nobody told me that pregnancy would be one long loss of dignity. I've had more men look at my private parts in the past few months than I ever had interested in them during college." She shook her head. "And you know what? Everybody keeps telling me it's going to get worse. I'm not going to get any sleep, I'm going to be leaking milk every time another baby cries. Oh, and apparently you get floppy down *there* and did you know there's even some kind of surgery called a husband stitch just to make your partner feel satisfied?"

North opened his mouth, trying to find the right words to say. He wanted to laugh but he knew that wasn't the right response. It was just that she looked so angry and sounded so West Virginian. She was also so damn cute that all he wanted to do was kiss her.

"A husband stitch?" he finally managed to get out. "What's that?"

"They stitch your vagina up to make you tighter for your husband."

"Shouldn't they just give the husband an enlargement?"

"Thank you!" She clapped her hands together. "That's what I said. Why would any woman want to push a head the size of a bowling ball through the smallest channel in the world and then go through the pain of having it all tightened again."

"I'm with you." He nodded.

"You know what else?" she asked him, on a roll now.

"No, but I'm excited for you to tell me." It was getting harder to not bundle her up in his arms.

"Kelly said she pooped when she gave birth. Actually pooped on the gurney in front of everybody." She lowered her voice. "And then she told me that wasn't actually the worst part."

It took every ounce of control he had to keep his expression neutral.

"Are you trying to not laugh?" Amber asked him.

This was the problem with knowing somebody inside out. Amber knew his tells. When he was lying, when he was sad, when he was trying to keep the inappropriate laughter inside.

"I'm just trying to show some solidarity," he told her. "It sucks that women have to go through all of this."

She nodded, as though satisfied with his response. "Thank you."

"Any time."

She started to walk out of the living room then stopped dead, turning to look at him, her face aghast.

"Did I really just tell you I peed myself?"

He frowned, trying to decide on the best answer. "Um... yes? No?"

"Can you forget about it?"

"It would be my pleasure."

"And never mention the poop thing to Kelly. She'd kill me."

He mimed zipping his lips. "It's our secret."

"Thank you. Now drink your coffee."

He did as he was told, sipping at the red paper cup with white snowflakes emblazoned on it. It was so quiet in here he could hear when Amber turned on the shower, when the cadence of the spray changed as she stepped under it, then again when she stepped out. By the time it turned off, he'd finished his coffee but still hadn't thought what he was going to say to her.

"So here I am, pee free," she said, her bare feet padding across the living room rug. Her hair was wet and balled into one of those buns all girls seemed to wear, and she'd put on a pair of yoga pants that looked exactly the same as the ones she'd presumably put in the laundry. Her top, though, that was what pulled him in.

She was wearing one of his old t-shirts. A black one with an old album on the front, and tour dates on the back.

He hadn't worn it for years. And seeing it on Amber did weird things to him.

"Nice t-shirt."

"Thanks. I stole a whole bunch from you."

"You did? What else have you got?"

She grinned. "I knew you wouldn't notice. They're just really comfortable, you know? I hate feeling rough things against my skin right now."

He tried to not grin.

"Stop it," she told him. "I didn't mean you."

"If I'm going to lose half my clothing, I can at least appreciate your double entendres," he said. "By the way, I want them back once you have the baby."

"They'll have boob imprints in them. You'll look like a woman."

He shook his head, still grinning.

Amber took a sip of her coffee—decaf—even though it had to be lukewarm by now. "So who's going first?" she asked, and he felt the dread come over him again.

"You?"

"Why not you?" she asked him. "What happened yesterday with your parents?"

"My mom called while we were showing you the house

and told me that my dad was in the hospital because he'd broken his hand."

"Oh no. Is he okay?" Amber's eyes widened.

"He's fine. The wall between their kitchen and living room isn't."

"He hit it?" she asked, horrified.

"Yup. They were arguing about whether the steaks mom was cooking were overdone, and then things apparently got ugly. Mom was screaming. He hit the wall, the cops were called by the neighbors, and he ended up in the hospital."

"Was your mom hurt?"

"No. But she could have been. If he'd hit her instead of the wall." North grimaced. "And yesterday when she told me, all I could think was that my dad and I have the same anger running through us."

She shook her head. "That's not true."

"It's what I've thought. And it's what scares me constantly. What if I end up being like that?"

"You won't. I know you won't," Amber whispered. She put her coffee down and reached for his hand.

Her fingers were soft and reassuring. But his stomach was still twisted.

"And then I realized something. That I had a choice if I want to be like that." He looked up at her. "It's no coincidence that Dad hit the wall and not Mom. He chose to because he knew the consequences if he'd actually battered her. In all these years he never has. He rants and shouts and hits walls because he could get away with it. That's a choice, right?"

Amber nodded.

He took a deep breath. "And it got me to thinking that I could control it, too. Get some therapy, decide to not get angry, whatever." She was tracing his palm with her fingers now, and he didn't want it to stop. "And then Kyle called you a whore, and I lost all control."

"No, you didn't. You stepped away."

"Only because you asked me to."

Amber's gaze was so soft it felt like a fuzzy blanket over his fears. "Does your dad stop because your mom asks him to?"

North shook his head. "No."

"Did he stop when you were a kid and begged him not to punish you?"

He shook his head again. His dad had never stopped until North was crying. That's when the satisfaction came. The feeling of power, of winning.

Of breaking another human being.

"Then you're nothing like him. And you know what? I like you standing up for me. I don't have anybody else to do that for me, apart from Kelly." She rolled her eyes. "And that's a blessing and a curse. But seriously, you're a friend and you take care of me. That's what friends do."

"I lost it with Mason when I heard he'd been messing around with Alaska."

"You two pranced around in the street like Hugh Grant and Colin Firth in *Bridget Jones*," Amber said, shaking her head. "Neither of you threw a punch."

"But I did punch Josh," he pointed out.

"When you were both kids. And he'd pulled Holly's panties out of his pocket." She leaned forward, threading her fingers through his and squeezing tight. "You protect people. That's who you are. You don't get angry because you want to hurt people. You get angry because you don't want those you love getting hurt. And I for one am here for that."

"I never want to hurt you," he told her, his voice low.

"And you never have. Ever." She was vehement now.

"You're my friend, North. My best friend. I know I'm always safe with you."

He reached for her. He couldn't help it. Her words were perfect but her body was life. He needed to hold her, to feel her, to know she meant what she said. His hands slipped around her waist and she scrambled over him, her legs straddling his thighs. He ran his palms over them again and again, just to remind himself that she was there.

"You don't need me to stand up for you," he told her. "You did pretty kick ass with Kyle yourself. And then Kelly topped it off, really hitting him where it hurt, banning him from the Tavern."

"He's gonna be pissed."

"Yeah he is. But it's not your problem." He lifted his hand, his fingers coiling a lock of wet hair that had escaped her bun. "And I'm always here if you need me."

"I know." She nodded. "And that's what I wanted to talk to you about."

He'd forgotten she had things to say, too. "Okay, tell me."

She took a deep breath, two tiny lines appearing between her brows. "I'm scared of losing you," she told him. "If this all goes wrong."

"This as in you and me?" he clarified.

She nodded. "Yes. You're my best friend. My family. We run a business together. If we crash and burn..." she trailed off, pulling her gaze from his. "Everything will be ruined."

"I'm not going to hurt you, I told you that."

"What if I hurt you?"

He blinked. "I'm a big boy. I can deal with it."

"I don't think either of us could. We need to really think about this, North. Because my heart won't survive if you're not in my life."

He cupped her cheek. "I'll always be in your life. However you'll have me."

"You can't make promises like that. I'm pregnant. I'm having another man's child. Neither of us know how things will go. We're running in the dark here, and there could be all kinds of hazards we can't see looming in front of us. I just think we should... I don't know. Be careful, I guess."

He said nothing, just cupped her face with his hand. He'd do anything for her, he knew that in his heart.

"I've got four months," she told him. "And then my whole world will turn upside down. Yours doesn't have to if you don't want it to. But mine, I have no control over it. I'm going to be a mom and that'll be the most important thing. You'll come second and I'm not sure that's fair to you."

"Of course I should come second." His voice was thick. "That's what good parents do."

She took another deep breath. "And the thing that I keep thinking is that it's okay for me to have my heart broken. But I can't let my baby get hurt in the process."

"That would never happen. I'd never hurt either one of you."

"What if he looks like Shaun?"

North lifted a brow. "Don't most babies look like Winston Churchill?"

Her lips twitched. "You know what I mean. It's hard enough that we have all this baggage." She waved her arm as though pointing at it. "But I'll have another man's baby, too. Do you know the likelihood of this working out?"

"No," he said honestly. "Do you?"

"I don't." She looked so sad. "But I'm guessing it isn't good."

"So what do we do?" he asked her. "Because I want to be with you. Both of you."

She ran her tongue along her bottom lip. "I guess we wait and see. And don't make promises we can't keep."

But he wanted to. He wanted to make her all the

promises. The ones that were battering his ribcage. He loved her. He wanted her. He never planned on hurting her.

Yeah, but who does? Did Shaun? Did your dad when he first got together with your mom?

"Do you want me to walk away?" he asked gruffly. "Because I will, if that's what you need from me."

"No." Her voice was small. "I don't want that."

"Then what do you want? Tell me how to make this work. I love you. I'll do whatever it takes."

"I want us to just... be together. For now. Until the baby comes."

"And then?"

"And then you can decide if you want to be part of my mayhem or not. When you see the dirty diapers and hear the screams and find out that I refused the husband stitch."

"I'm getting the enlargement, remember?"

"Hah." She rolled her eyes. "If anybody doesn't need an enlargement it's you."

"Thank you. I think." He gave her a crooked smile. "And as for the rest, I'll do what you need me to."

"You will?"

"Yes I will." He leaned forward, his lips brushing hers. "You can try to scare me all you want but I'm not going anywhere."

"North..."

"I know. No rash decisions. And I agree to your terms."

"Thank you." She wrapped her arms around his neck, kissing his jaw, his cheek, the corner of his lips.

"Any time." *Because I love you. And I'm not going anywhere.*

✺ 17 ✺

"We grow six different types of trees in the main farm," North was telling the group of grade school children gathered around him in the farm shop. "But we also experiment with about ten new varieties annually. Amber over there is our chief tree baby maker."

The children turned around to stare at her by the counter. The shop had been open for two weeks now and Wednesdays were the day that school visits were allowed. This latest group was from Charleston, and they couldn't have been more than six or seven. They were all wearing bright orange shirts with their school name emblazoned across the back.

"Hi!" she waved at them.

"Hello," they chorused back.

She tried to not grin, but they were so cute. "You'll see the greenhouse on your tour," she told them. "That's where I grow all my tree babies. And don't forget to come back at the end so you can all take a little living Christmas tree home with you. If you take good care of it, it should stay alive until the big day."

The kids started chattering excitedly between them. Then

North cleared his throat and they all craned their heads to look at him.

She smiled because he had to look like a giant to the kids. The weather was cooling, and he was wearing a pair of dark jeans and a white t-shirt with a black and red checkered shirt over the top.

His eyes caught hers and she felt her heart pound against her chest.

In the last two weeks they'd been almost inseparable, apart from when she was working at the Tavern or North was out in the fields. She'd only spent two nights apart from him in the last fourteen – one where she'd stayed over at Kelly's to watch Cole while Kelly's dad was out, and another when North had to travel to Charleston for a meeting.

She'd hated him being away.

And she was aware that despite all of her protests she was already getting attached to him. There was still that little niggle in her mind that this could all end in a few months when her baby made their appearance.

"So here's the deal," North was saying to the kids. "You follow me, you don't run off, and you don't touch anything unless I say it's safe to do so. Everybody got it?"

"Got it," the children chanted.

He walked through the glass door that led to the farm; the children following behind him like ducklings following their mother. It was even cuter because she knew he hated doing these tours. She was the one who usually did them, but she was just so tired today.

He'd offered, and she'd accepted gladly. You had to be on point when you were dealing with school kids, especially little ones. They had a habit of running when you least expected it.

Once they were out of the shop, she sorted through some boxes of decorations they'd packed away last year, pulling out the ones that she liked and putting the others away to donate.

There was a woman's shelter in a town past Marshall's Gap that they donated trees to every year, and there were never enough decorations to go around.

She was just closing up the last box when her phone rang. She picked it up, expecting it to be Kelly, but Shaun's name flashed up on the screen. Amber stared at it for a moment, the shock of seeing it making her body freeze.

He must have unblocked her. Which meant he had to know. Kyle had told him. The reality of the situation hit her like a ten ton truck. She clenched her teeth and accepted the call, slowly lifting the phone to her ear.

"Hello?"

There was nothing. She said it again.

And then she heard his voice.

"Is it true?"

Not even a hello. She flinched at the harshness of his tone. "Shaun."

A loud huff came down the line. "Kyle told me you're pregnant."

"I am, yes."

"And it's mine?"

She exhaled raggedly. "Yes."

"How do you know?"

"Because the dates line up. I conceived when we were together and I wasn't sleeping with anybody else." And yes, the last part was a jibe. But maybe he deserved it.

"I thought you were careful." He cleared his throat. "*We* were careful."

"I know," she mumbled. "So did I."

"Did you do this to trap me?" he asked, his voice low. "To make me come back?"

"No! If you'll remember, I was the one that ended things. It came as a shock to me, too. And I tried to contact you. You blocked me."

"I went away to forget about you. So what happens now?"

"The baby's due in January."

"It's too late to..." He cleared his throat. "Do anything about it?"

She paused, frowning. "Very much so."

He let out a low curse. "So what happens now? You want money?"

"No. I'm doing fine. I've moved into my parents' place. The nursery is ready. I've got a good obstetrician. I just wanted you to know that the baby is coming."

"So you're really doing this?"

She noted the word 'you'. It wasn't a surprise, but it still hurt.

"Yes, I am."

"I'm not sure I want to be part of it. I need to think." He let out a long sigh. "Fuck, Amber. Why didn't you just get rid of it?"

Something fluttered in her stomach. At first she thought it was just anger. But then she felt it again. Stronger this time. Something pressing against her skin. The baby was kicking.

She wasn't sure whether to laugh or cry. This was supposed to be a milestone. Something special. And all she wanted to do was shout at her ex.

"I need to go," she said. "A customer just walked in. Do you want me to send you some ultrasound pictures?"

"No." He sounded vehement. "I just need time. I'm not sure what I want."

"Well when you know, you know how to find me. Good-bye, Shaun."

She ended the call before she could say something cutting, because this baby was still moving and she didn't want him or her to hear an angry voice. She'd read that babies could hear at this stage, that their mother's voice was soothing.

Shaun didn't want to be involved with the baby. She'd known it in her heart but it still hurt to hear it. The baby would start life without a father who loved him or her. As they got older they'd ask questions. Where was he? Why didn't he want to know them? Why did they have to sit alone at Father's Day Donuts at school?

Kelly had given her enough of an insight into what it was to be a single mom. She'd insisted it was easiest when they were little. "Especially before they can ask questions, or before they look around and see a mom and a dad in every other family."

But Kelly was strong. Probably the strongest person Amber knew.

The door opened and the shop was filled with high pitched chatter as North, the children, and their teachers walked back inside. He caught her eye and she gave him a small smile. She didn't want him to worry.

And he did worry. She knew that. It was strange how much more she noticed now that she knew this man intimately. When they slept in the same bed he'd lay behind her, his hand cupping her stomach and it felt like he was shielding her and the baby.

It felt like she was safe.

"Okay!" she shouted out, cutting through the children's talking. "Who wants to tell me their favorite tree?"

They started shouting out different varieties as North walked behind the counter and helped her pass out the little potted trees they'd made for them. He looked at her, his soft eyes catching hers, as though he knew there was something wrong.

She'd talk to him later. When things were quiet and she'd gotten her head around finally hearing from Shaun.

"You going to tell me what's been bothering you all day?" North asked her, as he steered the car into her driveway. They hadn't talked about whose house to go to tonight, but from the way she'd been acting he knew she needed to be at her home. She felt most relaxed there, and he wanted her to feel safe.

She unclasped her seatbelt and stared vacantly out of the window. "Let's go inside."

He followed her in without saying anything. The first few times he'd stayed she'd asked him to move his truck to behind the house so that people wouldn't gossip. But she'd stopped asking so he'd stopped moving.

And he was aware it was a bit of a dick move. But he didn't care about gossip. He wanted people to know she was his. When she was around him he felt like a gorilla beating his chest, claiming what was his.

For a while he'd wondered if it was her hormones having an effect on him. He felt this weird need to protect her. To make sure she was safe. And it extended to the baby, because that baby was such a part of her. He loved touching her stomach knowing there was a child growing inside of her.

It brought out more feelings than he cared to admit to.

He was silent as she kicked off her shoes, putting her hand on the wall to keep her balance. Then she dropped her purse and slid her feet into her fuzzy slippers and walked into the kitchen.

"Shaun called me."

The mention of his name made North's jaw tighten. "What did he say?"

"Not a lot." Amber leaned on the kitchen counter. He walked around to join her, putting his arms around her from behind. She melted against him, and it felt like he could breathe again. "He wanted to know if it was his. How I could be so stupid. If I wanted his money. And then he said he wasn't sure if he wanted to be in the baby's life or not."

North swallowed hard. "Okay. How does that make you feel?"

"I don't know. Sad. Annoyed. Angry. But mostly with myself for putting the baby in this situation." She leaned her head against his shoulder. "I feel like I'm ruining their life from the start."

"You're not ruining anybody's life." He slid his hands down, cupping her stomach. "This baby is lucky to have you."

"You know the worst thing? I was about to rip him a new one and then I felt the baby kick. And I remembered what the books say about the baby being able to hear my voice."

"Wait a minute," North said, turning her around to face him. "You felt the baby kick?"

"That's what I said."

He grinned. "So you felt your baby move inside of you and you give a shit about what Shaun thinks? Aren't you getting this all the wrong way around?"

Her brows pulled together. "What do you mean?"

"I mean this is amazing. Your baby kicked you. He or she is growing, they're healthy, they're letting you know who's boss."

Her lips twitched like she was trying to not smile. "I think we all know who's boss. I don't get up to pee in the middle of the night for my own sake."

"I like it when you get up in the middle of the night. You're all snuggly when you come back to bed."

Her eyes narrowed. "Stop charming me. I'm trying to be annoyed."

He leaned forward to kiss the corner of her cheek. "Have you felt it since?"

"The baby?"

"Yeah."

"I think I felt them again this afternoon."

"Can I feel?" A crooked smile pulled at his lips.

"You can't feel anything from the outside yet," she told him. "I tried and nada."

"Let me try anyway," he said and she nodded. North dropped to his knees, pushing her top up and exposing her smooth, swollen belly.

Don't get hard. You're about to feel a baby.

He couldn't stop himself from kissing her skin. She smelled of strawberry body lotion, the stuff she rubbed religiously into her stomach to try to ward off stretch marks.

Slowly he moved his hands up, placing his palms flat on her stomach. It was warm and hard, but he couldn't feel any movements at all.

"Come on, baby, move for me."

"I don't think they kick on demand," she told him, but her voice was soft. She tangled her fingers in his hair.

And for one damn moment he knew what perfection felt like. In Amber's kitchen, on his knees, gazing at her stomach. Her fingers were massaging his scalp, his senses full of her.

"There," she breathed. "Can you feel it?"

"No." His brows knitted. "Where?"

She pulled her hand from his hair and he immediately missed her touch. She placed her hand over his, moving his palm until it was on the side of her stomach, where her hip flared out.

"I'm gonna need you to work harder, kid," North said to her stomach. "Let's make a pact. You kick for me, and I'll take you out for ice cream when you're older."

"Stop leading my baby astray," Amber told him, but there was a smile in her voice. "I think it'll be a couple of weeks before you really feel anything."

His thumb drew circles on her skin. "I guess while I'm down here..."

"What?"

She was smiling. He leaned forward to kiss her belly button, and the faint line that was etched into her skin from her navel to the hem of her yoga pants.

"Nothing." He gave her a grin then pulled her yoga pants down, revealing her blue panties stretching over the base of her curves.

"North..." She let out a sigh as he pushed his face against her and breathed in, his hands pushing her pants further down her legs. He couldn't get enough of her. "Don't smell me. I'm sweaty and I haven't showered."

"That's just how I like you." He hooked his thumbs into her panties, pulling them down her thighs. She parted them without him having to touch her. Like she knew what he wanted.

What he needed.

To make her his. He wanted to take her breath away until his was the only name she could remember.

He slid his tongue along her, the tip of it curling against her clit. Her thighs quivered as he licked her again. She couldn't move. Those pants were like shackles. Without a doubt, she was his willing captive.

And he loved it.

Her fingers were back in his hair, more vehemently this time, her nails scratching his scalp somewhere between pain and pleasure. He pushed his face closer, consuming her, his tongue teasing until her breaths became cries.

"North..."

He answered with his fingers, pushing two of them inside while his tongue continued its assault on her clit. He licked and sucked, feeling her steady herself against his head, her thighs pressing against his cheeks so hard he thought he might suffocate.

But what a fucking glorious way to die.

Her cries became louder. Her fingers tugged at his hair as though she didn't know what to do with them, her body rocking between his face and the countertop in a rhythm as old as time. And then she let out a long groan, her body stilling, her abdomen clenched tight as she reached her peak. He reached up to hold her waist to stop her from collapsing on the floor.

But he didn't stop kissing her there until she could breathe regularly again. Even then, he pulled his face away with reluctance. He couldn't get enough of her pleasure. Couldn't get enough of *her*.

Until the baby comes.

That's what she'd said. She wanted to be together until the baby comes. And then?

He'd just have to show her he could be here for the after, too.

"Do *not* come in," Amber warned, groaning as she tried to do up the stupid boots that came with the stupid costume. She could barely bend over now. Her bump was getting so big it was getting hard to do anything. How could she only be twenty-eight weeks pregnant? Surely she couldn't get any bigger? She'd fall over and never get up.

"C'mon, let me help," North said, his voice sugary sweet on the other side of the door.

"No, I've got this." But she didn't and it was driving her crazy. Whose stupid idea was it for her to dress as a pregnant witch, anyway?

Oh yeah. Kelly. Who also provided the boots. This was all her fault.

"Who ever heard of a pregnant witch, anyway?" she complained, knowing North would still be on the other side. "Weren't they all spinsters?"

North coughed. Or laughed. She wasn't sure, but either way, it pissed her off.

"Shut up," she told him.

"I said nothing."

"You thought it, though. You thought that I'm a spinster, didn't you?"

"Sweetheart, you're not a spinster. You're a gorgeous pregnant witch and I want to do all the dirty things to you."

"You can't see me. I look stupid." She gave up on the boots. Stupid things. "Why can't humans just lay eggs? I could put it in an incubator and not have to worry about looking like an elephant whenever I put on clothes."

"I like you looking like you do."

A smile almost caught her lips. That wasn't a lie. The bigger she got the more he seemed to like it. They'd had to start being creative now that her bump was huge and, yeah, she liked that too. Liked the way his eyes darkened whenever she walked into the bedroom naked.

He was all carnal desire and dirty talk.

"Have you done the boots up yet?" North asked her.

"Nope."

"Let me come in. I'll do it for you."

She let out a sigh, catching sight of her reflection in the mirrored closet doors. Kelly had adapted the costume for her, adding an elastic tummy panel so that it would fit over her bump. But because this was one of Kelly's cast-offs, it was still stupidly sexy. The neckline low and tight, pushing her oversized boobs together, and the skirt short and floaty around her thighs. She was wearing stockings that went to her thighs – orange and black stripes – and then she'd have these stupid boots if they actually did up.

"If you laugh at me I'll kill you," she warned.

The door opened and North walked in, letting out a low whistle as he looked at her. "Fuck. Maybe you'd better stay home."

Her heart dropped. "I look stupid, don't I?"

He slowly shook his head. "No. You look like you need to

be on your knees with me behind you, showing you exactly how naughty you've been."

"I'm not having sex in Kelly's outfit," she warned him.

"How about just the boots?"

She was smiling now. How did he do this to her every time? He was like her personal mood enhancer. Every time she felt like giving up, he was there.

He dropped to his knees in front of her.

"What are you doing?" she squeaked. She meant it about the costume, Kelly would kill her.

Probably.

"I'm lacing your boots," he said, his fingers deftly threading the laces through the holes. "Don't want you tripping."

She sat still as he finished, tying them both into a double knot. "I don't know why Kelly talked me into this."

They were taking Cole trick or treating. Kelly had wheedled her into it, telling her she should start being part of the parent community of Winterville.

"You sure you don't want to come?" Amber asked him when he'd finished. He was still on his knees in front of her.

"I mean..."

"To trick or treating." She rolled her eyes at him.

"It's okay. It's a you and Kelly thing. Anyway, I'm needed at the Inn."

He and his cousins always gave out candy from the porch of the Winterville Inn on Halloween.

"Why don't you ever wear a costume?" she asked.

"I am."

Amber frowned, taking in the jeans and flannel shirt he was wearing. "What are you going as?"

"The man that's gonna make you see stars later." He pressed his lips against hers. "Now go scare some kids."

She'd arranged to meet Kelly at her house. She'd planned their route out like a military operation. "So we have two hours," Kelly told her. "Between six and eight. We only go to the houses that have their porch lights on or pumpkins on the steps. And what do we do when they give us something, Cole?"

"Say thank you." Cole was resplendent in his Thor costume, his long blond wig flowing over his shoulders. He had his hammer in one hand and a bucket that looked like a pumpkin in the other.

"That's right. And if a house already has kids at it, we move onto the next one. There's plenty of candy for everybody."

"Do we get to go to the Inn at the end?" Cole asked. "That's where Noah's going."

"Yep. And then we come home and you get to eat one piece of candy and then you go to bed."

"Mom..." Cole whined.

"I'm serious, Cole. It's a school night." Kelly folded her arms across her chest. She was dressed as Harley Quinn, her legs encased in hot pants and pantyhose, a white t-shirt skimming her curves. She'd put her hair up in bunches and she looked totally bad ass.

Amber missed being able to rock a costume like that.

"Let's go," Cole said, pulling on Amber's hand. "Before all the good stuff goes."

The evening was warm for the end of October, and thankfully the sky was cloud free. As they walked down the streets, the sidewalks were full of Little Mermaids, Belles, Gandalfs, and Yodas. It was sweet watching them walk up each sidewalk, a little scared of the decorations but excited, too.

Amber had always loved this time of year. It reminded her

so much of being a kid, and her dad taking her and her friends out on hay rides around the farm, where he'd set up decorations and candy at each stop.

He'd loved any opportunity to spend time with her, and she'd loved it, too. She touched her stomach without thinking. It was one of her greatest regrets that her parents would never meet her baby.

Her mom would have loved to be a grammy, and her dad would've installed a baby car seat in the tractor. Her lips twitched at the thought.

"Okay, so the Mommy Mafia is up ahead," Kelly whispered. Amber looked at the group of women standing at the bottom of a driveway, talking to each other as their kids walked up it past scary witches and ghosts.

"The Mommy Mafia?" Amber repeated. "What's that?"

"The ones who are in charge of everything. If there's a party, they're running it. If there's a committee they're on it. If you want your kid to fit in you need to suck up to them."

"Do you suck up to them?" Amber asked her, frowning.

"Hell no. But they're nice to me because they use the Tavern for their book club on the last Monday of every month and I have all the dirt on them." Kelly wiggled her brows. "They drink a lot of wine."

"Hey," Kelly said as they reached the group of women. None of the moms were dressed up. They weren't watching their kids, either, they were too busy leaning over a phone and laughing.

The tallest of the moms looked up. "Kelly, hi." She glanced at Amber's stomach. "Hello," she said, looking suddenly interested. "You're Amber, right?"

"Yeah, that's right." Amber smiled at her, trying not to look intimidated. Was there really a hierarchy of moms? Did they actually have time for that?

"I'm Sondra." She reached out to shake Amber's hand. "I've seen you at the tree farm."

"North's farm?" one of the other moms piped up. "Hoowee."

"Right? It isn't' Christmas without seeing North Winter's muscles as he swings an axe."

"My favorite part of the season," another mom said.

Amber's smile wavered. "Well we hope to see you there soon."

Sondra winked. "You can count on it."

Kelly glanced at Amber and then took her hand, clearly done with the clique. "Well ladies, have a great Halloween. We'll see you later. Come on, Cole."

Cole willingly followed them to the next house. But Amber could still hear the conversation carrying on behind them.

"Did you hear that she's shacking up with him?"

"Who?"

"Amber. The woman with Kelly."

"No way. Is that his baby?"

"Nope. Some other guy's."

"So what does he see in her? The man could have any woman he wants."

"Maybe she's got something over him. Not that I can blame her. Who wants to be a single mom when you can have North Winter as your stand-in baby daddy?"

Kelly muttered something under her breath.

"Why are they like that?" Amber asked, trying not to feel hurt.

"Remember the mean girls at school?" Kelly asked. "They grew up and got meaner."

"Why do you put up with them?"

Kelly looked at her. "What am I gonna do? Go tell their moms they're being mean?" She shrugged. "I put up with them for Cole. Because I want him to have nice things. To be invited to parties and sleepovers and have friends to sit with at lunch. And unlike those bitches, I know that as he gets older, he'll choose his own friends and they'll have no influence. So I put up with it for now and then later I'll tell them what I think."

"That's one hell of a long game," Amber pointed out.

"Well, I'm here for it." She pulled a candy bar out of her pocket. "Want some?"

"Did you just steal that from your kid?" Amber asked her.

"Yep. He didn't even notice." Kelly grinned and snapped the bar in half, passing half to Amber. "I've got more where that came from. And now you know why I go out trick or treating with Cole every year."

"Will you stop checking your watch?" Gabe said, though he didn't sound annoyed. "She'll get here when she gets here."

"I don't know what you're talking about," North told him, putting his hand behind his back. "I was just stretching my arms."

"Sure you were." Gabe smirked. "Listen, I get it."

"Get what?" He wasn't planning on having this conversation with his brother. Sure, Gabe had been the one to make him think twice about his feelings for Amber, but they didn't talk about this stuff. They talked about football and whether the first snow fall of the year was going to be in November or December, and if the Dow Jones index would go up.

Nah, they didn't talk about the Dow Jones. But maybe they should. Anything was better than trying to talk about feelings.

"What's going on?" Their cousin Everley walked over to them, dressed as a fairy with sparkly wings. Finn was in a carrier in front of her chest. North reached down to stroke his head.

"North is getting anxious because Amber and Kelly haven't got here yet," Gabe told Everley, sounding gleeful.

Everley grinned. "Of course he is. That's so cute."

"I'm not cute." North raised a brow at her.

"You are when you want to be." She touched his shoulder with her wand. "By the way, have you invited her to Thanksgiving yet?"

"It's Halloween," North pointed out. "Thanksgiving isn't for another month."

"So that means no." Everley frowned. "If you want a job done, let a woman do it."

"She comes to Thanksgiving every year. I don't need to invite her." North shook his head. "Much like you don't need to invite me."

"That's because you usually host. But this year I'm hosting and it's only polite to invite her properly. Don't worry, I'll ask her."

North sighed. Lord save him from interfering cousins. "I'll talk to her. She may not want to come and she'll feel weird saying no to you."

"Why wouldn't she want to come?" Everley asked.

"Because her life is changing and she may want to change the way she spends holidays, too."

Everley blinked, as though she couldn't understand him. "But you two are together now. She always spends holidays with you. Which means she'll always be spending holidays with us, right? Unless you don't want to be with us." She pouted and he shook his head.

Growing up, Everley was always the chief mayhem maker of the cousins. But now she'd calmed down – though not completely. And when she wasn't exhausted from being a mom she was busy running the Jingle Bell Theater in town.

And apparently she still enjoyed interfering in his life.

"We're taking it slow," North said, his voice thick. "Amber wants to reassess how things are going once the baby is here."

"What do you mean?" Everley frowned. From the corner of his eye North could see Gabe frowning, too.

"I mean she doesn't want to tie me down. She's afraid I'll change my mind about us once she's a mom."

"You won't, will you?" Everley sounded aghast.

"No, but I don't want to freak her out by declaring that to her. She's adamant that I wait so I'll wait. But I'm not going anywhere."

Everley sighed. "Thank God. I was worried I'd have to hit you."

"That would be a bit of payback," Gabe said. "But seriously, why don't you tell her now?"

"Because she doesn't trust me, I guess." North shifted his feet. "I'll just have to prove it to her when the baby's here."

"How about Shaun?" Everley asked. "Where does he fit into this?"

North's jaw tightened. "I don't know. He knows about the baby and he doesn't seem interested."

"What if he gets interested once the baby's here?" Gabe asked.

"Amber's not interested in him, other than him being a dad to the baby. And she's right, he's the father. I'm not going to interfere with that."

Everley rubbed Finn's head. "But you'll still be a father figure, right?"

Hearing it said out loud made his heart feel raw. Yes, that was what he wanted. To be a partner to Amber and a father to her baby.

But she was so damn jittery, so unsure of herself. He tried to show her how beautiful she was, how lucky he felt to have her in his life, but she had no self-confidence.

He wanted to build it up, brick by brick, until she saw herself the way he saw her. And if it took a lifetime to do it, he was here for that.

"I'll be whatever she wants me to be," he said gruffly.

"Speak of the devil. Or witch..." Gabe was looking at the driveway that led up to the Inn. North turned to follow his gaze, his whole body relaxing when he saw her with Kelly, Cole between them holding a bucket overflowing with candy.

Amber had a hand on her stomach, and as her eyes met his, she grinned at him. Damn, he was a fool for this woman.

"Do you think he can still hear us?" Everley asked Gabe.

"Nope. Should we talk about him?"

"Nah. Let's save that for later."

Ignoring them, North walked over to Amber, taking her hand. "You okay?"

"Yeah." Amber nodded. "Though I feel like I've just gotten a university level education on how parenthood works in Winterville."

"She met the mommy mafia," Kelly explained. "They're bitches."

"Ouch." North grimaced, threading his fingers through Amber's. "What did they say?"

"It doesn't matter. I just know who to avoid now." She rolled onto her toes and kissed his lips. He blinked at the public display of affection, then curled his fingers into the hair at the back of her head. "Can we go home?" she asked. "I need to take these boots off."

"Yours or mine?"

"I don't care. Just wherever you are." She melted against him and he could see how tired she was. He slipped his arm around her waist and kissed the top of her head.

"Come on, let's go." He looked at Gabe. "You got this?"

"I got it." Gabe winked. "You two can leave."

"Don't forget to ask her about Thanksgiving," Everley yelled as he and Amber walked over to say goodbye to Kelly.

"Thanksgiving?" Amber asked, looking up at him.

"We'll talk about it later," he told her. "Let's take this one holiday at a time."

"Good idea." She nodded. "Because tonight I just want to curl up in your arms and forget about anything else."

🦋 19 🦋

"Sit." North pointed at the end of the bed. She teetered across the carpet, her feet throbbing from these stupid boots, her center of balance completely off kilter.

"Am I waddling?" she asked him as she collapsed on the mattress. "I'm definitely waddling, right? Like a duck."

"You're not waddling. You're just wearing stupidly sexy fuck me boots."

Laughter escaped her lips. "There's nothing sexy about my pregnant witch costume."

His eyes were dark as they caught hers. "I beg to differ." He strode forward, his gait so full of confidence it sent a shiver down her spine. Then he dropped to his haunches, his thick thighs pushing at the denim of his jeans. Her mouth turned dry, because this man was so damn attractive it was killing her.

His fingers were deft as he unlaced the boots he'd laced up earlier. She looked at him silently, taking in his eyelashes, sweeping up and down over those piercing blues, his nose, straight and strong, and his mouth that on paper might be just a little too feminine, but on him worked perfectly.

And the things he could do with it...

He pulled the first boot off and she let out a groan that sounded something like an orgasm. He smirked. "Normally, I'd ask you to leave these on," he said, taking the second one off. "But I think that's something we'll do another time."

"Do you have a thing for boots?" she asked. There were so many things she still didn't know about him.

"I have a thing for *your* boots. On you."

Oh. And then she had to spoil it. "The mean moms think I'm coercing you to stay with me."

He looked up at her, confused. "What?"

"I heard them talking as we walked away. They don't know what you see in me."

He winced. "They know fuck all. I see everything in you. I'm the one who wakes up every morning and has to pinch myself that you're still here." He slid his hand up her calf, his fingers pressing into her skin. "I'm the lucky one. And they're just bitches. So ignore them."

"I'm trying."

He looked at her for a moment, as though he was trying to find the right words. "I don't think you understand just how beautiful you are. Every part of you." He glanced at her bump. "Inside and out."

"There's nothing beautiful about pregnancy." She was fishing now, she knew she was. And yet she couldn't help it. She needed to hear this. Needed him to soothe the ache those moms caused.

"I've never wanted anything as much as I want you. And I've never had sex with a pregnant woman before, but..." He cleared his throat. "It gives me sensations I never knew I could get."

"What kind of sensations?"

"Amazing ones. At the base of my cock."

Her cheeks heated. "Because of my bump?"

"Yeah. It changes everything."

"Are you gonna hate it when it's gone?" she asked, fascinated now.

"No, because that means the baby will be here and that'll be great. And I know that it's causing you back pains and making you tired and I'm not enough of an asshole to want you to go through that for the sake of some sensations. But I'm not going to lie. I've fantasized about how quickly we can get you pregnant again."

"*Again?*" She lifted a brow.

He smirked. "As I said. Fantasies."

"I thought we weren't going to make any promises. Not until the baby's here."

His gaze caught hers. "No, I agreed you didn't have to decide. But my decision has never been in doubt. I want you and I want this baby. I want us together." He cupped her stomach, his palm warm through her dress. "But I know you're scared and I know you need time so I'm giving it to you."

Her heart was hammering against her chest. It was everything she wanted to hear, yet the fear was still there.

"I just can't face you leaving me..."

"I'm not going anywhere." He leaned forward and brushed a lock of hair from her face. He'd taken his flannel off when they'd gotten home, and his black t-shirt stretched across his shoulders as he reached out. She could smell the muskiness of him, the pine, and the fresh air.

He always smelled like that. Rain on a summer's day. Pine in the winter. Her outdoors man.

"I want you to take your clothes off," she told him.

He tipped his head to the side, taken by surprise at her sudden change in subject.

"Why?"

"Why do you think?"

His lips twitched. "I have a few ideas, but I want to hear them from you."

"I want to dance for you."

"You want to what?" He looked shocked, and she liked that.

"I want to seduce you. To see what you like. You've spent so much time learning what I need. I want to do it for you."

"I'm a simple man. I just want you."

She stood and pointed at the bed. "Strip and sit down."

He was grinning now. "Yes, ma'am."

It took him less than a minute to be naked and sitting on the end of her bed. And all thoughts of babies and mean moms and the future disappeared from her mind. It was just them. Just now.

She needed to stop overthinking. To stop worrying about what might happen. He was here, he was naked. And he was looking at her like she was the most precious thing he'd ever seen.

"If you laugh I'll kill you."

"I can promise you I won't laugh." He was deadly serious, his voice gruff. She glanced down and saw he was already hard.

"Don't touch yourself either."

"Now you *are* killing me."

She walked over to her phone, opening her music app, and scrolled until she found what she was looking for.

Sam Smith's "Unholy" came on. And yeah, she was taunting him. Trying to see if he'd laugh at the lyrics. She turned around and caught him staring at her, his lips parted, his gaze so full of lust it made her feel powerful.

She ran her hands down her chest. Her nipples were

already hard as hell. She felt oversensitive, full of need. She loved the way he couldn't stop staring.

Slowly, she danced over to him, placing her hands on either side of his hips, arching herself as best she could as he tried to kiss her.

"No kisses. They're extra." She pushed his chest with her palm and spun around, luckily keeping her sense of gravity as she slowly unzipped her dress. She let the shoulders hang loose and touched her chest again, slowly swaying her hips to the beat as his breath caught in his throat.

There was nothing sexy about her bra and stockings. Any idiot had to know that. Yet when she pulled her dress down and stepped out of it, he looked more turned on than ever. She put her foot on his knee, running it up his thigh, then grazed his cock with her toe before pulling it away.

"Amber..." His voice was gritty. Needy. She loved it.

But she didn't reply. Instead, she leaned toward him again, this time unclasping her bra. She slowly pushed one strap down and then the other, clasping her hands over her breasts to keep the fabric there.

And then she felt it. The wetness. What the hell, was she leaking now? Oh God, how embarrassing. She pushed the anxiety away. She was a mom-to-be. It was natural.

North was her friend. Her lover. He'd understand, right?

It was now or never. She dropped the bra on the floor and her heavy breasts hung loose. He couldn't take his eyes off them if he tried. He looked half crazed, his fingers gripping her bedsheets like he was afraid of falling.

"I want to suck them," he rasped.

"No." She tried to shimmy out of her panties, but it ended up being more of a tug-of-war. Not that it mattered, North didn't seem to care.

"Baby, please... I need you." He was begging now.

"You can't. I'm leaking."

She waited for him to look disgusted. But instead he just looked intrigued. "Milk?"

"Yeah. I think so." She grimaced. "Early milk."

"I still want to suck them." He gave her a lopsided smile. "Give them to me."

She let out a long breath, trying to work out what to do. "How about if I suck you?"

"That would be good. After I've had my turn."

"You really want to taste it?"

He nodded. Maybe it was all part of his fascination for her body. Something different, something new. She looked at him, trying to work him out.

Did he really find this attractive? Weirdly, she was starting to feel turned on by the thought. Maybe it was the intimacy of it. The way that everything she did seemed to fascinate him.

"Okay." She nodded.

His smile widened. He beckoned to her with his little finger, and she somehow managed to straddle his legs, wearing just her stockings and nothing else. He captured her lips first, his mouth soft and warm.

"You're the sexiest little thing I've ever seen," he told her. "You're gonna have to dance for me every night."

Little, she wasn't. She wanted to laugh at that. "I haven't finished yet."

"Good." He kissed her jaw, her throat, and then dipped his head to capture her nipple. His lips tugged and his tongue lashed and pleasure shot through to her thighs.

She could feel his hardness against her. Thick and long and as hot as she was. He let out a groan and moved to her other nipple, slicking his tongue over it and swallowing the wetness down.

"It tastes sweet," he told her. "Like you."

"You're a deviant," she murmured, stroking his hair.

"Never said I wasn't."

The song was reaching a crescendo now, reminding her she was supposed to be seducing him. Not that it was taking very much. She pushed away from him, somehow getting back onto her feet, running her hands up her sides, over her body, ruffling her hair.

"I love it when you arch like that."

"I'm a little afraid I might fall," she confessed.

He chuckled. "Then stop."

She shook her head and turned around, then bent over to slid her hands beneath the bands of her stockings. There was no possible way of making this look sexy. She tugged at the elastic, starting to pull them down her legs.

And then she felt his warm hands over hers.

"I thought I told you to sit down."

"I just need to touch you." He helped her roll the stockings down, and when they reached her knees she heard him drop to his own behind her, as he took over and rolled them to her ankles. She stepped out of the nylon one foot at a time, and he threw the scraps of fabric away.

"Go and sit down again," she told him. "I'm still going."

She waited until she heard the bed creak and then she looked at him over her shoulder. His cock looked thick and red, and he was leaking, too.

She turned slowly and sashayed over to him, then managed to drop to her own knees without falling over, using her hands on his thighs to steady herself.

"You've been such a good customer," she told him throatily. "I want to show you some appreciation."

"You don't have to... Christ..."

Her lips slid over him, taking in as much as she could. Then she pulled up again, and he groaned.

"Can I touch you?"

"That's extra." She looked up, a twinkle in her eye.

"I'll pay anything."

She smiled around his plush tip. "Then you can touch me."

She sucked him in again, loving how turned on it made him. It was turning her on, too. Knowing a slide of her lips could make his hips hitch, his voice stutter, his fingers tangle into her hair like he never wanted to let go.

She found her rhythm as the song ended and silence filled the room. On every up stroke she curled her tongue around his head, tasting him, loving him.

Never wanting this to end.

"Stop," he grunted. "I'm gonna come."

But she just started moving faster, her hand cupping him as she brought him to oblivion with her warm, velvety mouth. A low oath escaped his lips as he surged inside of her, his fingers sliding between her tresses as she swallowed him down.

And when she finally released him, she felt more alive than ever. Wordlessly he reached for her to pull her into his arms. His mouth found hers as though he didn't care that she tasted of *him,* and he kissed her like he never wanted to stop.

"Thank you."

"It was my pleasure." She curled her arms around his neck. There was a stupidly gorgeous smile on his face that she never wanted to leave. "Do you ever wish we'd realized how good this would be earlier?"

"Like earlier this evening?"

She laughed. "No. I mean all these years we've been friends. Best friends. Does it feel like a waste to you?"

His brows pulled in tight. "No. I liked being your friend. I still do. I just think we had to wait for the right time. Things can't be forced." He kissed her gently. "And maybe now is the right time for us."

Her heart did a little flip in her chest. "With me pregnant?"

"I think we've already established that I like you pregnant."

"And when I'm not pregnant..."

His eyes crinkled. "I think we've already established that I like you like that, too. Stop worrying." He cupped her jaw. "I'm not planning on going anywhere."

"Y ou and North are gonna have to tone down the PDA," Kelly said, shaking her head as Amber carried a tray of empty glasses to the bar. "Maybe I'm not sorry to see you leave after all."

Amber turned to look at North. He was sitting with his family at their usual booth. Gabe had suggested that they come in to celebrate Amber's last night working behind the bar of the Tavern, and they'd all been so sweet to come along.

North had refused to let her carry any drinks over to them. Every time she filled up the tray, he somehow knew she was about to come over to the booth, so he'd jump up and take it from her, kissing her softly in a way that set her blood racing.

"You'll miss me when I'm gone," she told Kelly, grinning. She didn't care if Kelly hated watching them kiss. She liked it and she planned on doing more of it.

Kelly stopped drying a glass and looked at her. "I will, actually. I know we have a full team now, but it's not the same. It's been so nice to spend some girl time with you in the last few months."

Amber's heart clenched. "It has," she agreed. It felt like the end of an era. Thanksgiving would be here next week and then, before they knew it, Christmas would be upon them.

And then she'd be having the baby and everything would be different.

Winterville was already in full-blown festive mode. The Tavern was bursting with tourists, and next week it would get even busier when the Jingle Bell Theater opened with this year's Winterville Revue. North's cousin, Everley was here tonight along with her husband Dylan, who'd persuaded his dad to babysit, but starting next week she'd be at the theater every night as co-director of the show.

"So you two are real tight, huh?" Kelly asked. "Have you talked about moving in together?"

"Not officially." He was pretty much at her place every night, anyway.

"But you're going to, right?"

"I think that's where we're headed. Maybe."

He was still looking at her, dammit. And she was molten chocolate inside. His appetite for her seemed to increase with the growth of her waistline. The most comfortable position now was spooning. At every doctor appointment she kept waiting for them to tell her she was having twins, or maybe a baby elephant.

She had nine more weeks to go, she was pretty sure she'd burst before then.

"Of course it's where you're headed," Kelly said, a grin on her face. "I bet you that he asks you to marry him as soon as the baby is born."

Amber's face must have been a picture of shock because Kelly burst out laughing. "I'm serious," she said. "He's going to ask."

"Can I get three bottles of Champagne and ten glasses?" Gabe asked, his voice low.

"Of course. If you tell me what they're for." Kelly's eyes sparkled. Gabe grinned at her.

"Come over with them and you'll find out." He looked at Amber. "You too."

"That'll be a hundred and twenty dollars." Kelly couldn't hide her glee. "I'll put a few more bottles on ice in case you want to keep celebrating whatever it is."

Gabe paid and waited as Amber and Kelly filled two trays with glasses, and then filled some buckets for the champagne. He helped them carry it all over, putting them on the table that his family was sitting around.

Amber looked at Nicole, Gabe's wife, and it was clear she knew what this was all about as she shifted on her feet.

"So, ah, Nic and I have something to tell you all," Gabe said, his cheeks pinking up adorably. "We're having a baby. Next summer. I knocked her right up."

Kelly snorted as she twisted the cage off the first champagne bottle, then pushed the cork out with a pop. "Those smooth-talking Winter boys," she said, shaking her head. "They get me every time."

Everybody was getting up and hugging each other. She watched as North pulled his little brother into his arms, whispering something in Gabe's ear that made him blush even more.

"Have you told your mom?" Everley asked him.

"Not yet," Gabe said when North released him. "We thought we'd tell you guys first. We're traveling to DC next week to tell Nic's folks. And we'll call mom and dad after that."

"Your mom's gonna be so excited." Everley clapped her hand together. "And maybe a little unbearable. My mom was like that with her first grandchild."

There was silence for a moment. Then Everley looked at

Amber, her face falling. "I mean... of course *you're* having the first grandchild..."

Amber smiled at her. "It's okay. I knew what you meant."

But Everley looked devastated. "I didn't mean it like that. I'm so sorry. You know that you and your baby are family. And..."

"Probably time to shut up, sweetheart." Dylan kissed his wife and shot Amber an embarrassed glance.

"Honestly, it's fine," she told them. The last thing she wanted to do was put a damper on Gabe and Nicole's announcement.

But then she looked at North and there was the strangest expression on his face. Was he upset that Gabe's child would be the first biological grandchild to his parents? She willed him to look at her but he didn't.

"You want a little taste?" Kelly asked, lifting her champagne glass toward Amber.

Amber shook her head. "No thanks. I'm all good."

Everley didn't mean anything by it. It was just a slip of the tongue. Some of it was Amber and North's fault, they hadn't exactly attempted to define their relationship to his family.

Everley walked over to where Amber was standing. There were tears in her eyes. "I really am sorry."

Amber hugged her. "It's fine. Honestly, it is."

"You're like a sister to me. You need to know that," Everley said, her voice urgent. "And you make North so happy. He's like a different man."

"He makes me happy, too," Amber told her. "But things are different for us than they are for Gabe and Nicole. I'm so happy for them and I know Gabe and North's mom will be, too."

"I can't believe we're going to have two new additions to the family so soon," Everley said, finally looking more relaxed. "Christmases are going to get busy."

"Yeah, they are."

She looked over her shoulder to see the line for drinks building up. "I'd better go help serve before there's a riot." Amber turned but her foot didn't make contact with the floor. Instead, her sole slipped against some ice that must have fallen out of the champagne bucket and had started to melt.

Everything went in slow motion as her legs were pulled out from under her, her body hovering in the air for a heartbeat before her back slammed onto the wooden floor. She groaned, stunned.

And then she noticed the pain. Her head. Her arm. Yeah, her arm more than her head. She screwed her face up, trying to not scream at the way her wrist was throbbing. And then the noise rushed in, people shouting, running, chairs scraping. She whimpered as she slowly opened her eyes.

North was leaning above her, his eyes darting over her face. "Amber?" He turned to the person next to him. "Dylan, do something!"

Dylan. Everley's husband. Yes, he was a doctor, but not for babies. Amber opened her mouth to talk to him but no sound came out.

"Amber," Dylan said, his voice soft. Less panicked than North's. "Can you hear me?"

Her ears were ringing but she nodded.

"Does it hurt anywhere?"

"The baby," she croaked.

"Your abdomen hurts?" Dylan tried to clarify.

"No. Is the baby okay?" she asked tearfully.

"Can I touch your abdomen?" he asked. She nodded but that hurt too, so she stopped.

His hands were so gentle as they carefully touched her bump. Then he smiled. "Got a kick," he said. "I think he's pissed off."

"It could be a she," she said softly. She went to touch her stomach but she couldn't pick her hand up off the floor.

"My arm…"

Dylan looked down. Then he said something to North that made him stand up and run out of her sight. Dylan slowly slid his fingers down her arm, asking what hurt and what didn't, and then he reached her wrist she let out a scream.

"I think it's broken," Dylan told her. "We're gonna need to splint you up and get you to the hospital. Do you have your obstetrician's number in your phone?"

"Yes," she whispered, because the pain was really too much. "But we don't need to call him, do we? The baby's fine."

"Just in case. You're going to the hospital, so you might as well have the full work up."

North knelt down next to him, passing Dylan the first aid kit that was always kept by the bar. Dylan checked her neck and asked her questions about a headache and whether she could remember her name and the date which she answered before he turned to look at North.

"There's no immediate sign of concussion or spinal injury. Can you try to sit her up for me?" Dylan asked. "Then slide in behind her. It's gonna be easier for me to splint and sling like that."

North nodded, his face so pale he looked like a ghost. Somehow between him and Dylan, North managed to get Amber sitting on the floor, her back braced against North's chest. Dylan moved around to her side to get easier access to her arm, his voice gentle as he warned her that it might hurt as he wrapped her wrist and forearm in a bandage, then added the split to it. North stroked her hair, kissing her softly as tears ran down her face.

Thank God Dylan had felt the baby kick. But she could

still have hurt the baby. The thought of it made her feel nauseous.

"I called nine one one," Kelly said, "An ambulance is on the way."

Dylan nodded. "How bad is the pain?" he asked Amber.

"Better now that it's splinted."

"It's always the way. Gravity's a great thing until you fracture a bone. Then it hurts like crazy."

North was still kissing her softly. His breath was tight, like he was finding it as hard as she was to get oxygen in. She wanted to press her hand against his chest, to feel his heartbeat.

Was it racing like hers?

"Can we get everybody back to their tables?" Dylan asked Kelly. "It's not ideal to have everybody surrounding us while we wait."

Kelly smiled. "Oh yes, we can definitely do that." She clapped her hands loudly. "Okay ladies and gentlemen. Show's over. Get back to your drinks or get the hell out of here!"

North paced the floor of Amber's exam room as she dozed fitfully on the bed. Her wrist fracture—a distal radius fracture, according to the orthopedic doctor on call, had to be adjusted before they could cast it. She'd panicked when they mentioned giving her a local anesthetic, scared that it could affect the baby, but the doctor reassured her that the dose was low and there shouldn't be any adverse reaction at all.

Still, she'd begged North to stay with her while it was done.

And now she was exhausted, and he was beating himself up because he should have put his foot down weeks ago. She'd been working at the farm six days a week, and at the tavern every weekend. There was no way her poor body could keep up with it all.

"Hi." An older doctor walked into the room, his eyes taking in Amber's sleeping form and North's pacing one. "I'm Amber's obstetrician. Doctor Cavanagh. You must be the father."

North opened his mouth to deny it, but nothing came out. It was easier to nod than do anything else. This way the doctor wouldn't try to make him leave.

Because there was no way he was walking out of here without her.

"North Winter." He shook the doctor's hand.

"It's good to meet you. So how is she?"

He glanced at her pale face. "Exhausted. But not in pain anymore."

"That's good." Doctor Cavanagh slid his finger on the electronic tablet he was holding. North assumed he was checking her charts. "I need to wake her up to check her over. And then she can go home."

"I'll wake her." North didn't want her to start panicking again. He walked to the gurney, the sound of her quick breaths filling his ears as he leaned over and touched her face. Her arm was in a sling. The orthopedic doctor had advised she use this for the first few days and then she should be able to ditch it.

"Amber." He stroked her cheek with his fingers.

"Huh?" Her eyes flew open. She blinked, her brows tight as she took him in. "Where? Oh, God."

"Your obstetrician is here," North told her. "He wants to check that everything's okay with the baby."

Her expression softened. "I didn't expect you to come in. I thought I'd just see the on call obstetrician."

"I don't let anybody else touch my babies." He smiled at her. "So, how did you fall? I'm guessing on your wrist."

Amber nodded. "I think so. It's a bit of a blur."

"Do you remember whether you put any weight on your abdomen as you fell?"

She frowned. "I think I landed on my side."

"Do you have any abdominal pain?"

"Not now, but if there was before, I didn't feel it over the pain in my wrist."

Doctor Cavanagh chuckled. "That's to be expected. The tech should be here in a minute to take a look at the baby for us."

"That would be great." Amber still looked pale.

"And then we'll get you home and you can get better sleep than you get here." He glanced at North. "It looks like Daddy's gonna be busy looking after you for a while."

Amber frowned "He's..."

"I'm planning on doing everything if she'll let me," North interjected, lifting his brow at her.

Ten minutes later, the technician was running the ultrasound wand over her swollen belly, pressing buttons and taking measurements. Doctor Cavanagh was leaning over the monitor, all the while reassuring Amber that everything looked good.

"Would you like to have a look?" he asked Amber.

"Yes, please."

"And I bet Daddy would, too. He hasn't had a chance to see the baby yet, has he?"

Amber looked at him. "Would you like to see?" she asked.

"Yeah." North's voice was thick. "I really would."

"Then come on over."

The technician turned the monitor so they could both see it. "It's a lot easier now that the little babe is getting bigger. That's the head, that's a leg, and that thing that keeps moving is the heart."

North wasn't sure he could breathe. Wasn't sure he'd ever seen anything so perfect. "Are those toes?" he asked.

"Yep, ten tiny ones," the technician confirmed. "And that's the nose."

North slid his hand into Amber's good one, squeezing her tight. His heart was banging against his chest.

"You still don't want to know the gender, right?" he asked Amber.

"I like the idea of getting a surprise," she said.

"It's old fashioned but I like it." The technician nodded. "Though I bet your friends don't."

"They all want to kill me."

The technician laughed. "What about you, Dad? How do you feel about not knowing the gender?"

Amber hadn't blinked this time at North being called Dad. But he was getting freaked out. Unsure how to deal with the emotions overwhelming him.

Because he wanted to be the father. Wanted to protect that perfect little baby growing inside the woman he loved more than he wanted to do anything else in the world. It felt so pure, so obvious.

How was it possible to fall in love with somebody he hadn't even met?

"I want what Amber wants," North said hoarsely.

Amber squeezed his hand. From the corner of his eye he could see her looking at him, her eyes concerned. Or maybe just curious. The technician finished the scan and wiped Amber's stomach, then wheeled the monitor out, leaving them alone with her obstetrician.

"Well, everything's looking great. Go home, make sure you rest for a few days, and make an appointment to see me at the office next week," Doctor Cavanagh told Amber. "The good news is that since you have nine weeks to go your wrist should be healed and the cast off long before your due date. So we won't have to adapt any of your birth plan."

"You have a birth plan?" North asked her.

"Kind of."

"She still hasn't put a birthing partner down," Doctor Cavanagh said.

"I'll be your birthing partner." North looked her in the eye.

"You don't have to do that."

"I want to if you want me to."

"I do." She smiled softly at him.

"Great." The doctor stood and stretched his arms. "Now I'm going home to drink some cocoa and get to bed. I'll let the charge nurse know all is set for discharge. They should be in soon with your paperwork." He stood and removed his gloves. "Look after her," he told North as he walked to the door.

North nodded. "I intend to."

The doctor left and North pulled a chair next to the bed. "Hopefully they'll be in to discharge you soon," he told her.

"I'm sorry about that," she said, her cheeks pink.

"About what?"

"Him assuming you're the dad."

"It's okay. It's an easy assumption to make. And I didn't exactly tell him I wasn't."

"Why not?"

He shifted in the chair. "I don't know. Maybe I thought it was none of his business. Maybe I want to be."

"Want to be?"

"The baby's father."

She pulled her lip between her teeth. "North..."

"I know. We've had this discussion. You're wary and that's okay. But I want to be there when your baby's born, because I intend on being a big part of his or her life so they'll need to get used to my smell and my voice. I want to help, baby. I want to do everything a father would do to support you. And if you don't want that, then okay. But if you do secretly want that but you're afraid of saying it out loud then this is me telling you it's what I want."

"I want that," she told him. "I just don't want you to regret it."

"I know you're scared," he said, "But you have to know I won't let you down. Not ever. You're mine, and this baby will be mine too, because I'm gonna love him or her so hard and deep. Just like I love their mother."

"I love you, too."

He nodded. "I know."

They looked at each other silently. Then she nodded. "I want you there."

He grinned. "That's good. You've stopped fighting me."

"I figure if anything's gonna put you off me for life it's watching me squeeze a baby out through one of the places you love the most."

"Why would you try to put me off?"

"Just keeping it real, Winter."

He kissed her, a smile still pulling at his lips. She was okay. The baby was okay. That's all that mattered to him right now.

❧ 21 ❧

"I hear you caved on North's helicopter idea," Gabe said, handing Amber a glass of orange juice. They were at Everley and Dylan's sprawling house on the outskirts of town. The rooms were filled with family and friends – Everley had invited everybody from the Jingle Bell Theater who had nowhere else to spend Thanksgiving – and the walls echoed with the sound of chatting and laughter.

"I kind of had to. There was no way we could get all the trees ready in time with me not able to pull my weight." She lifted her casted arm up. It had been a week since she'd fallen at the tavern and she was still getting used to only having one fully functional arm. Her non-dominant arm at that. At first it had been completely embarrassing as North had to help her dress and undress and even use the bathroom.

But at least she could do that by herself now.

"But we've only contracted it for a few days," she told Gabe. "Along with a pilot."

"North will be gutted he can't learn to fly it in a few days."

"Don't." She shook her head. "He's talking about getting his license ready for next year."

"Of course he is." Gabe grinned. "I bet he's already started googling for lessons."

The man himself was in the corner, having been cornered by little Candace, who wanted him to help them with a wooden jigsaw puzzle. She was sitting cross legged next to him as he patiently passed her the pieces. Finn was nestled into his lap, sucking on his fingers.

"Shouldn't you be over there getting some practice?" Amber asked him.

"Shouldn't you? You're gonna be a mommy long before I'll be a dad," Gabe pointed out.

"I'm scared I'll hit them with this." Amber lifted her cast. "I rolled over in bed the other night and whammed North on the chest. You should see the bruise."

Gabe grinned. "Are you getting used to it, apart from using it as a lethal weapon?"

"Mostly. I can't drive, of course, which I hate. And every-thing takes twice as long. But the good news is it'll be gone before the baby's here, so I'll be able to hold her and change her."

"Her?"

"Her or him. It just takes so much longer to say that."

"North thinks you're having a girl," Gabe said.

Amber blinked. "He does? Why?"

"I don't know." Gabe shrugged. "He just said something about it the other day when Mom was on the phone. She wanted to talk to us all, including Kris, once I told her about the baby."

She hadn't expected that. Hadn't expected North to talk about her to his mom at all. And yet it was natural, wasn't it? If the baby was naturally his, he'd be talking about it all the time.

"How did your mom take your news?" Amber asked him.

"She was ecstatic, as expected. Talking about being a grandma twice in one year."

"And your dad?"

"Was his usual self." Gabe raised a brow. "He doesn't like the attention being taken from him."

No, he didn't. One reason Amber loathed him. That and the fact that he tried to sell this town to the highest bidder, one that planned to knock the entire place down.

And yes, North, Holly, and their cousins had stopped him from doing that. But it showed his true colors.

"And Kris was on the line?"

"Yeah." Gabe's smile widened. "He's talking about coming back here next year. For the winter."

"He is?"

Kris had lived in London for a long time, working in the money markets over there. He rarely visited Winterville. She'd gotten the impression he didn't love the place like the rest of his brothers and cousins did.

Still, it would be nice for North if he came back. She knew North missed him.

"So he says." Gabe shrugged. "I'll believe it when I see it. I think he'll get bored within a week."

"We have a lot of interesting things to do here," Amber protested. "Especially during Christmas time."

"Ah yeah, but you forget, Kris hates Christmas."

"The turkey's ready for carving." Everley walked into the living room and lifted Finn from North's lap. "Honey," she said to Candace, who was leaning on his shoulder, "I need to steal Uncle North for a minute."

"No." Candace put her arms across her chest, frown lines crinkling her tiny face.

"But he needs to carve the turkey. If he doesn't do that we won't eat."

North always carved the turkey. It was a Winter family

tradition. But Candace didn't look like she cared about traditions right now.

"Don't like turkey." She stomped her foot.

Amber tried to not laugh. Even little girls fought over North Winter.

North leaned forward and ruffled Candace's hair. "We can finish this later," he promised her.

"No. Now." Her face looked like thunder.

"Excuse me, young lady?" Holly walked in, giving her daughter a pointed look. "We don't talk to people like that, do we?"

"Stay here with me." Candace looked at North. "Please?"

Amber almost lost it when Candace battered her eyelids. Where did she learn that from? Definitely not Holly, because she was as down to earth as it got.

Maybe it was just innate. She could remember being able to charm her own dad into submission with a wheedled word and a smile. Her mom used to watch on, shaking her head, but saying nothing.

Would it be the same with her baby and North? She was so aware that he was more related to Candace than he would be to her child. By blood, at least. And she didn't know why that upset her so much.

She felt so protective of her baby. She never wanted him or her to feel less than everybody else. Didn't want them to watch the Winter family at get-togethers like this and not feel part of it.

As though he could sense her thoughts, North stood and walked toward her, his gate strong and sure. She loved that man so damn much. Loved the way he loved his family, the way he loved her. He was the center of her world.

And yet she was still afraid this could all come crashing down.

"Want to help me carve the turkey?" he asked when he reached her, brushing his lips against her cheek.

She lifted her cast up. "I'm not sure I'll be much help."

A half smile pulled at his lips. "Let me rephrase. Want to come watch me do manly things so it drives you crazy with lust so you'll jump on me as soon as we get back to your house?"

"Yeah." She nodded, grinning back at him. "I'd like that very much."

The sound of the helicopter blades were deafening overhead, but the way the pilot worked alongside the crews on the ground was something amazing to watch. Harvest began a couple of weeks ago, when they'd been doing their usual cut and load onto the trucks that would bring them back to the farm to be netted up and sent to their customers.

But their deadline was coming fast and they had too much work to complete.

Every year their customer base was getting bigger. It didn't just include the people who visited the farm, or shops in the local area. They supplied trees to big box stores throughout West Virginia, Virginia, and the Carolinas, as well as to Washington DC and Maryland.

And now she was out of action. North was right, they needed to get this done in the simplest, quickest way possible. And if it included using the ultimate toy that he'd always wanted? Well it made him happy.

And that made her happy, too.

She was beyond busy in the shop, along with the seasonal staff they'd employed to help them through to Christmas, but every now and then she'd peek out of the window to see how they were getting along. It was an amazing process, even when the helicopter wasn't involved. They still had to cut down each tree by hand – which was why North had a crew of lumberjacks working with him out in the fields far away from the farm shop. But rather than carry them by hand to the trucks like they usually did, they loaded them into piles and the helicopter sent down a winch, which they attached to the trees.

The helicopter then lifted the trees up and over to the truck beds, before moving onto the next pile.

Just that simple addition to the process meant they could do in days what usually took weeks. North was right, it was expensive, but it was necessary to keep up with the demand. This was their third day of harvesting this way and they still had two more to go, but they were able to process about twenty times as many trees as they could by hand in that time.

If North had his way, by next year they'd have a helicopter of their own. And she wasn't opposed to it. She loved seeing him so worked up. Loved teasing him.

She loved him. That was the thing. It was as scary as it was comforting.

The rest of the day was taken up with helping customers and working with the delivery drivers to give them their drop off routes for the next day. Some of them were local, some of them would drive through the night to other states.

At least there were no school visits. They didn't schedule any after Thanksgiving, mostly because the farm was too dangerous then. With the chain saws and the heavy trees being carried they didn't have enough eyes to keep it safe.

When she was a child, people bought their Christmas trees close to the big day. Mostly because they hadn't bred ones that would keep their needles for longer than a week. Now if it was cultivated right and given the right kind of care, a cut Christmas tree could last for a month or longer.

The last driver left at four, just as the shop was quietening down. She could still hear the sound of the helicopter blades cutting through the air though. North told her he'd be working until dark and Kelly had offered to give her a ride home on her way to the Tavern.

Amber couldn't wait until this damn cast was off. She hated being a burden on people.

She was replying to a few emails, which took some effort using a single hand, when the bell over the door jingled. She didn't bother looking up – she still had three staff members working to serve customers, but then she felt a shadow fall over her.

"Amber."

Her fingers froze on the keyboard at the familiar low drawl. Slowly, she lifted her gaze.

Shaun was right in front of the counter, looking tan and relaxed.

"When did you get back?" she asked, trying to not sound accusing. And also trying to not freak out because she was not prepared for this.

"Yesterday." His gaze dipped to her stomach, half hidden by the countertop. Only half because you really couldn't miss the huge swell that started right below her breasts.

"I thought you weren't planning on coming back until next year."

"Yeah, well I changed my mind."

"You could have called," she pointed out. "Unless you still have me blocked."

He leaned on the counter, his jaw tight. "What happened to your arm?"

She looked at her cast. "I fell. Fractured my wrist."

"The baby okay?"

She wanted to laugh. "Do you care?"

"I don't know. Do I? How do I even know it's mine?"

One of their temporary staff was at the register next to where Amber was, scanning some decorations for a customer. Her head was inclined as she listened to every word.

Amber let out a long breath. What should she do? If North walked in right now he'd probably lose it. She felt like she was losing it, too. And then because God must hate her with a passion right now, she saw Kelly's beaten Corolla pulling into the parking lot.

"What do you want?"

"To talk to you."

"Okay." She nodded. As much as she wanted him to disappear, he was her baby's father. She owed him this. But more than that, she owed the baby this. They deserved to have her do whatever it took to have Shaun in their life.

Even if it was the last thing she wanted to do.

"Can we do it somewhere that's not here?" she asked him.

"Like where?"

"Where are you staying?"

"I'm back at my house with Kyle." He shrugged. "Kinda like old times."

"Right. So could I come there?"

Shaun wrinkled his nose. "Probably best not to. It's... not in the best condition. Dean and I have a lot of stuff we need to clean."

She hated to think what state the house was in. "Then you'll have to come to mine."

"The farm house, right?"

She nodded.

The door opened and Kelly walked in, then stopped suddenly when she saw who was standing in front of Amber. Her brows pulled tight and she smashed her lips together in a furious thin line.

"Come over at eight," Amber suggested.

"Ah, we have a game tonight. I promised Kyle I'd play."

"A poker game?" It was hard to not laugh. At least she knew exactly where she stood on his list of priorities.

He lifted a brow. "Yep. Does tomorrow work?"

"Does tomorrow work for what?" Kelly had obviously decided to not keep her silence anymore.

Shaun grimaced at the sound of her voice. "We're talking here."

"Yeah, and so am I." She looked at Amber. "Everything okay?"

No, it wasn't. People were watching them. She pushed her laptop shut. She'd just have to work on the emails later. "How about we do this now?"

"Do what?" Kelly raised her voice. "What's going on? Why are you back? Why haven't you called? She's been going through so much shit, thanks to you."

Shaun blinked.

"Honey," Amber said, looking at Kelly. "It's okay. I've got this."

"He needs to know what you've gone through. With the apartment and the tavern and your wrist. Oh, and about how you're growing his damn baby in there."

"A baby I didn't ask for," Shaun pointed out.

Amber's cheeks flamed. She could live with him talking badly about anything but her baby. "Okay, that's it. You both need to get out."

"I'm driving you home, remember?" Kelly asked.

"Yep. So go get in the car and I'll be with you in a minute." She looked at Shaun. "If you actually want to talk, meet me at the house in half an hour."

He looked at his watch like he was doing her a huge favor. "Okay, but I can't stay long."

"Asshole," Kelly muttered.

"Get in the car." Amber widened her eyes at Kelly, who sighed then turned on her heel and walked out.

Dear Lord, could this get any worse?

She grabbed her bag with her good hand and put it on the counter, then tried to slide the laptop into it. It took three tries before she got it situated. And Shaun just stood there watching, of course.

"You can go, too," Amber told him as she walked around the counter and picked the bag up, hitching it over her shoulder.

"Christ, you're huge."

Apparently, yes, it could get a lot worse.

"This looks different," Shaun said as he walked into the hallway. She'd got Kelly to leave by promising her a full blow by blow account once Shaun had left. "You've done a good job."

"Thanks." She kicked her shoes off, leaning against the wall to keep herself steady. And then the baby kicked her right in the bladder. "Oof."

"You okay?"

"Yeah. Just the baby kicking." She rubbed her stomach. She could make out a rounded foot pressing against her skin. It was amazing how much her baby was turning into a contortionist. But she loved being able to communicate with them through touch.

"Can I feel it?"

She blinked. One thing she hated about being pregnant was how people saw her body as public property. They'd try to touch her without even asking. But at least he'd asked.

And it *was* his baby. That was the thing. "Okay." She moved her hand and he put his large one over the spot she'd been touching. "Can you feel that?" She knew from the pressure on her abdomen that the baby was pushing out right there.

Shaun's brows pulled together. "Yeah. What is it?"

"Most likely a foot."

"It feels long. How big is it anyway?"

"I'm thirty-three weeks. The baby's around four pounds. The size of a pineapple the doctor says."

Shaun blinked. "That's big. How long do you have left?"

"Until my due date?"

"Yeah." He pulled his hand back and stared at her stomach.

"About two months."

"Okay." He nodded, pushing his tongue against the inside of his cheek. It reminded her of the way her belly looked when the baby kicked. "I want to find out if the baby's mine before the birth. My mom looked it up. There are online tests you can do, just a swab and some blood. The results come back in four days."

She hadn't known that. Hadn't thought to look. "There was nobody but you."

"I need to see it with my own eyes. And if we do it now, then I can be a part of it. Rather than waiting for the test after you give birth."

"What do you mean be part of it?" Amber frowned.

"Be at the birth."

"Is that why you came back?" she asked him. "Because you want to be there?"

He shifted his feet. "I dunno. My mom said I should do it."

"Your mom did." Her voice was deadpan. "Funny how I haven't heard from your mom or you this whole pregnancy."

"Yeah, well I only just told her." He shrugged.

"I don't know that I'd want you at the birth," Amber told him honestly. "I can only have two people."

"I'm guessing Kelly is one of them." Shaun rolled his eyes. "No, but North is."

Shaun laughed, though there was no humor behind it. "So you want him to be there and not me?"

"He's been here for me throughout the pregnancy. So yes, I want him to be there."

Shaun's eyes narrowed. "But he's not the father, is he?"

She wasn't prepared for this conversation. She'd been an idiot to think it would all be easy. Maybe it had been easier to ignore Shaun's existence than to think about how she was going to explain about her and North.

"We're together, North and I."

"What?"

"Did Kyle not tell you?"

"No he fucking didn't. You and North? I knew it." Shaun raked his fingers through his hair. "I told you that he wanted you." He blinked. "Is that why you called things off with me?"

"No," she croaked. "It's a new thing."

"Is the baby his?" Shaun asked, not listening.

"No! I told you, there was nobody else when we were together."

"Yeah, well I'm definitely gonna need that test now." Shaun paced up and down the hallway, then turned to look at her. "Are you two fucking? While my baby is in there?"

Her stomach turned. "That's none of your business." Amber wrapped her hands as best she could around her protruding belly to protect her baby.

He started to laugh, though there was no humor in it. "I guess you hooked yourself another chump, huh? What kind of mother are you anyway? Spreading your legs for the first guy who comes along. Ah, don't answer that. You're a terrible one, like you'd have been a fucking crap wife."

She felt dirty. The kind of dirt that a shower couldn't scrub off. And she hated Shaun for making her feel that way.

Because what she and North had wasn't grubby. It was beautiful and made her feel loved and safe.

Thank God he was still working at the farm and not listening to this. Yes, he had better control of his anger these days, but this would push him to the edge.

"You need to stop this. While you're pregnant with my kid. You need to keep him away." Shaun was agitated, shaking his head.

"Shaun..."

"I mean it. Keep him away from my kid. I don't want his dirty body anywhere near it."

She couldn't believe this. "You keep saying it might not be yours and then you turn around and tell me what I can and can't do? Sorry, but it doesn't work that way."

Shaun screwed his face up. "So that's it. I get no rights? If I'm the dad I should have a say over this."

"No. You get a say over our child, but not over me."

"They're the same thing right now," Shaun said, his voice tight. "Ah fuck this." He stalked to the door, wrenching it open as cool air rushed in. "I'm talking to a lawyer. And I still want that damn test."

"You'll get your test." Her hands were shaking. She knew he was just making threats. He wouldn't go to a lawyer, would he? He didn't want this baby, he'd made that obvious. But it didn't stop her chest from feeling like she was one gasp of air away from not being able to breathe.

Shaun didn't reply. Just stepped out onto the porch and slammed the door behind him, leaving Amber staring at the space where he'd been standing.

"That little fucknugget," Kelly said, shaking her head as she passed Amber a cup of tea. "I want to wrap my fingers around his balls and squeeze them so tight he'll be singing soprano for months. You're pregnant and he launches all this at you. Just goes to show what he really feels about the baby." She sat down on the chair next to Amber's. "So what did North say?"

"I haven't told him."

"Why not?"

"Because I don't want *him* turning Shaun into a soprano." And maybe because part of what he said had hit a nerve. He'd called North a chump. The same way those moms at Halloween had laughed at her, saying she was using him as a surrogate baby daddy. Is that what everybody thought?

It hurt deep inside. She hated feeling so vulnerable about it.

"Oh I do. I'd pay good money to see that." Kelly lifted a brow. She'd driven back over here to the house, even though she was supposed to be at the Tavern right now. Amber had protested but she'd shooed her off.

"Yeah, well I kind of like him on this side of the law. And anyway, he needs to focus while he's finishing up at the farm. We've got two more days of harvest to go, and being pissed at my ex while using chainsaws isn't exactly the best combination."

Kelly sighed. "You're right. Boring but right. So what are you gonna do? Wait until after the harvest to tell him?"

"No. He'll find out Shaun's back anyway, you know what this town is like. I need to tell him that much. I'm just not going to tell him exactly what Shaun said." She was already feeling anxious, she didn't need anything more to worry about. She just wanted North to know it changed nothing.

Or it changed nothing for her.

"You're gonna tell him about the paternity test though, right?"

"Yes, of course."

"And the lawyer threat?"

"Shaun won't go see a lawyer," Amber said.

Kelly lifted a brow. "You sure about that?"

"I think so. But it doesn't matter. He can't take the baby away from me, can he?"

"You're talking to the wrong single mom. I don't hear from Grady ever. And I don't get child support from him either, but that's a small price to pay for having him out of our lives."

But that was the thing. She wanted Shaun to be involved. She just wanted North to be there, too.

But maybe she shouldn't. She was so confused.

"Was I stupid for thinking this could work?" she asked Kelly.

"What do you mean?"

"I just thought that it would all work out for me. With North. And Shaun, I guess. That we'd be amicable, and he'd see the baby when he wanted, but that North and I would be... more."

"You two are more."

"He's going to be hurt when he finds out that Shaun wants to be at the birth."

"He wants to what?" Kelly shouted. "You told him no, right?"

"Kind of."

"What do you mean, kind of?"

Amber swallowed hard. "I told him that I can only have two people at the birth and North was going to be one of them."

Kelly frowned. "I thought you could only have one."

"I only want one," Amber told her. "That's the difference."

"I would have done it for you." Kelly pouted.

"I know. And I would love for you to be there after the

baby comes. I just thought it would be good for North to, I don't know, bond with the baby, just the three of us."

"Oh, honey." Kelly patted her arm.

"Please don't be sweet. It's going to make me cry and I don't want to."

"You don't have to have anybody at the birth that you don't want."

"I know. But it is Shaun's baby, too. He deserves to meet him or her." She sighed. "This is such a mess."

"I know. But it's going to be okay."

"I hope so."

Amber's phone buzzed, North's name appearing on the screen.

We're done for tonight. I'm going to head home and shower. You want me to pick you up or should I come to yours? –North x

"Is that North?" Kelly asked as Amber typed out a reply.

"Yep. He's finished for the night."

Come to mine. I'll make you some dinner. –Amber x

And she'd feel better telling him about everything here. This house felt like their space. North had done most of the work on it, along with his family. And their relationship had started here. Grown here. It felt like home in so many more ways than one.

"Did he mention Shaun?" Kelly asked. Damn, that girl lived for the drama sometimes.

"Nope. He'll be here in about an hour," Amber said. "And you probably need to get back to the Tavern."

"Ah they'll survive without me." Kelly grinned and sat back in her chair.

Amber lifted a brow. "You're not going to be here when I tell him about Shaun."

"You're such a spoilsport." She sighed loudly. "You know, you could secretly Facetime me in."

"Kelly!"

Kelly lifted her hands up as though in surrender. "Okay, I get it. No friends allowed. You just need to know that if I'm ever mixed up with drama you'll be the first to get a front row seat."

"Great." Amber rolled her eyes. "More drama is just what I need."

***

Harvest time was always the most exhausting yet exhilarating time of the year. North was on a high as he drove over to Amber's house. From the speed they'd been loading up the trucks they only needed one more day to finish the harvest for their December deliveries. Yes, they'd probably cut more trees over the next few weeks, but the volume would be lower and they'd do it by hand.

It had taken him less than thirty minutes to get showered and changed. It was weird how he couldn't wait to get out of his house and go to hers. The place didn't feel like home anymore.

Because *she* was his home. His own place was just bricks and mortar.

There was smoke curling up from the chimney when he pulled into Amber's driveway. Though it was still on the Christmas Tree Farm, it was on the other side of the huge expanse of trees from where his own place was built. A ten minute drive at least. But it calmed him to see so many trees, snow capping their tips, all lined up and thriving.

He hadn't created the farm. But along with Amber he'd made it thrive. For a long time that had been enough for him. To have his family, the business, the town that he held a stake in.

But now he knew he'd been kidding himself. Being with Amber was like Dorothy landing in Oz. She'd opened his eyes to see that life could be glorious Technicolor. She was all he wanted. Her and the baby.

Everything else faded into insignificance.

He grabbed the pot from his truck bed. It held a little tree he'd found growing next to the bigger ones. A self-seeder they hadn't expected. Usually, it would end up in the mulch because it was too much work to pot and move to the area where their saplings grew.

Yet he hadn't been able to bring himself to leave it. It looked too vulnerable. So he'd taken precious time when he should have been cutting trees to pot this little baby tree. And then instead of planting it where it should go, he knew what he needed to do.

Bring it here, to Amber's house. Decorate it. For the baby.

She opened the door before he even got up the steps. Damn, she looked tired. They needed to talk about her stopping working and soon. He knew she hated staying at home when they were short staffed at the shop, but she needed to take care of herself and the baby.

"Hey." He kissed her cheek. The soft scent of her enveloped him like a warm blanket. "I missed you."

She curled her arms around his neck and hugged him hard, her face buried into his neck. "I missed you, too." He felt her lips moving against his skin and it sent a shot of pleasure to his groin.

"I found this," he said, lifting up the tree. "I thought we could decorate it. Put it in the nursery."

She pulled back reluctantly, then looked at the tree.

Her face crumpled.

North blinked. "We don't have to. If you'd rather wait until next year."

A sob cut through her words. "It's not that."

A sudden fear took over his body. "Is it the baby? Is there something wrong?"

She slid her good hand down her stomach. "The baby's fine. Moving constantly."

Thank God. "Then why are you upset?"

"Shaun's back."

He took a deep breath. "As in back in Marshall's Gap?"

She nodded.

"Have you seen him?"

"He came to the shop. Wanted to talk. I told him to meet me here."

North's mouth was dry. "When?"

"Earlier today while you were out harvesting." She was twisting her fingers, not quite meeting his gaze.

"Why didn't you call me?" The thought of that asshole being here, with her, alone, made his teeth grind together. "Did he upset you?"

"He..." She let out a long breath. "He wanted to know more the baby." She looked afraid. He hated it.

North pulled her into his arms, his mind racing. "It's okay," he whispered. "It's gonna be okay."

She was shaking. It wasn't right. He hated that she was feeling like this. "Let's go sit down," he suggested, sliding his hand into hers. He led her to the sofa, sitting on the end, Amber curled next to him, her hand still tightly gripping his.

"Did he say how long he's back for?" North asked, stroking her hair softly.

"For good, I think."

"I guess we knew that would happen eventually, right?"

Her eyes met his. He was a fool for this woman. He'd do anything for her.

"Yeah, but it's still a shock, you know? I thought I'd have some notice. This is a small town. You'd think somebody would have given me a heads up."

"Maybe it's better this way, get it all over with at once. So what did he say?"

"He wants me to take a paternity test."

"That figures. And then what?"

"Then if it's his baby he wants to be at the birth."

North looked at her carefully. The thought of Shaun being there when she was vulnerable made his stomach twist. "And what do you want?"

She ran her tongue over her dry bottom lip. "I don't know. I'm... I guess I don't want him there. But it's his baby, too. How can I say no to him if he wants to see his child come into the world?"

"Because the birth is about you. It's about what you want, nobody else. And whoever is there with you is secondary because they're not going through the most transformative, emotional time of their life."

"I'm scared," she told him. "What if he insists on being in the room?"

"He doesn't have the right to insist. Nobody does." He kissed her brow. "This is all about you and the baby."

She sighed, leaning her head against him. "I don't know what to do."

"You don't have to do anything right now. You don't have to make any decisions," he told her softly. "You're exhausted. Let me cook us some dinner and then you can get to sleep."

"I said I'd cook for you. You've been in the fields all day."

"And you've been growing a baby." He gave her a soft smile. "You win."

"Why are you so nice to me?"

"Because I love you." It was simple yet so true. "You and this baby. We'll work this out."

"You make everything feel better," she mumbled.

"That's my job." He kissed her brow, the truth of his words surprising him. That's what he wanted to do. Make her feel better. Make life better for her and the baby. Protect them from harm.

"I don't want to lose you." She sighed.

"I'm not going anywhere." He hated how vulnerable she sounded. It wasn't like her. She was his strong Amazonian, but right now she was scared.

"Promise?"

"I promise."

She was sleeping, but it was fitful. Though that made her one up on North because he couldn't sleep at all. And that was dangerous, because tomorrow he needed to be out in the fields with hazardous equipment and that would take all of his energy.

He turned in bed to look at the time. It was only just past eleven. He'd insisted on them going to bed right after dinner, and Amber hadn't protested at all. She seemed to welcome the opportunity to curl her body against his, and he'd felt the same damn way.

He stared up at the ceiling, thinking about their conversation.

Shaun wanted to be at the birth. And that was his right. North knew that. And yet he couldn't help feeling sick about it. He was furious that the guy had upset Amber—again—and yeah, the thought of him there in the delivery room made him want to punch something.

Not because he was jealous—though he was—but because Shaun didn't care. Not enough to come back and take care of Amber when she was at her most vulnerable. And now that he was back, his first thought was to make demands and not to make sure she was okay.

He glanced over at her arm in the cast. At the swell of her stomach beneath the sheets. What kind of man would see that and come in to make demands?

And that was why North wouldn't push her. Yes, part of him wanted her to tell Shaun where to go, that there was no way he'd be in the delivery room when she gave birth.

But he wasn't lying when he told her it was her decision, and hers alone. She didn't need any more men trying to pull her apart.

He wanted to keep her together.

There was still a part of him that wanted to pull on his clothes, drive over to wherever the hell Shaun was staying, and beat the hell out of him for making her cry. But he knew that would only make it worse.

Shaun would get riled, and he'd upset her even more. He was the baby's father. He had rights and North had none.

Fuck, he would never get any sleep if he kept thinking about that guy.

He sat up, raking his hand through his hair to pull it away from his face, and tried to imagine both him and Shaun in the delivery room with Amber.

It would be carnage.

Because yeah, he had better control of his anger these days, but Shaun would be sure to push him to the edge. Just hearing the man's name was enough. Having to share a small room with him while Amber was vulnerable and all North would want to do was protect her...

Okay this wasn't working. He pulled on the t-shirt he'd discarded on the floor and padded out to Amber's kitchen. Grabbing a glass from the cupboard, he poured some water from the filtered jug in the refrigerator, and drank it all down, the cooling liquid doing nothing to calm his ire.

But he needed to stay cool. For her sake. And he needed to get some sleep if he wanted to use the damn chainsaw without causing injury to himself or anybody else tomorrow.

When he crawled back into bed Amber had moved, her arm outstretched as though she was searching for him in her sleep. He gently lifted it so he could lay down, kissing her palm, and just that connection was enough to soothe his soul.

They'd work this out together. He'd do whatever it was she needed him to do. And somehow he'd get used to having Shaun in their lives because he was the father and North wasn't.

Even if he wished he was with his whole heart.

❧ 23 ❧

"Where are you going?" Amber asked as North took a right instead of a left at the end of her driveway. "The farm is the other way."

"Thank you for the lesson in Winterville geography." North smiled. "I need to go pick something up from town first."

"What?"

"Nothing important."

"Then how about you drop me off at the shop first?" Amber suggested. "We're due to open in half an hour and I need to check all the deliveries."

But he carried on driving. "It's out of my way."

She frowned. "It's literally two minutes in the other direction. There's no point in me sitting in the car for half an hour while you go pick up something that's unimportant." She lifted a brow at him and he completely ignored her.

"Relax. I got Sara to open up for us. She'll handle the deliveries."

"Sara? She only works during the week."

"Well she's working on a Saturday for me as a favor."

North pushed his foot on the brake as they joined a line of cars all trying to enter the town. It was early in the morning but it was also close to Christmas and Winterville was teeming with tourists. She looked at him, expecting him to be annoyed, but he had the most serene expression on his face. He flicked the radio on and Nat King Cole's voice filled the air.

"Why aren't you annoyed at the traffic?" she asked him. "You're usually bitching about it by now."

"They're all paying customers." He shrugged. "It's good to have them here."

"But we're going to be late."

"Yep." He nodded and damn if he didn't look pleased with himself. She wasn't sure if it was just her hormones talking, but he was looking more delicious than ever right now. She wanted to climb across to the driver seat and kiss the smirk right off his lips. Was he doing this to annoy her? He knew she hated being late. She hated arriving at the shop when customers were already inside, too.

She was a planner. She liked to be prepared. And North was messing everything up. Didn't he know they only had two weeks until Christmas? The shop was going to be mayhem all day.

"There's nowhere to park," she pointed out as they finally made it into the town square. He had to drive slowly because there were people everywhere, spilling out from the sidewalk into the streets. "You want me to jump out and get whatever it is you can't live without?"

"Nope. Sit."

She flopped back onto the seat. "Ugh."

Eventually, he found a space about a hundred yards from the square, pulling in and killing the engine. North jumped out of the driver's side then walked around to where she was sitting, pulling her door open. "Come on."

"I'll wait here."

"You're really in a grump mood today," he said, that smile still playing around his lips.

"Yeah, well you try carrying around a five pound baby in your belly," she said. She didn't bother to point out that she also had broken a wrist and then her idiot of an ex-fiancé had come back to demand a damn paternity test only to ghost her again when it had come back positive.

Yep, despite all those demands he'd made of her last week, as soon as the test came back showing he was most definitely the father, Shaun had decided to ignore her calls and texts.

He was such an idiot.

"If I could carry it for you I would." North slid his arm around her shoulder, pressing his lips against her brow. "You know that."

"Yeah, well you get to do all the work when he or she is here," she said.

He didn't blink an eyelid. "I'm looking forward to it."

Her heart did a little clench because he wasn't joking. She'd caught him watching YouTube videos the other day on how to burp a baby with colic. She knew how lucky she was to have him. Not every man would be this excited about his girlfriend having her ex's baby, yet his enthusiasm was genuine.

Every now and then she'd catch him gazing into the distance, as though he was deep in thought about something. But when she asked him what it was, he'd just brush the question off and talk about which monitor she was thinking about buying, and whether they should look at the video ones so they could watch as the baby slept.

They were about to pass the Winterville Tavern when he stopped walking. She frowned again. This was getting weird. "Don't tell me you need a beer before you pick up whatever it is you need to get?" she said.

He lifted a brow. "You finished bitching?"

"Nope. I forgot that I also haven't been able to drink a beer for months. I can't sleep for more than two hours without needing to pee. Oh, and I'm stupidly horny at all the wrong times."

He looked at her, his head tipping to the side. "Why didn't you say something before we left the house?" he asked her, his eyes dark. "You know I would have helped you."

Yeah, he was still up for meeting all her physical needs. More than up for it. She'd expected him to baulk at the way her stomach was now the size of a beached whale, and that she was leaking more milk than she'd expected. But dammit the man just seemed to love every part of her and it made her...

Ugh. Why was she mad about that?

"You may want to smile in about three seconds," North whispered in her ear, pushing the door to the Tavern open and ushering her inside.

"Surprise!" The loud sound of at least twenty voices filled her ears. The tavern was gloomy, and it took a few seconds for her eyesight to acclimatize. And then she saw them, her friends, North's family, and everyone else important to her standing in the center of the room. The walls were covered with pink and blue banners and balloons, and on the tables were pretty white Christmas trees with pink and blue ornaments.

"Happy Baby Shower," Kelly said, walking forward to hug her.

"It's eight o'clock in the morning," Amber said, still trying to work out what was going on.

"I know. But it's almost Christmas and this was the only time everybody was available. So, sit down and enjoy, okay?"

"You knew about this?" She tried to look annoyed as she

caught North's eye, but it was impossible. This man made her light up.

"He was the one who suggested it. We were all trying to figure out when on earth we could fit this in," Kelly told her.

"We could have waited until after Christmas," Amber pointed out.

"Yeah, but we didn't want to." Kelly shrugged. "Anyway, you'd have ended up buying everything yourself if we didn't do this in advance. I know you, you're a planner."

Amber sighed. This was all too much. "Thank you," she whispered.

Kelly pointed at a chair and Amber sat down reluctantly, as her friends all surrounded her. Somebody put on Christmas music as North brought her over a mimosa. "It's non-alcoholic," he told her. "But don't worry, they all are. We decided that alcohol and early mornings before everybody has to work wasn't a good idea."

She opened her mouth to reply but then Dolores came over with a gift in her hand. "I had no idea what to get, so I figure this would work."

Amber opened it to find a beautiful hand-crocheted blanket and a gift card for the Cold Fingers Café inside.

"I figured something for the baby and something for mommy when she doesn't get any sleep would be perfect," Dolores confessed. "Any time that munchkin causes you problems, you come into the café and I'll bring you a drink and rock him or her back to sleep."

"Thank you." Amber threw her arms around Dolores. "That's so kind."

For the next hour she opened so many gifts it was overwhelming. Clothes and bedding and diapers and things to bathe the baby. Holly had bought her the baby monitor she and North had decided on, and that's when it dawned on her. "You've been planning this for weeks," she said to him. "All that talk about what we should buy for the baby, you were making a registry."

"People kept asking what they should get." He shrugged. "So I told them."

His eyes held hers for a moment. Was it possible to feel lost and found at the same time?

"Thank you," she breathed.

"No, thank *you*." He cupped her stomach, his expression so serious it made her heart hurt. "For making my life better in every way."

His lips met hers just as the baby gave an almighty kick, as though to remind them that there were three people here right now. He grinned because he'd felt it, too. "Both of you make my life better," he murmured.

Yeah. Well ditto, buddy.

***

"So the idiot hasn't called her yet?" Kelly said as North helped her load clean glasses onto trays. Amber was out of earshot, sitting with Everley, Alaska, Nicole, and Holly on the other side of the Tavern.

"Nope." He shook his head, knowing exactly who Kelly was talking about. "Not a word."

"I'm surprised you haven't gone to see him." Kelly passed him a bottle of the non-alcoholic champagne he'd insisted on. "I'll pour the orange juice. You top it up, okay?"

"Got it." He smiled. "And I want to talk to him. I want to do a lot of things. But Amber doesn't want me to."

Kelly opened the orange juice and started pouring. "Well, somebody needs to talk to him. He's such an asshole treating for her this way. Maybe I should, especially after what he said about her."

"What do you mean?" North topped up the glasses slowly, the bubbles rising as he poured.

"About her using you."

North blinked. "Using me?"

Kelly sighed. "She didn't tell you."

"Nope. But I hope you're going to."

"Okay, but you didn't hear this from me," Kelly said, turning to look at him. "He told her she was using you as a surrogate baby daddy. And that she was dirty for having sex with you while she was pregnant with his baby. He told her she's a terrible mother."

He could feel his pulse speed up, his blood run hot. "He said that to her?"

Kelly nodded. "Can you believe that? The guy disappears for months, ignores her even when he knows she's pregnant, and then has the nerve to tell her that she's a terrible parent? And the worst thing is she probably believes him. And now he's messing with her again. One minute he's threatening lawyers on her, the next he disappears again, leaving her anxious and worried."

"He threatened her with a lawyer?"

Kelly shifted her feet. "She's going to kill me. But yeah, he said he didn't want you near the baby. Started threatening her with legal bullshit. She's scared he's going to take the baby away."

He raked his hand through his hair. "He can't do that."

"I know." Kelly nodded. "But he's trying to scare her and it worked."

"That fucker."

"Right?" Kelly nodded. "I should have gone over there. Slapped him stupid."

The image of Kelly—all five feet of her—slapping Shaun would have made him laugh at any other time. But right now, he wanted to do the same.

A lot worse, actually.

What kind of man deliberately scared a pregnant woman? Especially when she was carrying his child?

"You know what the worst thing is?" Kelly asked, her voice low. "What if he's like that to her in the delivery room? What if he upsets her and the stress causes problems with the birth? I wish he'd never come back."

"Stress can do that?" The little hairs on the back of his neck stood up.

"Yeah. It's scary enough trying to push a baby out of the smallest hole in your body," Kelly said, wrinkling her nose. "But to have a man who trash talks you standing there while it happens? Staring at you when you're at your most vulnerable and not caring about your feelings at all? That's so horrible."

Ah fuck. North rubbed his face with the heels of his hands. He could feel it now, the red mist. And if he was there with Amber when Shaun started acting like a fool – when she was giving birth – it was going to be a bloodbath.

"I wish he'd just stay gone," North said.

"You and me both," Kelly agreed. "Maybe one of us should talk to him about that."

He looked at her carefully. "Amber would be hurt if we interfered." But he couldn't let Shaun ruin things for her either. He just couldn't. She was a great mother already, and she was going to be amazing when the baby was born. The thought of Shaun making her birth experience less than she wanted, of him making her feel like she wasn't good enough, made North want to hit something.

No, somebody.

And he wouldn't. He knew better than that. Even riled up he knew that it would only make things worse, but not doing anything was killing him.

"I'll go talk to him."

Kelly blinked, surprised. "You will?"

"Man to man. Tell him that if he's going to be at the birth then he'd better keep his damn mouth shut and be there to support her." And yeah, North was pretty sure that Shaun would take it poorly, but what was the alternative?

"What if he doesn't like that?"

"Then Amber will get a lawyer, too." He glanced over at her. She was laughing with Holly as Candace tried to do a little dance on the floor. His heart clenched at how beautiful she was. "Josh knows enough of them, we'll hire the best we can get."

"She'll hate that I said anything."

"Then don't tell her."

"Don't you tell her either," Kelly said, giving him a dark look.

"Okay."

Kelly nodded, pressing her lips together. "You're good for her, you know? I can kind of see what she sees in you. Behind that big hulking exterior, you're pretty sweet."

"Thanks for the compliment. I think." North lifted a brow.

She shrugged. "That's the best you're going to get from me. Now get pouring, big man. We have thirsty guests out there."

❦ 24 ❧

"I need to go to the barn," Amber said when she and Sara had finally cleared the long line of people waiting to pay for their trees. "Brian is due in ten minutes, do you think you could cover until then?"

"Sure. Go ahead. I've got this." Sara smiled at her. The woman never frowned. She was the perfect employee for the farm. She even wore a Santa hat every day without being asked. Amber had heard rumors that she also watched Hallmark Christmas movies year around.

If only she was feeling as lighthearted. Her sleep last night had been interrupted at least four times by a full bladder. She was pretty sure the baby was playing soccer with the damn thing.

"You're a lifesaver." Amber blew her a kiss and grabbed her coat. Snow was falling every day in the mountains now, and the ski runs were finally open, much to Gabe's delight. The roads around Winterville were full of tourists, traveling for their Christmas fix of sleigh rides and the Christmas Revue at the Jingle Bell Theater, followed by singing around the huge tree at the Winterville Inn.

The baby kicked her, and Amber winced. He or she must be getting pretty cramped in there now. She rubbed her stomach and a foot poked out again, making her smile.

Because despite the aches and the toilet runs and the lack of sleep this little thing was worth it. She couldn't wait to meet them. Couldn't wait to hold him or her in her arms.

And yeah, she was annoyed because Shaun still hadn't replied to her message about the paternity test. But whatever, that was his problem.

A small crowd was gathered to the left of the farm shop. Mostly women. Then she heard the chop of an axe against a trunk and she knew what was happening.

North was chopping wood again.

One of the women let out a sigh and Amber recognized them. The Mommy Mafia from Halloween. Wearing chic coats and cute wool hats, their cashmere gloved hands curled around their to-go coffees from the Cold Fingers Café.

Through a gap she could see North talking to one of the farm workers. He was just wearing a t-shirt, despite him always getting on her for going out without a coat. Even from here she could see the tautness of his muscles as he gripped the axe again and swung it down, the sound of wood splitting filling the air.

She looked down at her bump. At her cast and her hands – the uninjured one was swollen and red from working non-stop in the shop. She was wearing a pair of old jeans and a sweater she'd stolen from North.

Everything about her looked decidedly un-chic.

Walking over to the barn, it took her twice the time it normally did to unlock the huge padlock. It was frozen and stiff and her fingers couldn't turn the key. When it eventually budged, she had to put all her weight against the door to push it open.

Why was everything so difficult?

Flicking on the lights, she looked around the barn. It was a mess. They'd tidy it up in the spring once the shop was closed, but for now they didn't have time. Still, she had to find these boxes before five. So she walked down to the aisle where she'd put them last year, sighing with relief to see the marked cartons still on the bottom shelf.

They were marked with the words, *Wheeler Foundation*. The charity ball in Charleston that they supplied the décor for every year. It was Amber's baby. She'd started the tradition ten years ago, persuading North that it was good publicity to provide trees and garland for such a prestigious cause.

Plus she liked going to Charleston to decorate the ballroom. It really felt like Christmas when she arrived with the truck driven by the farm team. They'd descend on the hotel where the ball was to be held early in the morning and spend all day fixing the décor before disappearing right as the guests arrived.

She went to grab the first carton and realized she had a problem. Damn, she hated this cast. With her free hand, she somehow shimmied the carton to the edge of the shelf then hooked her arm around it, almost dropping it to the floor.

At this rate it was going to take her all day to get the decorations ready. The baby kicked again, as though annoyed at being jostled by the box.

"Sorry, sweetie," she whispered. "Just another twenty boxes to go." She reached for the next one, hooking her arm around it again.

"What are you doing?" North asked. She jumped because she hadn't heard him come in.

He gently took the box of decorations from under her good arm and put it on the floor.

"I'm trying to find all the decorations for the Wheeler Foundation."

"When's that happening?" he asked. He'd put his jacket back on, though it was wide open over his t-shirt. His face was flushed and he smelled of trees.

"Tomorrow. I've arranged with the truck driver to leave at six in the morning. They'll be loading up tonight so I need to have these ready to go so we can set off on time."

North shook his head. "You can't do that."

"Why not?"

"Because you're eight months pregnant. And your arm is in a cast. You can't sit in a truck for four hours then spend the next eight decorating a ballroom. Why didn't you tell me it was happening this week?"

"I did. You didn't listen. And anyway, this thing has always been my baby."

"Honey, you can't do this." North's voice was soft. "You know that."

"It's too late to cancel on them," she told him. "The ball is tomorrow night. I can't let them down like that."

"I'll do it."

Amber blinked. "You hate decorating." He was outdoorsy, hands on. For years they'd had a sideline decorating for big customers, and he'd grumbled every time. For the past couple of years they'd reduced that size of the business, except for their charity work.

"I know. But I hate the idea of you traveling all that way even more."

"Don't you have work to do here?" she asked him. She still wasn't sure about this. Elinor Wheeler, the rich patron of the Wheeler Foundation, was a stickler for perfection. North would hate that.

"I can leave for one day. We have enough people to cover the chopping out there." Though most of their harvesting had been done earlier in the month, they still allowed people to choose their own trees and then one of the staff would cut them down. That was North's area of work, while Amber's was always supposed to be the shop.

Until she'd broken her damn wrist.

"I hate that I'm so useless." She sighed and nudged the box with her foot. She couldn't wait for this cast to be gone.

"You need to take it easy," North told her. "You're still healing, you don't want to break your arm again."

"I just want to be normal." She hated relying on other people.

He grinned. "That's never gonna happen."

She narrowed her eyes at him. "Careful, Winter."

Ignoring her stare, North walked over to the piles of decorations. "How many more boxes are there?"

"About eighteen. They should all be on these shelves."

It took him less than five minutes to get them all ready. She knew it would have taken her at least an hour. And even though all she was doing was pointing at the boxes she still felt breathless.

She had to lean on the shelves to catch her breath.

"You okay?" He frowned.

"The baby's just doing some gymnastics in here," she said.

"You look exhausted. You should go home."

"There's too much to do." She let out another long breath. And dammit, she needed to pee again.

"What time is the truck getting here?" North asked her.

"At five."

"I'll get Greg to load up the trucks. Is it the usual number of trees they need?"

"Yes."

He winked at her. "In that case, your work here is done. It's time to go home, princess."

"Sara needs me in the shop."

"Sara has everything handled. You look exhausted. Let me

take you home. I need to head over to Marshall's Gap anyway."

"Why?" she asked. North never left the farm during business hours. Not at this time of year.

"I just need to pick something up. I'll drop you at home on my way."

Her stomach lurched again and the fight went out of her. She really did feel tired. Maybe a nap would help. "How about I go home for a few hours then come back to supervise the truck being loaded?"

"How about you let me take control for a change? The baby needs rest, too."

She nodded. He was right but she hated it. "Okay. Thank you." She'd just get Kelly or Holly to bring her back later. No point in arguing now.

"Come on." He put an arm around her shoulder. "Let's get you home."

He hadn't told her exactly what he had planned in Marshall's Gap, mostly because he didn't want to worry her. She looked exhausted – she had for days – and he wanted her to rest for a change.

After she'd gotten settled into bed, he climbed back into his truck and drove toward the bigger town on the other side of the mountain.

Shaun hadn't been difficult to track down. He was back working for Walker Woods in their mill on the other side of town. North had waited to see if he'd finally contact Amber before deciding her ex had taken way more than enough time. So now he was heading to Shaun's workplace, parking his truck in the lot behind the low warehouses where the wood was processed.

The air was filled with the high-pitched buzzing of the saws as North made his way to the warehouse, where he knew Shaun used to work. He'd been to this mill more than a few times and knew his way around. He also knew just about everybody that worked here, a few of them waving or calling out his name as he passed by.

But he didn't have time to stop and talk. He wanted to have this conversation and walk away.

Pushing the warehouse door open, he stepped inside, the aroma of freshly cut wood filling his senses. It was a different smell to the pines that he worked with. Walker Woods mostly dealt with hardwoods—not the soft pines that they grew on the farm. Sure, sometimes their interests overlapped—but mostly North tried to keep out of the family's way.

There was no love lost between his family and the Walkers.

A big burly man looked up from a standing desk, his eyes narrowing when he saw who it was. Sam Walker was Kyle and Dean's dad, a man around North's own father's age. But unlike North's dad, he was still working, still running his family business, and wily as a fox.

"What are you doing here?" he asked.

"I'm looking for Shaun."

Sam folded his arm across his barreled chest. "I don't want any trouble here."

"And I don't want to give you any. Just point me in his direction and I'll be an angel." North came to a stop in front of him. He'd give Sam a moment to help, but he'd search down every aisle if he needed to.

He wasn't leaving until this conversation was done.

Sam scrutinized him, his body unmoving. Then he shrugged. "Why can't you have this conversation on his time? At his house?"

"Because I want to have it while he's sober."

Sam's mouth twitched. "Well, that's fair. He's over at the docks." He pointed at the huge floor-to-ceiling doors that opened up to the truck loading bay. "You've got ten minutes. We're busy and I don't want him slacking."

"Thank you." North gave the older man a nod.

"And North?"

He turned back to look at the older man. "Yeah?"

"No violence. Because I don't feel like beating your ass today."

North shook his head, the ghost of a smile shadowing his lips. Sam might be built like a tank but wouldn't be any competition against North. But Sam was old school and North figured he'd give it his best shot, anyway.

He was the boss around here and everybody knew it.

"And put some goddamn ear protection on!" Sam shouted, throwing him a pair. "At least until you're outside."

North did as he was told–this was Sam's kingdom, the same way the farm belonged to him and Amber, and what Sam wanted was what he'd get. He slid the snug headphones over his head and walked down the closest aisle, past rows and rows of pallets of different sizes, filled with treated wood ready to be sold.

Shaun was easy to spot. North had spent the last few years watching him spend time with Amber, after all. He was scowling at something on the clipboard he was holding, while a truck driver was talking rapidly, pointing at a pallet in the middle of the road.

He looked up as North approached, his eyes narrowing. "What the fuck ever," Shaun said to the driver. "Just take it. We'll bill you if it's wrong."

"Asshole," the driver muttered, but he lifted the handle on the pallet jack and began to pull it across the blacktop. Snow had begun to fall again, and though the roads around the mill were cleared daily, little flakes were sticking to the dark surface.

Shaun's jaw was twitching as North walked up to him. "Fuck off."

North shook his head. "We need to talk."

"Like hell we do. Can't you see I'm busy? The boss'll fire me if I slack on the job."

"He says you have ten minutes," North said, keeping his voice even.

"The old man said that?"

"Yep."

Shaun rolled his eyes. "Not here," he said, turning on his feet and stalking away from his station beside the trucks. He didn't ask North to follow him but he did anyway. Snow fell lightly on his head and face as they walked toward the smoking area at the corner of the building.

Shaun stopped abruptly, folding his arms across his chest and scowling at North. "You got five minutes," he said. "I'm taking the other five as a break."

"Why haven't you called Amber?"

Shaun blinked. "Why's that your business?"

"Because you asked her for a paternity test and then ignored the results. She's carrying your baby and you're messing around."

"So it's my baby now?" Shaun let out a huff. "Did you think about that when you were fucking her?"

North gritted his teeth. He wasn't going to let this piece of shit get him riled. "She's got a month to go, she needs to make plans. Do you still want to be at the birth?"

"As I said, this has fuck all to do with you. I'll talk to Amber when I'm ready."

North curled his fingers against his palm. "You're hurting her. Which means you're hurting the baby. It's your kid, man, why would you do that?"

"You have no idea what I'm doing," Shaun hissed. "Or what I'm going to do. And the first thing I'm going to do is make sure that you don't go anywhere near my kid."

"That's not your choice."

"Damn right it is. You think I want an asshole like you bringing my child up?"

"I won't be bringing your child up. Amber will. I'll be supporting her like any good man would do." North took a step closer, his jaw so tight he could probably cut all the wood in the mill. "And I'll be making sure she's treated the way she should be."

"What does that mean?"

"It means you don't get to talk shit to her. Not if you don't want to deal with me. You don't get to belittle her, you don't get to call her names, and you sure as hell don't get to use the kid to make her cry."

Shaun opened his mouth and shut it again. "I have rights."

"Yes, you do." There was a bitter taste in North's mouth. "But you also have responsibilities."

"I'm not giving her a goddamned dime."

He would have laughed if this wasn't so serious. "I'm not talking about money. I'm talking about taking care of the mother of your baby. Making sure she's doing okay because that means your child will be okay. I mean, you asked for something and she did it. At least acknowledge that she has for God's sake. She wants to know if you'll be there at the birth. She wants to make plans. She's about to go through one of the hardest things a woman has to do and you're fucking her around."

"I don't want you at the birth."

North looked at him. "Amber wants me there. And that's good enough for me. Did you know if a woman is stressed it can cause problems with the birth?"

Shaun scrunched his nose up. "I don't care. It's my kid. I don't want you there. I'll get a lawyer involved if I have to."

"I'm not going anywhere," North told him.

Shaun gave him a sour smile. "We'll see about that."

"And I'll be making sure you don't hurt her again. Especially at the birth."

"I'm not planning on doing anything, not unless you push me. But you're not going to be there." Shaun lifted his chin. "Because if you are, I'm gonna make sure you regret it."

Christ, he wanted to punch the lights out of this man. But he was here for Amber, and she'd hate that. He took a deep breath, trying to push the anger down. "I'll do whatever Amber wants me to do," he told Shaun, his voice thick. "Because she's the important one in this. Not you, not me. Just her and the baby."

Shaun wrinkled his nose. "Whatever."

"I'm serious," North said. "This is about her. So don't you insult her, don't you upset her, and don't you dare do anything to ruin her birth experience."

"And if I do?"

North narrowed his eyes. "Try me."

He couldn't look at Shaun anymore. Not without wanting to hit something. More specifically, his smug jaw. So he spun on his feet and walked back toward the loading bay, sliding the ear protector over his ears so he couldn't hear if Shaun was still talking.

He'd made it through a conversation with Shaun without resorting to violence. So that was good, right?

Now he just had to make it through the birth.

―――――――――

Amber was waiting by the door when she saw North pull up in the driveway. It was dark – she'd slept for three hours and when she'd tried to get Kelly to drive her back to the shop Kelly had refused, telling her that North had told her to say no.

So of course she'd tried to call North and he hadn't answered, which drove her crazy. But all of that was eclipsed by the other phone call she'd gotten about an hour ago.

As soon as he walked into the living room North could tell something was up. "Hey." He frowned. "Are you feeling okay?"

"Shaun called," she told him.

North swallowed. "Right."

"He said you went to see him."

North looked at her carefully. "Yeah, I did. I was going to talk to you about it after dinner. I bought some chicken, thought I'd make enchiladas."

"He said you threatened him." Amber's heart was doing weird things in her chest. She'd been scared of Shaun's threats for weeks. And now North was making threats too.

She was angry. Not just because North had done this without talking to her – that was bad enough. But because Shaun had been the one to call and tell her what was going on.

"I didn't threaten him. I told him to step up and be a man." North kicked his boots off and carried the brown grocery bag into her kitchen.

His expression was soft as he put the bag down and turned to look at her. "Go back to bed. I'll call you when dinner is ready."

"If I went to bed every time I felt like this I wouldn't get up until after the baby is born." She let out a long breath. "Why did you talk to Shaun without speaking to me first?"

"Because you would have told me not to."

"Exactly." She threw up her hands, the stiffness of her casted wrist reminding her why she wasn't supposed to do that. "What if you two had fought? You realize he could bring a lawyer into this, don't you? What if he tries to take the baby?"

"He won't."

Oh, she wished she was that certain. "You don't know that. He started hinting at it on the phone."

"Then we'll get a lawyer and fight him."

He sounded so calm and she hated it. "You don't get it, do you? I'm scared, North. I'm walking this damn tightrope between you, me, Shaun, and the baby. And it feels like nobody is thinking about what I want."

"I think about what you want every day." His voice was low. She could sense the anger rising in him, too, yet she couldn't stop herself.

"You were thinking of yourself when you went to see him. I had it under control. You had no right going in there and messing things up."

"No right." He swallowed. "Yeah, I get that. No rights. That's me. No rights over you because you won't let me in. No rights over the baby because as much as I'm in love with you, I'm not the dad. And now I have no rights to defend my fucking girlfriend to the douchebag making her life miserable."

Tears stung at her eyes. "You knew all of this. You said it was okay. You said you'd wait to see how we both feel after the birth. You knew Shaun was the father and I'd want him to be in the baby's life." Why was he being like this? It was hurting her.

"Yes I knew it all. But you didn't tell me what he'd said. You didn't tell me everything he said to you. How he made you feel dirty for being with me while you're pregnant."

Her breath caught. "Kelly told you that."

"Yep. So don't talk to me about communication. I went there because you won't stand up for yourself."

A ragged breath escaped from her lips. "You think I'm weak."

"That's not what I said."

"It's what you think though, isn't it? The same as everybody else. That I'm not good enough to be a mom. That I can't stand up for myself and the baby. That I'm using you because I can't do this alone."

"I don't think you're weak," he told her.

She said nothing. Because somewhere deep inside she knew he did. She'd told him she could stand up for herself and he didn't listen.

One of the baby's limbs hit something inside of her. Something that hurt badly. She groaned.

"You all right?" North asked.

"I'm fine." Tears stung her eyes. Everything about her felt useless. She couldn't even pick things up because her damn arm was still in a cast.

No wonder Shaun said she was a bad mom.

A heavy weariness came over her. She had to lean on the wall to keep herself upright. Her head felt like she'd been through a spin cycle in the washing machine. All these thoughts were rushing through her head but she couldn't quite grasp them.

And then to top it off a wave of nausea came over her. Her throat felt tight and tingly. "You should go," she whispered. Before she said something she regretted. She was cranky and tired and still so stupidly angry.

North stared at her, uncomprehending. "Where?"

"To your place. I just need to go to bed."

"Amber..."

She shook her head. "I need to be alone for tonight. I need to think." The baby kicked again, and it made her breathless. "Please, just go."

"I don't understand why you're so pissed with me," North

said, looking at her confused. "All I did was talk to him. I didn't hit him, I didn't hurt him, I just stood up to him because you won't."

The nausea was rising. "I'm tired, North. So tired of all of this. I just want to go to bed."

"Let me stay with you." His voice was soft.

"Not tonight." She swallowed. "You have to get up early. We'll talk when you're back from Charleston."

"This is bullshit." North shook his head. "I want to stay with you. Make sure you're safe."

But she'd never felt more unsafe in her life at this moment. "Please let me be alone." She needed it. She craved it. North shifted his feet, his brows pinching.

"This isn't right," he told her. "None of it."

She pressed her lips together. There was nothing right about her life right now. And this anger she felt toward North was almost painful. She wanted to sob, to lash out, to do something.

But she couldn't.

"Goodnight," she whispered. It was her last stand. If he tried to persuade her again, she'd relent because she couldn't stand to see the pain in his eyes.

But he didn't try again. He just nodded and turned, then stalked down the hallway toward the front door.

And she collapsed back on the sofa and let the tears overwhelm her.

🌸 25 🌸

D espite the exhaustion suffusing her body, Amber didn't sleep a wink. The night was filled with crying jags, with recriminations. But most of all with missing North.

She'd been an idiot to send him away. She was going to tell him that. She was just so afraid of everything right now. Of the baby coming into the world and being torn between her and Shaun. Of Shaun's threats that he wanted to keep North away from them both.

And deep down she was still so afraid that North wouldn't want them anyway. It was too much to ask, for him to take on another man's baby. Would he love them? Would he be able to?

She wanted to call him, just to hear his voice, but he was leaving for Charleston early and she didn't want to interrupt his sleep. So she lay, cupping her stomach, looking at the clock until five forty-five came around.

She picked up her phone to message him, but saw that he'd beaten her to it.

· · ·

I love you. Let me come see you when I'm back. –
North. xx

That was enough to make her want to cry again. But she
blinked the tears away. She was calmer now. The fear was still
there but it had lessened.

I'm the one who's sorry. I love you, too. I should never
have said all those things. – Amber xx

Two ticks appeared next to her message. And then her phone
started to ring. She picked it up, her throat tight.

"Hi."

"Baby."

Just the sound of his voice was enough to make her chest
ache. "I'm sorry," she whispered.

"I'm in the truck with the guys," North told her.

So he couldn't talk. But he could listen, right?

"I shouldn't have made you leave."

"It's okay." His voice was cajoling. "Did you get any sleep?"

"No. You?"

"Not much."

She should have called him.

"I'm sorry," she told him. "I'm just so tired. And this is all
such a mess." She felt overwhelmed. Her head was pounding
from a lack of sleep. At least the baby had settled down in her
womb.

"It's not a mess," North told her. "You're just upset. It's
okay, we'll talk later."

She let out a long breath. Tonight felt like a long time
away. "Thank you."

"Try to take it easy," North told her. "You had a hard day yesterday. Take care of yourself and the baby."

"I'll try," she promised. She really would. Sara could do most of the work, she'd just supervise and make sure she ate and rested. The baby needed her to be sensible.

"And Amber?"

"Yes?"

"Try to not beat yourself up. We'll work through this. Together."

She wanted to talk to him for longer. Wanted to tell him over and again how sorry she was. How afraid she was. How she wasn't ready for this baby, wasn't ready to be the mom she wanted to be.

But he was in a truck with the guys. It would have to wait.

"I love you," she whispered.

"Right back at you."

A little rush of hope warmed her skin.

"Are you feeling okay?" Kelly asked over the phone. Amber had managed to calm herself down and take a shower. She was about to pull on a pair of pregnancy yoga pants and an oversize shirt.

"I'm fine. Can you give me a ride to the shop this morning?" She still hated asking. She was going to owe people rides for a lifetime once this cast was off.

"I thought we could go out for coffee," Kelly said. "I called Dolores and she's agreed to reserve our favorite table."

"Aren't you beyond busy at the tavern?"

"I just want to spend some time with my bestie," Kelly told her.

"Has North called you?" Amber asked. Because nice Kelly made her feel suspicious.

Kelly cleared her throat. "He might have. And for what it's worth, I'm sorry I told him what Shaun said to you. And encouraged him to go talk to Shaun."

"You encouraged him?" Amber blinked. She felt worse than ever.

"Yeah. I just wanted him to stop hurting you. And North's a big guy, you know. If anybody can stop Shaun he can."

"I gave North hell," Amber told her.

"So I hear."

"And I made him sleep at his place."

"Ouch. I guess maybe you both needed some space though. I'll be over in half an hour if that works for you?"

"Yeah." Amber agreed. "That would be nice. Thank you."

"No problem. Love you."

"Love you too." Amber hung up and pulled on her clothes, having to rest on the end of her bed between movements. She was so lucky to have friends like Kelly and North. She couldn't believe she'd gotten so upset last night.

She put on a slick of lipstick and glanced at the clock. She had ten minutes before Kelly was due to arrive, so she walked into the nursery, smiling at the cool cream walls and the warm wooden furniture North had bought for the baby.

Her chest ached looking at it. He'd done all of this for her. She was going to have to find a way to thank him. She loved him so much, she'd do whatever it took to make him feel a part of this birth and this baby.

He deserved it. He was her rock. She wanted to be his, too.

Picking up a tiny yellow striped onesie that Kelly had given her, Amber smiled as she pressed the soft cotton fabric to her cheek. She'd spent last week laundering all the clothes in a gentle detergent so it would be ready for when the baby was born. It smelled clean and fresh and – she imagined – all things that babies didn't smell of. She held it out, amazed that the little thing growing inside of her would fit into it soon.

They'd be a real person. A boy or a girl that she loved. Somebody who relied on her completely and utterly for survival. But she wasn't alone. She had friends, and she had North. She needed to stop fighting this thing between them.

She'd still try to keep things civil with Shaun, but it was up to him, too. If he kept making threats or hurting her, she'd have to put her foot down.

Not leave it to North to do.

Feeling determined, she opened the closet to hang up the onesie, but as she tried to thread it onto the hanger her weak hand dropped the fabric too soon and it floated down to the floor.

Groaning, because picking things up from the floor was so not an easy option at eight months pregnant, she managed to get down onto her knees and grab the onesie before somehow getting herself up again.

Her back protested against the movement, and she groaned again, gritting her teeth against the pain. Nobody had warned her about the back aches, or the fact she couldn't sleep on her back or her front and trying to sleep on her side with a giant ball attached to her was a losing game.

Finally, she got the onesie onto the hanger and closed the door. She checked her watch. Crap, now she was running late. Waddling into the hallway, she somehow got her boots on—pull on ones because laces were beyond her right now—and slid her good arm through the sleeve of her oversize coat. As she reached for the door, she felt her back spasm again. This time, it was even more painful. Or maybe she was just a wimp. All she knew was that when the time came, she was going to ask for all the epidurals she could get.

As she reached for the door, her phone pinged. She pulled

it out of her purse and shook her head when she saw North's name on the screen.

Stop beating yourself up. We're going to face this together. I love you–North xx

The man could read her mind. The faintest of smiles pulled at her lips.

I'll try. But I'm also going to make it up to you later. I promise you that.–Amber xx

Will it involve another lap dance?–North xx

Definitely!––Amber xx

I'll hold you to that.–North xx

Her back was still hurting as they walked into the Cold Fingers Café. She rubbed it and Kelly frowned at her.

"How long has your back been hurting?"

"Since last night," Amber told her as they reached the table Dolores had saved for them. She'd told them to sit right down and she'd bring over hot chocolates and cookies. She really was the best. "I think I slept on it weirdly. All that tossing and turning and thinking about what a bitch I'd been to North."

"You weren't a bitch. You were scared." Kelly lowered her voice. "And if a guy had gone behind my back like that, I'd probably get annoyed too."

"But you encouraged him," Amber said, shaking her head.

"Yeah. I never said I was consistent." Kelly shrugged.

Another twinge hit her as Dolores gave them their drinks and cookies.

"You should call the doctor," Kelly said. "What if you're in labor?"

"It's my back, not contractions." Amber sighed. "My body's breaking down bit by bit. First my wrist, now my back..."

"And soon it'll be your vagina."

Amber grimaced. "Stop that."

"Just telling you the truth." Kelly broke off a chunk of cookie and slid it between her lips. "So give me the deets. Tell me exactly what happened with you and North yesterday."

She sipped at her hot chocolate as Amber told her about their argument, the way she'd blown up at North, and how he'd left the house.

"Ah, that's normal," Kelly said. "You two are still trying to work out how this thing between you is going to go. There are bound to be teething problems."

"I just hate that he's on his way to Charleston. I want to say sorry to his face."

"It's only a few hours," Kelly reminded her. "You'll see him soon. And I know for a fact he cares about you. After all, he's the one who asked me to take you out today."

"I wish he was this baby's dad" she said, rubbing her stomach.

"He is. He will be. Dads are made, and he'll be a great one."

Amber smiled softly. "Yeah, I think he will."

———

Snow was falling as Kelly dropped her off at the cottage. They'd ended up making a day of it, having lunch at the café, then heading out to the mall for Amber to pick up a few last minute gifts. It felt like a precious gift in itself spending time with her best friend, one she had North to thank for.

"I'll come in with you," Kelly told her. "Make sure you're okay."

Amber gave her a soft smile. "I'm fine, and you have to go pick up Cole." She leaned over to give her friend a hug, but it was only a half-one because her stomach was in the way.

Kelly checked her watch. "Are you sure?"

"I'm certain. I'm all good. Now go."

The sun was already beginning to slide down from her anchor in the sky, the mountains casting long shadows over the fields of trees beyond the cottage. Amber watched Kelly's truck turn around, and slid her key into the lock right as her back spasmed again. She'd managed to ignore it for most of the day, but this time it knocked the wind out of her, making her want to double over in pain. She had to put her hand on the wall to steady herself, her breath short as she tried to capture oxygen in her lungs.

When she tried to straighten up and push herself off the wall she couldn't. She was too breathless, too shocked.

Too afraid.

What if you're in labor?

That's what Kelly had said earlier. But Amber had waved it off. And this couldn't be labor. Wasn't labor supposed to make your stomach cramp so hard it brought tears to your eyes?

She wasn't cramping at all. At least she couldn't feel any cramping.

When the next spasm came, she gingerly put her hand on her stomach. It was rock hard. She couldn't be. It was too early, she wasn't ready.

North wasn't here.

This couldn't happen.

After a minute she managed to catch her breath and make her way inside the house. Icy cold wind whipped her face as she finally opened the door, bringing tears to her eyes. She stumbled inside, breathless, afraid.

"You stay right there," she whispered to her stomach. "I'm not ready for you yet. You're not even supposed to be born this year."

There was no response. No kick. Nothing. And that made her more worried than ever. She should just call her doctor. Make sure everything was okay. She wouldn't worry anybody until she'd spoken to him.

26

"Back labor is a thing," Doctor Cavanagh said, as Amber sat in the kitchen, talking to him on the phone. "Can you tell me how long it is between your spasms?"

"Um, I think it's around ten minutes."

"And how long are they lasting for?"

"A minute or so?"

"Okay." The doctor sounded so calm it made her feel slightly better. "And when did you first feel the pain in your back?"

"It was achy last night, but then this morning it really started to twinge when I tried to pick something up."

"Did the spasms come regularly then?"

Amber shook her head. "No. Just a few through the morning and afternoon."

"But now they're regular, yes?"

"Yes." And they hurt like hell.

"I'd like you to come into the hospital so I can examine you."

"Is there something wrong?" Amber asked, fear clutching

at her chest. "It's too soon, isn't it? And aren't contractions meant to be in the front?"

"It could be that the baby's in the wrong position, but it could also be back labor. The best thing we can do is examine you, do an ultrasound, then hook you up for monitoring. Try to not be scared, even if you're in labor the likelihood is that it's going to take some time for the baby to come, and you're far enough along to deliver. You did the right thing in calling, now let me make sure everything's okay for you."

"Thank you." Her voice wobbled.

When Doctor Cavanagh hung up she took a deep breath and pulled up North's number. It rang twice before he picked it up, breathless.

"Hey, sweetheart. How are you feeling?" His voice sounded like an echo. He must still be in the ballroom putting up the decorations.

"Um, I'm not so good." She took a deep breath. "I need to go to the hospital."

"What? Why? Is everything okay?"

No it wasn't. She was scared as hell. But this time she wasn't going to lose it. "I might be in labor. I don't know. The doctor just wants to check me out."

"What do you mean you don't know?" he asked, his voice lifting. "Can't you tell?"

"No." She felt like a failure. "I've got back pain and he thinks it could be because the baby's in the wrong position or something."

"Shit." North sounded like he was panicking. "Who's with you now?"

"I'm on my own. At home."

"You can't be on your own. What if the baby comes? I'll call Gabe."

"No! It's okay, I'll call Kelly."

"If she doesn't answer, call Gabe, okay? I'm going to leave Charleston right now."

"You can't leave until the ballroom is ready. And there's a team of you. You all have to get home tonight."

"We're almost finished anyway. We'll be out of here in twenty minutes. I'll meet you at the hospital."

"Thank you." She let out a long breath. "But drive carefully. The likelihood is it's a false alarm." She ran her tongue along her bottom lip. "North, I'm going to need to call Shaun, too. Just to let him know what's happening."

She hated telling him that. She wished she didn't have to. But there was no way she'd do it behind his back.

Not after everything they'd been through.

He was silent for a moment. Then he cleared his throat. "Yeah, you do. I'm going to hang up now so I can hurry this along and get out of here. But I'll call you back when we're on the road. Try to keep calm. For the baby."

"I'll try." She hadn't thought it would be like this. She'd imagined her water breaking at the farm shop, North whisking her into his truck and holding her hand as he drove her to the hospital. Him by her side every step of the way, as she gave birth to the child they both wanted so much.

And yeah, Shaun was in there, too, but she could cope with that if North was with her.

"Drive safely," she whispered.

"I will. I love you."

Her heart clenched. "I love you."

"He's gotten a little too comfy in there," Doctor Cavanagh said, pushing at Amber's stomach with his warm hands.

"It doesn't feel comfy. It's... oh..." Another contraction—because yes, that's what they were—overwhelmed her. She squeezed her eyes shut and tried to count to ten like they'd taught her in her class, but the pain was too much. She let out a long, aching groan.

"Remember your breathing exercises," Kelly urged, squeezing her hand.

"The contractions are five minutes apart," the nurse murmured to the doctor.

"Okay," the doctor said. "We have a decision to make, Mommy. Because the baby is breech and with their back to you, I think we should get prepped for a c-section."

"Can't you turn them?" Amber asked.

"It's not something we recommend. You're in active labor and the baby is four weeks pre-term. A c-section is the best way to make sure he or she is born healthy."

Amber let out a long breath. She never imagined her delivery would end up like this. Laying on a bed in the hospital with Kelly holding her hand, North somewhere on the road in a truck, and Shaun—as always—nowhere to be found. She'd called twice and left a message on his phone, but he hadn't turned up.

"You should go," she told Kelly. "You need to open the tavern."

"Honey, I'm not going anywhere," Kelly told her.

"When would you do the c-section?" Amber asked the doctor.

"Soon. I'd like to get you prepped and into the operating room in the next half hour."

Fear gripped her heart. "What if I don't have a cesarean?" she asked him. She needed to know the worst.

"A breech birth isn't guaranteed to go well." He looked serious. "And with the baby being four weeks early, I'd be extremely worried that they would go into distress."

"A cesarean is okay," Kelly whispered. "My mom had one with me."

"Can we wait?" Amber asked. "Until the father... my boyfriend is here?" The thought of doing this without North made her blood run cold. After everything they said last night, she wanted him to be involved.

Wanted him to see their baby being born.

"How far away is he?"

"A few hours."

The doctor let out a long breath. "I'm not sure we can wait that long. Let's get your spinal tap done and then we can discuss again. We'll keep monitoring your labor, but if it's progressing as quickly as I think it is, we'll need to get you in there sooner rather than later."

Amber's phone rang, the way it had been ringing every ten minutes since she'd called North from her house. Kelly answered it for her, then passed it to Amber.

"How are you feeling?" he asked.

"The doctor thinks I need a cesarean. The baby is breech and too little to turn." She was trying to not cry, she really was. But she was so scared something might hurt the little one in her stomach. So scared about everything that could go wrong.

"Then that's what you should have."

"But he wants to do it now. I don't want to do it without you. I want you here for the birth."

"Yes you can. Baby, you've got this. Think of all the things you've done. You've grown this little thing inside you. You've fought for them. You've made a home for them. You can do this."

"I've asked to wait for you to get here."

"Is that safe?" North sounded wary.

Kelly was looking at her, and Amber knew that if she lied Kelly would tell North the truth anyway. That was the trouble with having a big mouthed friend.

"He thinks we should do it sooner, but you won't be here."

"Can Kelly go in with you?"

"Yes she can," Kelly shouted. Damn North's loud voice.

"How about Shaun? Has he turned up yet?"

"No. But I don't want him in there with me." She wanted him. She wanted to give him this gift. To show him she trusted him more than anything.

"Then he won't be. This is about you and the baby, nothing else. I'll get there as fast as I can, but you need to be strong, baby. Let Kelly come in with you and I'll be there before you know it."

The door opened and a man in green scrubs walked in, carrying a case in his hand. He walked over to Doctor Cavanagh and the two of them talked softly.

"Amber, this is Doctor Greene, the anesthesiologist. He's going to give you a spinal block. We're going to need you to end your call though, so we can get you situated."

Kelly took the phone from her. "It's me," she said into the phone. "Yeah I know. I will." She paused as the nurse helped Amber to a sitting position, her back facing the anesthesiologist.

"North says he loves you and you've got this," Kelly told her.

She wasn't sure she had anything, but then she didn't have any choice. This baby needed to be born and she needed to make sure he or she was born healthy.

"Tell him I love him, too."

27

The traffic on the interstate was all backed up. North stared out at the road ahead, frustration making his teeth grind. They'd packed up as quickly as they could, but it was still a long drive in a rig like this at the best of times. And this sure wasn't the best of times, not when he was supposed to be with Amber, making things better for her.

His phone screen lit up and he quickly answered the call. This time Kelly was using her own phone.

"Is there news?" he asked.

"No. I told Amber I was going to the bathroom but I thought I'd call you out of her earshot."

"Why? Is there something wrong?"

Kelly paused for a moment. He could hear the tap of her shoes on the hospital tiles. "She's doing great. Honestly, North, she's so brave it's killing me. But I just heard through the grapevine that Shaun's finally on his way."

A sour taste filled his mouth. "So he finally crawled out from under his rock."

"Yeah, unfortunately. I just thought you should know

before you get here and see him. How much longer will you be?"

He looked at the GPS. "Too long."

Kelly sighed. "I'm sorry you won't be here for the birth. I know Amber wanted you here. She's so sorry about what happened. She hasn't stopped talking about apologizing to you."

"She already apologized. And it was my fault, too."

"Yeah, well go easy on her. She loves you."

This was his fault. He shouldn't have left town. Not when she was so upset. He should have stuck around, should have insisted that the team do the décor without him.

Because now he was going to miss the baby's birth. He hadn't realized how important it was for him to be there until he couldn't be. He wasn't the baby's father, but at least he'd have been there from the beginning. Been there to support Amber, been there to hold her baby, been there to show her that he wasn't planning on letting her go through this alone.

Except she wouldn't be alone. Shaun would be there. And that made him feel even worse. The thick heat of jealousy at the thought of Shaun watching his child being born was consuming him. He didn't want that man near Amber or the baby.

And yet he had more right to be there than North did.

"Try to take as many pictures as you can," North said. "And just make sure Amber is okay."

"Of course I will." Kelly's voice was soft. "I asked if I could take my phone in and Facetime you through the delivery but they don't allow it."

He wasn't sure he could cope with that anyway. Seeing her go through any pain or anguish while he was hours away unable to do anything for her. "So you're going in with her, right?"

"Yes. Shaun will have to wait outside."

Good. He hated himself for thinking like that, but it was true. Shaun was so damn unreliable and Amber deserved somebody who was always there for her.

"Take care of her," he told Kelly. "Don't let anything happen to her or the baby."

"Of course. Just make sure you get here in one piece, okay? Don't do anything stupid. I can be there for the birth, North, but it's you she'll want with her afterward."

The sky was dark and snow was falling heavy and thick by the time they pulled in front of the hospital. North had to jump out of the cab at the end of the drive because there wasn't enough room for the truck to turn around and get out again – it was too big and ungainly for that.

He held his phone in front of him, unable to take his eyes off the picture Kelly had sent. Amber wearing a white and blue gown, her arms cradling the tiniest of babies. A little girl, just like he'd predicted.

He'd managed to speak to Amber for about thirty seconds before the baby was whipped down to the neonatal ICU and Amber was moved into post-op, waiting to be recovered enough to spend time with her daughter.

It was just a precaution to take the baby down there, according to Kelly who'd taken over the phone when Amber was fading to sleep. They wanted to keep the baby in the NICU for observation overnight, but if all went well then she should be able to join Amber in her room in the morning.

"Does she have a name yet?" he asked Kelly.

"Nope. She says she wants to name her once you're here."

Yeah, well he was here now. And he wasn't leaving her again.

Snowflakes stuck to his face as he strode across the blacktop, the wind whistling around the building as the glass doors opened on his approach. Two lit up trees stood sentinel on either side of the doorway. But before he could step inside a shadow to the left of them moved.

North blinked when he saw Shaun standing beneath the shade of the roof, his coat zipped right up to his chin.

"What are you doing out here?" North asked. "Is Amber okay? The baby?" Shaun had seen the birth through an observation window, according to Kelly, and then the neonatal doctor had offered for him to accompany the baby down to the NICU while Amber was in recovery.

But he wasn't in the NICU, he was here. And North felt his anxiety rising.

"I'm leaving," Shaun said.

"Who's with the baby?"

Shaun shrugged. "The baby's asleep. She doesn't care if anybody's with her."

"Did you at least tell Kelly you were leaving?"

Shaun wrinkled his nose. "Why would I tell her?"

So that the baby wasn't left on her own. North knew Amber would hate that. Her child had only been in the world for an hour and it was a damn scary place. "Go back in and do what you agreed to," he said, lifting a brow at Shaun.

Shaun looked at him like he was crazy. "I got somewhere else to be."

"Somewhere more important than being by your child's side?" North tried to keep his voice even, but his fury was rising. "You're her dad. She needs you."

Shaun stepped back, shaking his head. "She's so fucking small. I don't know if she's even gonna live. That baby doesn't need me. She needs a doctor. I didn't ask to be a dad. I don't want any of this."

"Then why are you here?" North asked.

"Because my mom told me to be. But I wish I hadn't." Shaun shook his head. "I don't want to be here."

North's skin was crawling. What kind of man left a vulnerable baby alone when he could be there, looking after her?

"You can be her father," Shaun said. "That's what you want, isn't it? That's what you've always wanted. To push me away, to have Amber. Well, now you've got her and my kid. You should be happy."

"I'm not happy that her dad's walking away from her. I want the best for her."

Shaun frowned, as though he was trying to take in North's words. "What do you mean?"

"I mean, if what's best for Amber and the baby is to have you in their lives, then that's what I want." Even if it meant he had to see Shaun's face every day. If it made his girls happy, then he'd live with it.

Because he loved them.

Shaun's eyes narrowed. "I don't get you. You should be happy I'm walking away. That I'm such a fuckup. It makes you look better, doesn't it?"

North sighed. "Just don't make any rash decisions. Leave if you need to, but don't walk away from your kid forever. She could be the best thing that ever happens to you."

Shaun stared at him for a moment longer, then walked past him, into the dark and the snow, leaving North shaking his head.

Once an asshole always an asshole, but he didn't have time for that now. Amber and her daughter needed him. And he wasn't planning on letting them down.

"Okay," the nurse said, smiling at Amber. "We're almost ready to take you down to meet your little one." There was a wheelchair beside her bed because they wouldn't let her walk anywhere until the effects of the spinal tap had completely worn off. They'd stitched her up and let her have a sip of water and some buttered toast, which she'd awkwardly eaten with her uncasted hand.

But none of that really mattered because she was going to see her little girl. She opened her mouth to tell the nurse that she was beyond excited and then she saw North standing in the doorway.

Her body suffused with warmth as their eyes caught. He'd taken his coat off but there were still snowflakes in his hair. Was it snowing hard outside?

It was difficult to remember what the weather had been when she'd gotten in here.

"Hi." His eyes were soft as he walked toward her. The nurse stepped back from the bed Amber was laying on.

"You must be North," the nurse said, patting her hair.

But he didn't hear her. He was too busy looking at Amber.

"You okay?" he asked as he stood by her bed.

"I'm so sorry," she whispered. "For last night. For you missing the birth. I wish you'd been here."

"I wish I had too. But I'm here now. And I'm not going anywhere." He leaned down to press his lips softly against hers. "And it makes sense that you were so cranky. All those hormones getting you ready to give birth."

She wrinkled her nose. Maybe he was right. "Can I blame the hormones for the next twenty years?" she asked him.

His eyes caught hers again, and he smiled at her so warmly it made her chest ache. She loved this man so much. Loved that he fought for her – even when it was her he was fighting.

"You can do whatever you'd like," he told her. "You just

brought a baby into the world. You're a damn walking miracle."

But she didn't feel cranky anymore. She felt happy. In love. Complete. And a whole lot of that was down to the man standing in front of her.

"Okay then," the nurse said, "Let's get you in the chair and wheel you down."

It wasn't the easiest of movements for her. Her whole body ached, and the spinal block had worn off enough for her to feel the painful pinch of her abdominal stitches. But it hadn't wore off enough so that she was stable on her feet. North's hands were soft and gentle as he helped the nurse move her to the wheelchair.

"You ready?" he asked.

She nodded. Her body ached to hold her daughter. She'd hated being separated from her even for a short time.

"Then let's go."

It was only once they were in the hallway that she realized she hadn't told North who was down there with the baby.

"North?"

"Yes?"

"Shaun's down there."

North cleared his throat as the nurse pressed the button to call the elevator. "Ah, he's actually not. I saw him outside when I was walking in."

"He's not down there? She's alone?" Amber's voice rose an octave.

"I sent Kelly to be with her," North told her. "I don't think they'll let her in, but she promised to make funny faces at her through the window.

The elevator doors opened and the nurse wheeled her inside. She hated that she had to sit in this thing. Her arms ached to hold the baby, she just wanted to run to her.

"You'll see her in one minute," the nurse told her, as though she could read Amber's mind.

When they reached the NICU, she could see Kelly doing exactly what she promised, standing in front of the window, grinning from ear to ear.

"She's doing great," Kelly told her.

"Let's take mommy in first," the nurse said. "We can get her settled and then daddy can come in too."

"I'm not—"

"That would be wonderful," Amber said. She wanted him in there with her. It didn't matter if he was daddy or uncle or friend. He'd stood by her side through all of this. She wanted him to meet the baby. The nurse showed Amber how to scrub her hands, then laid a gown over her chest and lap before taking her into the NICU.

The door closed behind them as the nurse wheeled her to the closest warming bassinet. Amber held her breath as she looked at her baby. She was so tiny and perfect. Her onesie – newborn size – looked huge on her, as she waved her hands around, her legs curled up to her stomach like she was still in the womb.

"Here we go, sweetheart," the nurse crooned, picking her up and looping the tiny tubes over her arm. "Here's your baby. She's a tough little thing. She doesn't need any supportive measures. These wires are just to make sure there are no issues. And if you look right there at that monitor, you can see her heart rate and oxygen are perfect."

Amber held her free arm out as the nurse placed her little child inside it, keeping her casted arm far away from her vulnerable daughter. Her breath caught in her throat as those wide, innocent eyes met hers. She was warm and smelled good and Amber placed her against her chest, emotions rushing through her.

She'd fight ogres for this little girl. Move mountains. Kill for her. Do whatever it took to keep her safe.

"I'm going to get Daddy. I think this is a Kodak moment," the nurse told her. "You doing okay?"

Amber nodded. "I'm great." And she was. After everything that had happened. All the fear and shock and pain, her child was here and she was perfect. She just needed to continue to grow.

The nurse opened the door and beckoned North inside. He was gowned up, his gaze soft as it landed on her and the baby. He took the seat next to her and she let out a sigh.

"Would you like to hold her?" the nurse asked him. "And then after that we should see if she will eat. We're hoping if she does she can come back to your room with you," she told Amber. "Because she seems to be thriving in here."

North swallowed. "I don't want to hurt her."

"You won't," the nurse told him. "She's a fighter. I can already tell that."

"You okay with me holding her?" he asked Amber.

She nodded. She was more than okay with it. She wanted him to know her daughter. She wanted the baby to know him, too.

And as the nurse scooped her baby up and got her situated in North's arms, she felt her face flushing. His thick, muscled arms cradled her daughter as she blinked and looked up at him.

"You see that?" the nurse whispered to Amber. "She loves him already."

It felt like her chest was about to burst. Watching the two people she loved the most staring at each other. Getting to know each other.

Bonding.

It was everything she'd wanted. Tears sprung at her eyes.

"Let's take a picture," the nurse murmured. North

reached into his pocket while still cradling the baby, before handing his phone to the nurse.

"Smile," she told him.

And he did. Amber did, too. She wasn't sure she would ever stop.

He didn't leave her side all night. They wheeled her and the baby to the maternity ward two hours after they'd gone down to the NICU, having removed the monitors before they placed her in a tiny see-through bassinet on wheels.

Amber had tried feeding her, but she couldn't latch on, and having only one arm made it even more difficult. The nurse had reassured her it was normal, and that her sucking reflex would get stronger as she grew. In the meantime, she'd shown Amber how to pump her milk, and they'd fed the baby using a bottle so tiny it looked like it belonged to a doll.

"We're going to have to stop calling her baby eventually," North said when they got back to her room.

"I know." She let out a breath. "I just don't want to choose the wrong name. She's gonna be saddled with it for the rest of her life."

"What are your thoughts now that you've seen her?"

She'd already come up with a long list that she'd shown him a month ago, when they'd first talked about names. But she'd been adamant that she'd know the name as soon as she saw her.

Of course she didn't. But maybe, just maybe...

"What do you think about Willow?" she asked, looking at her daughter's bright blue eyes. "I kind of thought it might work."

"Willow." He played with the name on his tongue. "It's beautiful. Yeah, she looks like a Willow."

Willow let out a cry, and North jumped up before Amber could even react. "Is she hungry again?" he asked her?

"I don't know. We should try, I guess?"

He helped Amber get Willow situated on her lap, the way the nurse had shown them, and passed her a bottle which she put to Willow's lips. Willow frowned and moved her head, her little face scrunching up in anger.

"She's feisty," North said. He was grinning.

"It's your fault. She's spent the last few months in the same house as you," Amber told him.

"Nah, she's just like her momma. As cute as her, too." He brushed her cheek with his lips just as Willow let out a long-drawn out yawn.

"I know how you feel," Amber whispered to her. "It's been a long day."

"Want me to hold her while you sleep?" North asked.

"Would you?"

The corner of his lip quirked. "Been patiently waiting for my turn again."

"What if she poops while I'm asleep?" Amber asked.

"Then I'll change her diaper the way the nurse showed us."

She bit down a smile, because North had been so damn excited about learning how to do everything. She loved the way he tried–and failed–to wrap the diaper around Willow's tiny legs before she peed all over the changing table.

And now he was sitting in the easy chair next to her bed, his arms wrapped around her daughter, who stared right up at him. Willow blinked, her thick lashes sweeping down over her cheeks, and then she blinked again before closing her eyes completely.

"Sleep," he whispered to Amber. "You need to recover."

"I'm too busy looking at you two."

"We'll be here when you wake up," he promised. "Now close your eyes. I've got this."

"Spoilsport," she muttered, but she did as she was told. And within a minute, she could feel herself drifting away.

"Five and a half pounds."

North's deep voice broke its way through her dreams. Amber blinked her eyes open, taking in a mouthful of air. North was still in the easy chair, Willow's tiny head cradled in his elbow, her body resting against him as he held up his phone.

"That's a good size for a preemie," the female voice on the other end said. Amber recognized it as North's mom. "Did they say when you all can go home?"

"Forty-eight hours or so. Just to make sure both Willow and Amber are okay. It's major surgery. They want to make sure she's healing properly, too."

"That makes sense. Maybe we can come visit you both soon." There was a pause and then a man's voice echoed out.

"Why would we visit? It's not his kid, is it? I don't know why he's even holding her. He's a goddamned chump, if you ask me."

Amber was wide awake now. But she didn't move. She didn't want North to know she was listening in. He didn't move either—he was too busy making sure Willow was asleep and comfortable.

"Stop it!" his mom said. "That's so rude."

Through a gap in her eyelids she saw the sharp set of North's jaw.

"If I hear you say that again, especially when Amber or Willow are around, you won't have a mouth left to speak out of." North's voice was low when he finally replied. But there was no doubt as to the vehemence in his tone. "She's a few hours old and I already love her more than you ever loved me or Gabe or Kris. And you know what? I feel sorry for you. Because you missed out on this. On the feeling that you'll never let anybody hurt your child. That you'll do whatever it takes to protect them from the world because that's what they deserve from a parent."

"Yeah, well say that when they're a teenager and a little punk," his dad scoffed. "When she's mouthing off and telling you you're nothing."

"I will. Because even if she doesn't think she wants my love, she'll still get it. Because that's what good parents do. That's what you should have done."

There was silence for a moment. Then his mom's voice came through the phone. "He's stormed off."

"I'm not letting him talk to Amber or Willow like that, Mom. Not ever."

His mom breathed heavily. "He's still your father."

"No. A dad takes care of his kids. Loves them. He doesn't make them feel like crap. I couldn't stop him from coming near me growing up, but he won't ever come near my girls."

Amber's heart clenched.

"And if that means you don't want to come see us, then don't," North continued.

"Of course I want to see you all. I'll talk to your father."

"Whatever. But I'm serious, Mom. I won't stand for anybody treating my kid like he treated us boys."

Amber held her breath. Her heart felt so full it could burst.

"I understand. She's so precious," his mom whispered. "That picture of the two of you... the expression on your face."

Amber let out the mouthful of air she'd been holding.

North turned his head, his eyebrows lifting when he saw she was awake.

"I've got to go," he told his mom, ending the call before she could reply.

"You heard," he said.

"Yeah." Amber nodded.

"How much of it?"

She pulled her lip between her teeth. "Quite a lot. I heard what your dad said. And what you said."

North pressed his lips together in a hard line.

"I heard you say she was yours."

"I'm sorry. I shouldn't have done that."

"I liked it," Amber said softly. "I like that you called us your girls. I like knowing you're always on our side." She reached for him, her fingers curling around his arm. "I like knowing that even when she's a teenager she'll have a daddy who loves her."

"She already has a daddy," North said. She could see a swirl of emotions in his eyes.

"And now she has two. Isn't she lucky?" Amber smiled. "Because I think she is. We both are."

"Does that mean you're okay with this? That you want us?" North asked. She could hear the hope in his voice.

It echoed with the joy in her heart.

"Yes. I've always wanted you. You're everything to me. I'm so sorry I made you leave when we fought."

"It's okay. We've both said we're sorry. And maybe we've learned something, too."

"That hormones make me moody?" she asked.

He grinned. "No, that we need to keep talking. To keep telling each other how we feel. If we're afraid or if we're angry, we need to say it."

"We do." She nodded. "And since we're being open, I want you in our lives. I want to wake up with you every morning. I want to curl up with you every night. I want you to protect us and love us and always be there for us," she whispered.

"I want that, too." His voice was gritty now. Still low. Willow smacked her lips together, sleeping through it all.

"Good." Amber smiled at him. And he smiled back, his eyes shining, his beautiful, beautiful face lighting up.

"You're it for me," he whispered. "I don't think I could go anywhere even if I tried."

"Then don't try."

He leaned over the side of the chair. She scooted to the edge of the bed as best she could, her stomach complaining at the movement. But it was worth it to feel his lips brushing her brow, her cheek, her jaw, before coming to a stop at her mouth.

"Have I told you how amazing you are?" he asked, before capturing her lips in the softest of kisses.

"No. Tell me again," she breathed against his mouth.

He smiled. "I intend to. Every day for the rest of our lives."

🏵 28 🏵

S he was too comfortable. Here in the cocoon of her bed
she was too warm, too cozy, too... alone.

Wait! She sat up, her eyes seeking out the crib next to the
bed, but Willow wasn't there. Nor was North, though there
was an indent in the mattress next to her showing that he had
been in here until recently.

They'd come home from the hospital two days ago. North
had carried Willow out in her brand new car seat, a smile on
his face as he fixed her into the backseat then helped Amber
into the car. She was still on pain meds from delivery, and
Doctor Cavanagh had given her a big lecture about not lifting
anything heavy or overdoing things. She had to take things
easy for six freaking weeks.

And of course North was taking this serious.

He refused to let her pick anything heavier than Willow
up, and even then he had to help her thanks to her cast. He
also refused to let her cook, let her clean, let her do anything
other than take care of her baby and rest. Secretly, she liked
the way he was taking care of her, but she didn't want to let

him know it. So she grumbled and he grinned and it felt like they were finding their new normal.

Slowly, she rolled onto her side and angled her legs out of bed, her feet hitting the rug on top of the wooden floor. She was still wearing maternity clothes – Kelly told her to get used to them, they'd be her friend for a few more weeks– her nightdress doing little to hide the strange in-between state of her body. She wasn't pregnant but she definitely wasn't back to normal either.

It was as though they were living in a bubble. One with just her, Willow, and North inside. Maybe it was having a baby at Christmastime that did it. The snow was falling regularly outside and they had enough food to feed an army thanks to all her friends making casseroles and sweet treats. The three of them could probably survive the winter without having to step outside the house.

North wasn't in the living room when she peeked around the door. She closed it gently and padded down the hallway to the kitchen, but they weren't there either. That's when she saw the gentle glow coming from beneath the nursery door. They hadn't used it yet – Willow had been sleeping in the crib in their bedroom since they brought her home. Amber pushed at the door and when it opened she smiled, because the two people she loved most in the world were together.

He was sitting in the rocking chair, his long legs stretched out as he gently pushed to rock the chair back and forth. Willow stared up at him, her pretty bow-shaped lips sucking at the tiny bottle of milk that Amber had expressed last night.

Her hand was clutching North's t-shirt like she never wanted to let go of him, and there was such a look of peace on her face that it made Amber's chest clench.

But it was the expression on North's features that stole her breath. He was staring down at her little girl with adoration, a half smile pulling at his lips. He loved her already, she could tell that from the way he held her so gently, the way he whispered to her when he tried to get her back to sleep.

From the way he always beat her to the crib when Willow was crying.

"Hey." She curled her fingers around the door jamb. "You should have woken me up. I didn't hear her cry."

He looked over, his smile widening when he saw her standing there. "You were down for the count. I wanted you to sleep."

"I got six hours."

"That's pretty good, right?"

"I'd say we're killing it as new parents."

Willow let out a little mew. She hadn't found her voice yet, and they both laughed every time she sounded like a cat. She cried out again, and North recentered the nipple of the bottle, stroking her hair and cooing at her.

The lucky girl. Only a few days old and she was already so loved. Amber knew how she felt.

"You're a natural," she said, walking over to them. He reached for her, and somehow she managed to balance on his legs without squashing him or Willow. His arm curled around her waist, and she nestled her side against him, leaning down to kiss her daughter's downy head. It was awkward with her cast, but somehow it worked.

"She's easy to love," North told her. "Like her mama."

Warmth rushed through her. "You're pretty easy to love, too."

"Don't tell lies." He winked at her. "I'm messy and difficult."

"If you say so. I'm not arguing with you anymore." She grinned and he shook his head. Emotion washed through her. She felt so happy right now. So contented. She was with her baby and the man she loved, and nothing else mattered.

Yes, they still had hills to climb. It was almost Christmas and they hadn't wrapped any gifts—or even bought anything for their surprise baby. They had to call in all the favors they could find to have proper staff in the shop for the next few days before things got quiet again, and of course they had the steady stream of friends and family visiting to deal with.

And then there was Shaun. He hadn't come to see Willow since they'd been home, despite being invited. He'd claimed he was busy working, then told her he was going away for the holidays. Kelly had heard through the grapevine that he was planning to travel again.

He didn't want to be a father to Willow, that much was clear. And though it hurt Amber's heart, she knew that Willow wouldn't suffer. She was so loved by everybody else. By her mama and North and all of his family. She wouldn't know what it was like to be lonely or afraid because they'd all take care of her.

"She's asleep," North whispered. "Shall we take her back to bed?"

"Sounds good." Amber didn't even know what the time was. It was still dark outside, so she assumed it was early morning. Too early for the sun to have risen above the mountain tops.

She slowly climbed off his lap. They walked back to the bedroom and North laid Willow gently down in the crib, then inclined his head at the bed. Amber climbed in and so did he, pulling her toward him. "Are you in any pain?" he asked her.

She shook her head.

"Good." He stroked her hair softly, then kissed her brow with his warm lips. He smelled so good. Like pine trees in the summer rain. Her little piece of home. She tipped her head and captured his mouth with her own, moving her lips against his.

He cupped the back of her head, deepening the kiss, then she felt him hard and thick against her.

"Oh."

He blinked. "Ignore it."

"It's too big to ignore."

"Well thank you." He shook his head, smiling. "But seriously, it's all fine. Ignore it and it'll go away."

"What if I want to take care of it?"

His eyes caught hers. "No."

"Why not?"

"Because you're four days post op and your baby's in the crib next to us."

"You do realize she's going to be in the same house as us for the next eighteen years at least?" Amber asked him. "We're gonna have to take some risks." Or be completely frustrated.

He gave her a goofy grin.

"What?" she asked him. "What did I say?"

"You said we're all going to be living together for eighteen years. I liked it, that's all."

"You might not like it when we're both PMSing together," Amber whispered.

"Then we're just gonna have to have a boy and even things out."

Her brow lifted. "What makes you think I'm going to go through all this again?"

North stroked her face softly, tipping his head to the side. "I don't think anything. These are all things we can work out in the future. If you want ten kids or no more kids, I'm here for that."

Damn this man knew how to sweet talk her. "I want at least one more. Maybe two."

His lip quirked. "Then that's what you'll get. Do you think Willow will hate it?"

"Hate what?"

"Not being an only child?"

It was her turn to smile. "I think she'll be okay. Because we love her and I know that having more kids won't change that."

"I never want her to feel loved less than. Just because I'm not her biological dad."

"She won't. I know you won't let her." Amber traced the line of his jaw. "As far as I'm concerned, you're her dad in every way that matters." She pulled her lip between her teeth. "If that's okay with you."

He nodded. "It's more than okay. I want her. I want this, I want you." He pressed his lips to hers and she could feel the passion in it. "I'm in love with you. I've been in love with you for longer than I can remember. And now we have our girl and it's all I've ever wanted."

Tears pricked at her eyes. "I love you, too," she whispered.

And yes, it had taken them a while. But maybe they preferred the scenic route and not the highway. But now they were here together, with their perfect little girl and a beautiful future stretching out in front of them.

That little seed of friendship they'd planted all those years before had grown into love. And that was all she wanted.

***

Two days later they were finally getting into the swing of things. Amber still found picking Willow up awkward, but thankfully North was there to help. She couldn't wait to get the damn cast taken off. A few more weeks and she'd be free. Sure, she'd have to work on strengthening her muscles, but she was so excited at the thought of being able to do the everyday things she'd always taken for granted.

But it was all worth it when the three of them were

together. North was so gentle with Willow it made her heart hurt.

And right now the two of them were dozing in the chair next to the fireplace.

There was a knock at the door and she pushed herself up, wincing at the twinge in her abdomen. According to the nurse her stitches were healing nicely, but it would still be weeks until she was able to drive or move about freely.

She pulled open the door, expecting to see a delivery man there. They'd had so many gifts and flowers sent in the past couple of days that North had joked they should buy shares in UPS.

But it wasn't a delivery driver. Not unless Shaun had changed jobs. He was standing on her porch wearing a thick plaid shirt and a beanie. Her heart dropped.

She hadn't heard from him since Willow's birth. She wasn't going to chase him. He knew where she lived, where they all lived.

If he wanted to see his baby she wouldn't stop him.

"Hi." He shifted awkwardly, his engineer boots slapping against the tiled porch. "I... ah... wondered if we could talk."

She looked over her shoulder. "Willow's asleep."

He frowned. "Willow?"

"The baby." Of course he didn't know her name. For some reason that made her heart hurt. Shouldn't every father know their kid's name?

"Oh. Right." He nodded, looking more awkward than ever. "It's okay, I didn't come to see her."

Amber knew she should invite him in. But she didn't want to. Not when North and Willow were sleeping. This was their sanctuary, it didn't feel right having him invade it.

"What do you want then?" It didn't come out as harsh, but she felt it anyway.

Shaun let out a long breath, the vapor escaping his lips

and dissolving into the frosty air. "I wanted to let you know I'm leaving town again. After Christmas."

Amber swallowed. "Okay. But if you want to see Willow before you go you'll—"

"I don't want to see her," he interrupted. "That's what I came to talk to you about. You seem to have everything covered. You and North. You don't need me."

"You're her dad."

"I know." He blew out another mouthful of air. "But you have North now."

She was confused. "I don't understand. That doesn't stop you from being her dad. People have parents and step parents all the time."

"Yeah, but maybe it's best for her to just have you two. I've been thinking about it and I want to sign away my rights."

She felt his words like an iron fist against her chest. She didn't understand them. How could somebody say that?

How could somebody have a child and not want to be with them?

"You don't need to do that. We can work it out. If it's about money I don't want any. I won't chase you for child support."

He shook his head. "It's not about the money. I just think... ah... I don't know." He raked his hand through his hair. "I just don't want to be a dad. And maybe she deserves better than me."

Amber wasn't going to argue. She was too tired, too achy, and maybe there was too much water under the bridge right now.

"What if she wants to know you when she's older?" Because there was no way she'd ever lie to her child. If Willow wanted to know where her real dad was then Amber would support her.

The ghost of a smile flitted over Shaun's lips. "Then she can come find me. If I'm still alive."

Oh Shaun. "You're the one who'll miss out," she told him. "Not her."

"Yeah. I know that."

Amber pulled her lip between her teeth. There were too many thoughts flying through her mind right now. "Think about it," she said. "There's no rush."

"Yeah, I want to get it sorted before I leave. Make it a clean break." He swallowed. "I've already spoken to a lawyer. They'll be sending you some documents after Christmas. You just need to sign and send them back, I'll do the rest."

It had started to snow again, though Shaun was sheltered by the overhanging roof of their porch. "Does your mom know about this?"

He shrugged. "It's my decision."

"I know. I just wondered."

Shaun kicked his boot against the floor. "I'm not going to change my mind. I just want to leave this all behind. I made a mess, I know that."

"Willow isn't a mess," she told him. "Not at all."

"I'm not talking about Willow. I'm talking about me. About you." His eyes caught hers. There was a softness there she hadn't seen for more than a year. "I lost the best thing I had. And now I'm paying for it."

"Shaun..."

He shook his head. "It's okay. I know there's no way back. I just wanted to see you before I go." He took a step backward. "Take care of yourself, Amber. And the baby." He was out in the exposed air now, snow falling on him. He blinked away some flakes that landed on his eyelashes. "I'll see you around." Then he turned and ambled down the steps toward his beaten down truck, while Amber stared at the footprints he'd made in the freshly-fallen snow.

Then she closed the door and let the warm air of the cottage envelop her. When she walked back into the living room North was slowly waking up, though Willow remained fast asleep.

"Everything okay?" he asked her when she leaned over to kiss him.

"Everything's fine. More than fine." She'd tell him about her conversation with Shaun later. She was almost certain it would make him happy and mad in equal measure. But more than anything it would make him determined. To be there for Willow and for her whenever they needed him.

His eyes crinkled as he smiled up at her. "Yeah it is, isn't it?" He pressed his lips to Willow's soft head. "Everything's perfect."

Christmas Day arrived so fast it felt like he had whiplash. North wasn't sure he wanted to leave the cocoon the three of them had been nestled in for the last few days. But Amber was desperate to get outside, and Willow had slept for four hours without waking, so they all loaded into his truck and he pulled out of the driveway to head over to the Winterville Inn, where they always spent Christmas Day.

The snow was falling lightly, tiny wisps of flakes that barely touched the windshield before they melted away. He glanced over at Amber, who was staring out of the window, a smile playing at her lips.

Damn she was beautiful. He had to pinch himself at least once a day to make sure he wasn't dreaming. Just a year ago he'd thought she was lost to him forever. That he'd lost his chance with the only woman who'd ever touched him deep in his heart.

But now she was sitting beside him, their baby safe in her car seat in the back of the cab, and life was good.

He and Amber had talked for a long time a couple of nights ago about her visit from Shaun and his desire to sign away his parental rights. She'd been shocked and upset, but also there was some relief there. Shaun was so unreliable.

And North was determined to make up for it. To be the one that Amber and Willow could always rely on. To be their rock whenever they needed him.

To make them happy, the same way they made him feel complete.

When they arrived at the Inn the parking lot was so full he had to drive around twice to find a spot. He parked outside the kitchen, then walked around to help Amber out. She pulled the kitchen door open with her free hand as he unlatched Willow's seat from the back of his cab.

Willow looked up at him, her wide eyes taking everything in. A tiny snowflake landed on her nose and she blinked before letting out a little tiny cry.

"It's snow," he whispered to her, wiping the icy flake from her nose. "I'm afraid you're gonna have to get used to it. You'll be seeing it a lot."

Her little forehead crinkled as though she understood him.

"But it's okay, it's warm in the summers. You'll be able to play outside with your cousins. And we'll go to the beach at the lake. You'll like it around here, I promise."

The kitchen was in full Christmas morning chaos so they walked quickly through it and into the main reception area of the inn. Somebody had put the radio on, and "Feliz Navidad" was blasting from the speakers, making the kitchen staff have to shout louder.

It smelled so good. Of honey roasting ham and holiday

spices. His stomach did a little lurch as they pushed the door to the reception area open and walked through.

He knew every inch of this place, he'd practically grown up here, working for his grandmother and then in the past few years spending time with his cousins here.

It warmed his heart to know that Willow would get to know the Inn, too. That she'd be part of a big family who loved her and wanted to take care of her. She was so tiny right now it was hard to imagine her being big enough to run around the rooms, ducking behind trees and jumping out at her mom.

Having snowball fights with her cousins as their parents looked on with wry smiles.

He slid his arm around Amber's shoulders. She was still slow moving, even though she protested every time he tried to help her. She was getting stronger by the minute, though, and he knew he'd have to force her to put her feet up later today while the rest of them worked, taking care of the guests until the evening.

Because the evening was for his family. The one he'd grown up with and the one he'd made with Amber. It was when they ate their dinner together, when they toasted their grandmother who'd built this community from nothing. When they finally got to relax and look forward to the future together.

Alaska was behind the desk, wearing a Santa outfit. Everley was next to her, holding Finn in her arms. Their eyes lit up as they saw North and Amber walking toward them.

"You came! I win the bet." Everley rubbed her hands together.

"Was there any doubt?" Amber asked, leaning forward to kiss her cheek.

Everley cooed over baby Willow. "She makes Finn look

huge." She wrinkled her nose. "If I look at you any more I'm going to get baby fever and I do *not* want that."

Gabe and Nicole were talking to some guests by the Christmas tree. They waved over at them, Gabe cupping Nicole's stomach protectively, and North waved back. Then Holly walked out of the office with her husband Josh and their daughter Candace, who squealed when she saw Willow laying in her car seat.

"Me have baby," she said, running over, then she tripped and flew across the floor, landing on her hands and knees. She let out a cry and Josh picked her up and kissed her.

"Be careful with the baby," he whispered to her. "She's little."

"But I'm big girl," Candace protested.

"Yes you are, sweetheart." Josh rolled his eyes, but he looked so damn infatuated with his daughter anyway. North knew how he felt.

Not wanting to be left out, Finn toddled over to join them. But then he tripped over his shoes and let out a wail so loud it made them all wince. No mewing like a cat for him.

"You sure you want more kids?" Amber whispered in his ear as mayhem broke out in the Inn from all the little ones.

"I'm sure," he told her.

She grinned. "Me, too."

And for a moment he could picture it. Being surrounded by a gaggle of little girls and boys, all desperate for his attention. Them growing up on the farm, learning from him and Amber as they took them on hayrides and taught them how to nurture the trees they'd planted with love.

In the space of a year his life had become pretty amazing. This woman and their child – because Willow *was* his child – were the best Christmas gift he'd ever been given.

And he couldn't ask for anything more than that.

EPILOGUE

Six months later...

Amber was wearing a slinky red dress, and damn if it didn't make him hard just looking at her. Seated at the bar, her pretty legs dangled down, high-heeled silver shoes making them look even longer, as she sipped on a mimosa.

North stood and watched, taking his time to drink her in with his eyes. This woman ruled every inch of him. She looked as good wearing short jean shorts with Willow strapped to her stomach as she did when she dressed up and had her hair done and sent him a cryptic message telling him to meet her at the Tavern.

"Hi," he murmured, slipping into the stool next to her. "Do you come here often?"

Her eyes lit up as their gazes met. "I'm sorry, have we met?"

"I'm North Winter." He held out his hand. She took it in her smaller one, shaking it lightly.

"What's a beautiful woman like you doing drinking alone at a place like this?" he asked her.

She lifted a brow. "Looking to get laid."

"I think that's a guarantee in that dress." It would have been a guarantee without it. He hungered for this woman.

She tipped her head to the side. "Is that right?"

"Yep. I'd like to volunteer as tribute if you're looking for one."

Her lips curled. "I'm not that easy, Mr. Winter. You'll have to seduce me first."

"Oh baby. I'm looking forward to it." He ran his finger down her bare arm and it made her shiver. "Speaking of babies, where's ours?"

"She's at Holly's. She and Josh offered to watch her for the night."

"All night?"

"Yep."

North nodded. "She knows that she still wakes up at least once a night, right?"

Amber grinned. "Yep. I've given her the run down. Don't worry, Daddy, your baby will be fine."

Kelly walked over, leaning on the counter. "What'll it be?" she asked North. "A long comfy screw or a screaming orgasm?"

"I'll just have a beer."

"Spoilsport." Kelly leaned down to grab a bottle. "By the way, do you like Amber's dress?"

He looked at the tight red fabric covering his favorite curves again. She still moaned about them, but he thought she looked amazing. "I love it," he said, his voice gritty.

"I love you," Amber mouthed. And he felt it right down to his toes.

They rushed through another round of drinks and then dinner at the new restaurant next door. Funny how neither of them had much of an appetite. They only had a main course each, turning down the offer of dessert or coffee.

He just wanted to take the woman he loved home. Fulfill her every damn desire.

The night was warm and sultry as they stepped outside. He slid his arm around her waist, loving the feel of her against him. Then he pulled her down the narrow alleyway at the side of the tavern and turned them both until her back was against the wall, her body sandwiched against his.

Her breath caught. "Mr. Winter, what are you doing?"

"Just want to show you how much I like this dress." He tipped her head up and kissed her hungrily. She kissed him back, arching her body into his, tangling her fingers into his hair.

He was hard and she knew it. She slid her palm between them, cupping him, squeezing him softly until he let out a groan.

"You're killing me," he told her, his voice thick.

"That's not the plan," she whispered, kissing his neck. "I need you alive for what I have planned tonight."

"And what's that?"

She slid her hand under his waistband. "Showing you exactly how much I want you." Her warm palm encircled him and he closed his eyes. God, she felt good.

He moved his own hands down her body, then pulled at her dress, lifting it up her thighs, giving him access to where he needed to be the most. His fingers moved up, reaching the edge of her panties.

"Lace," he murmured.

"They're new. Red to match the dress."

He wanted to see them. But he needed to touch her first. His fingers slid along her neediest part and she let out a sigh. He moved again, this time hitting her nerve endings, and she had to steady herself against him as he circled her again and again.

"North..."

"Hold onto me." He was moving faster now, his thumb brushing her as his fingers slid inside. Uncurling her fingers from him, she put both of her hands on his shoulders to steady herself. He captured her mouth with his, swallowing her sweet sighs.

He wasn't going to fuck her here. He'd do that when they were home – alone. But he wanted her to know how irresistible she was, how beautiful she looked. How much he appreciated her arranging for them to be alone.

"I'm going to..." She clenched around his fingers. Her breath was shallow, her beautiful eyes shining bright in the moonlight.

"Yes. Now." He flicked her clit with his thumb, his fingers still inside of her as he kissed her again to swallow her cries.

He had to use his other hand to hold her up, she was shaking so hard. She'd never looked more beautiful. More his. He loved the way she called out his name, the way she arched and cried out, her body boneless in his arms.

He loved her more than he could ever put into words.

And when she recovered enough to speak, she put another smile on his face.

"Take me home," she whispered. "I need to feel you inside of me."

North Winter was glorious when he was dressed, but spectacular when naked. His muscles were strong, defined, and his skin tan from a summer of working outside. She looked up as he walked toward her, completely unembarrassed by his nakedness, his thick cock heavy and engorged as he feasted on her with his eyes.

This wasn't the first time they'd had sex since Willow was born. She was almost six months, after all. But it was the first time they'd been able to do it without keeping an ear out to listen for her cries.

It was the first time he'd been able to strip her in the hallway and kiss and lick her to a second orgasm before she finally dragged him into the bedroom. It was the first time they'd been able to take their time.

He climbed over her on the mattress, his body dominating hers. There was a dark look in his eyes that she loved.

Strong North. Angry North. Happy North. She'd seen them all. Every shade of this man.

And she loved every one of them.

"Make me yours," she whispered.

He dragged his length along her. She was so wet from his touch it wasn't funny. Then he stopped. "Shit. I need a condom."

"No condoms," she told him.

His eyes caught hers. They'd been talking about the right time to try for another baby. They'd both agreed they wanted to do it soon. They wanted small age gaps between their kids, the same way North and his brothers were.

But instead of pushing inside of her, he scrambled off the bed and grabbed his pants, sliding his hand into the pocket. She frowned. Did he not hear what she just said?

Oh God, was it the wrong time to suggest it? She opened her mouth to tell him it was okay, but then she saw what he was holding.

It wasn't a condom.

It was a ring box, a dark one, velvet by the looks of it. He opened it up, his eyes meeting hers.

"If we're gonna try for a baby, I want this on your finger," he told her.

She wanted to laugh because that was so North. "Are you asking me something?"

He blinked. "Uh, yeah. Sweetheart, I love you. So damn much. I want to grow our family together. I want to make you all so happy. And more than anything I want to be your husband. The one who gets to take care of you."

"As long as I get to take care of you, too," she whispered.

"Is that a yes?"

"If that was a proposal," she teased.

He grinned. "It was. It was a crap one, but it was definitely a proposal."

"Then it's yes."

He slid the ring on her finger, his eyes shining with emotion. "Have I told you how much I love you?"

"Every single day."

"And Willow, too."

"Our daughter loves you right back." She had such a thing for North. Not that Amber could blame her. She kind of had a thing for him, too.

She adored him.

He was such a good father to their little girl, and she was so thankful for that. Shaun hadn't changed his mind – his lawyer had sent the forms he'd promised after Christmas and he'd officially surrendered his parental rights.

North had already told her he wanted to adopt Willow. There would be some legal hoops to follow but he was determined to be her father under the eyes of the law. But the paper didn't matter to her, or to Willow. As far as Amber was concerned they were already a family.

And she loved it.

Just over a year ago she'd run away from her own wedding, unaware that she was actually running into his arms. And she wasn't afraid of getting married to him. She wanted it the same way she wanted him.

Completely. Forever.

"Let's do it soon," he whispered, capturing her lips.

"Yes," she murmured. "Now get inside of me."

He smiled against her mouth. "Your wish is my desire." He curled his hands around her hips, kissing her again as he filled her completely, her body stilling to accommodate him.

And then he was making love to her. Maybe making a baby, too. Not that she minded if he didn't.

They had the rest of their lives to get this thing right. And as he kissed her and kissed her, their bodies moving as one, she knew she'd found the perfect shade of North Winter.

The one that was hers.

DEAR READER

**Thank you for reading Every Shade of Winter!
If you're not quite ready to let North and Amber go,
check out this bonus epilogue for a glimpse of their
wedding and happy ever after by putting the following
address into your browser>>
https://dl.bookfunnel.com/55vonwrupa**

**The next book in the Winterville series is MINE FOR
THE WINTER - Kris and Kelly's story**

WANT TO KEEP UP TO DATE ON ALL MY NEWS?

Join me on my exclusive mailing list, where you'll be the first
to hear about new releases, sales, and other book-related
news.

To sign up go to this webpage:
https://www.subscribepage.com/carrieelksas

I can't wait to share more stories with you.

Yours,

Carrie xx

ALSO BY CARRIE ELKS

THE WINTERVILLE SERIES

A gorgeously wintery small town romance series, featuring six
cousins who fight to save the town their grandmother built.

Welcome to Winterville

Hearts In Winter

Leave Me Breathless

Memories Of Mistletoe

Every Shade Of Winter

Mine For The Winter (Coming Soon)

THE SALINGER BROTHERS SERIES

A swoony romantic comedy series featuring six brothers and the
strong and smart women who tame them.

Strictly Business

Strictly Pleasure

Strictly For Now

ANGEL SANDS SERIES

A heartwarming small town beach series, full of best friends, hot
guys and happily-ever-afters.

Let Me Burn

She's Like the Wind

Sweet Little Lies

Just A Kiss

Baby I'm Yours

Pieces Of Us

Chasing The Sun

Heart And Soul

Lost In Him

THE HEARTBREAK BROTHERS SERIES

A gorgeous small town series about four brothers and the women who capture their hearts.

Take Me Home

Still The One

A Better Man

Somebody Like You

When We Touch

THE SHAKESPEARE SISTERS SERIES

An epic series about four strong yet vulnerable sisters, and the alpha men who steal their hearts.

Summer's Lease

A Winter's Tale

Absent in the Spring

By Virtue Fall

THE LOVE IN LONDON SERIES

Three books about strong and sassy women finding love in the big city.

Coming Down

Broken Chords

Canada Square

STANDALONE

Fix You

An epic romance that spans the decades. Breathtaking and angsty and all the things in between.

If you'd like to get an email when I release a new book, please sign up here: https://www.subscribepage.com/carrieelksas